Of Greeks, Virgins, and Tectonic Jive

OF GREEKS, VIRGINS, AND TECTONIC JIVE

A novel by Romaine Riley

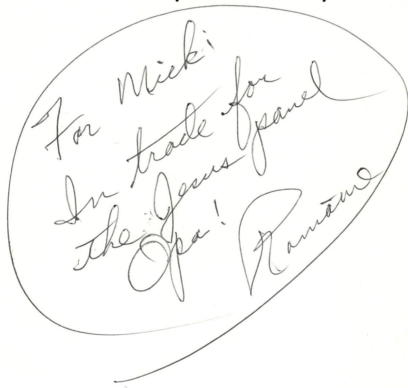

For Mick:
In trade for
the Jesus panel
the Opa!
Romaine

iUniverse, Inc.
New York Lincoln Shanghai

Of Greeks, Virgins, and Tectonic Jive

iUniverse books may be ordered through booksellers or by contacting:

iUniverse
2021 Pine Lake Road, Suite 100
Lincoln, NE 68512
www.iuniverse.com
1-800-Authors (1-800-288-4677)

ISBN-13: 978-0-595-40067-6 (pbk)
ISBN-13: 978-0-595-84452-4 (ebk)
ISBN-10: 0-595-40067-1 (pbk)
ISBN-10: 0-595-84452-9 (ebk)

Printed in the United States of America

Boss…it did really happen, didn't it?

PROLOGUE

▼

The patrons had wasted no time in leaving after the incident. It had stunned them all, the suddenness…the finality.

Though they had heeded Captain Bateman's request to vacate KYLIX and go to their homes a few of them had loitered outside on the sidewalk, apparently feeling the need for some kind of additional closure. They withdrew eventually as did the authorities and except for the lone squad car out front the neighborhood returned to normal.

Alexander Cassidy and Yorgos Papanikolas were alone at the bar now, silent, sipping ouzo beneath the melancholic glow of red blue and gold ceiling spotlights. An unreal light. Almost violent.

Yorgos sat at the counter with his head cupped in both hands. Cassidy glanced at him covertly as a single loud sniffle broke the silence. "You okay, Yorgos?"

Yorgos grabbed his gut abruptly, got down off the barstool and stood behind Cassidy, clasping a hand to his shoulder.

"Gotta go, Alekko. Can't stand this shit anymore."

"I'm good here, Yorgos. Go home."

"You're sure? I mean the kid'll be all right with my family until Erica gets here."

"I'll take care of it. Bateman left her a message. She's gonna call this number."

"Bateman gonna get pissed if I leave?"

"Naw, it's cool. Go on home."

"Okay, you know where I live. *Kahleeneekhta.*"

The KYLIX felt oppressive after the door closed behind Yorgos. For the first time since he knew the place Cassidy was alone there and it was deathly quiet, uncharacteristically so. He downed what ouzo was still in the glass. The fire was in his throat, then spread quickly to his innards. He took a club-like hold on the bottle, got down from the barstool and moved aimlessly between the tables, four chairs to each with red-checkered tablecloths, the votive candles now extinguished.

He stopped, gazed around listlessly. Exhaustion overcame him. He dropped heavily into the nearest chair, put his forearms on the table and rested his head. Time passed him by as though in a vacuum. His ears felt hot, the back of his neck cold. The dead weight on his forearms caused them to tingle. He adjusted them in response and became distantly aware of upending the ouzo bottle. He snapped awake and put the ouzo bottle upright.

He allowed his gaze to drift around KYLIX; to the hundred empty wine wickers which hung in a decorative line around the walls; to the revolving Art Deco ball of mirrors which hung from the ceiling above the dance floor. As in a daze he focused on the coloured prisms of light which reflected from the mirrored ball down onto the dance floor, a hypnotic circle of moving reds blues greens and white, silent and never ending. Then abruptly he got to his feet and made his way to the kitchen where he lowered his head to the sink and splashed cold water on his face.

Somewhat relieved Cassidy wandered uncertainly around KYLIX while waiting for the expected phone call. He studied the Greek figures on the muralled walls. He might as well have been standing in a taberna in Athens as one in Santa Barbara, California. There were classic ruins, shepherds in the fields, ancient patriarchs at the backgammon board. Young men, drunk and carefree dancing in a taberna; fishermen on their boats, and his own favorite…the portrait of a beautiful girl on the kylix, or drinking cup. The trademark.

Suddenly he was startled out of his reverie by *the table*, still askew, one leg shattered by the impact. Nausea seized him. He lifted the sagging table, braced it with a chair and backed away. He stared at the dark spot on the dance floor, still evident though Yorgos had worked hard to remove all the traces.

Cassidy's face lost its composure by degrees and settled into a pained expression. He knelt down and brushed his fingertips across the spot in curiosity. His mouth opened as though to speak then closed without a sound. He tried again and the intimate soulful words of the Greek love song A HEAVY SILENCE FELL punched out haltingly one word at a time…"*Épefté vathia shopé… sto palio mas vaso.*"

He faltered, stopped singing. The muscles in his jaw tightened and determination replaced the pained expression. He tipped the bottle and saturated the spot with ouzo, allowing time for the powerful liquor to permeate the wood. He grabbed a tablecloth and scrubbed frantically but nothing happened. The spot was stubborn. More ouzo, more frenetic scrubbing, but again to no avail.

"*FÉ-YÉH-TÉH*," he shouted, but the stain would not 'go away'.

Angrily he got to his feet and hurled the tablecloth down at the stain just as his obsession was interrupted by the harsh ring of the telephone.

He crossed the floor and watched the phone ring several more times, then snapped a look at the wall clock. It was three a.m. in Santa Barbara, six a.m. in Philadelphia. He picked up the receiver with a certain dread.

CHAPTER 1

▼

New Year's day came clear and tranquil to the lovely seaside town of Santa Barbara. The air was pure and the streets glistened with heavy dew, a nightly gift from the sea. A few early sailboats were the only movement out on the Pacific, benign in its immense flatness.

Marta Tosca hesitated as she drove past the twin towers of the old mission church, standing dominant and alone on the crest of the hill. The early mass had always been her favorite, particularly on the holidays when there seemed to be a special feeling of friendship and togetherness among the celebrants, many of them descendants of the early Spanish families who were prominent in local history. She pressed on, more concerned about Tina than herself.

Turning onto Alameda Padre Serra Road she began the uphill drive to her home. The community of homes on APS was special, resembling to a degree that of the French Riviera, a label sometimes given it. She pulled into the driveway and began the steep climb to her house. As she brought the car to a stop she experienced a peculiar kind of peace, a sense of satisfaction. She sat in the car for a moment and observed the town below, sprawled out from the base of APS to the shore of the Pacific.

These were the most pleasant hours of the day for all who lived on APS, those quiet hours before the young men in their freaky low-riders began to shatter the solitude of the narrow twisting road, each one a champion race driver in his own mind if as yet undiscovered.

Usually seven a.m. was the latest hour she could return from her periodic rendevous with her boyfriend Chuck without being monitored by her snoopy neighbors. But it was Tina that bothered her most. She felt guilty about leaving her daughter alone all night, though the neighborhood was considered a safe one.

She had seen Tina through some tough years. Besides, Chuck was her first and only lover since her messy divorce from Reuben 'Padro' Tosca three years earlier, and though not a puritan she was of a generation that took the selection of a bed partner seriously.

After dealing with the incredible macho of Padro for the fifteen years of their marriage she considered herself fortunate to have the easygoing and gentle Chuck, but truth was luck had nothing to do with it. Marta Tosca was a handsome Cuban woman of good background and an attractive figure a little on the pudgy side. Though her long black hair was now tinged with gray it was striking along with her large startling blue eyes. It had been this comeliness and her easygoing nature that had attracted the jaded Padro in the first place. A sensual and giving woman who would do anything he asked and come back for more. A woman who confirmed his manliness before the world.

She closed her car door softly so as not to attract undue attention and smiled as she reflected on the nicely balanced New Year's eve just spent with Chuck. A math teacher at Santa Barbara High School, Chuck had taken her to the annual dinner and celebration at the home of Bernard Boxwell, school principal. After the midnight rush of champagne and kisses they had quit the party and gone to Chuck's house where they welcomed in the New Year properly, in each other's arms.

As she unlocked the front door her thoughts shifted to her young daughter Tina and the New Year party at the KYLIX taberna. She would not have worried unduly except for the large age difference between her daughter and Alexander Cassidy, Tina's escort for the evening. One could never tell about older men. She was anxious to discuss it with Tina, and hoped they had behaved properly. Given that, the worrisome situation would likely go away in the brightness of the first day of the brand new year.

But noticing her daughter's bedroom door standing ajar (it was always closed when Tina was at home), Mrs. Tosca's breathing missed a pull. She peered inside cautiously. The bed cover was unwrinkled, the pillow cold and plump. The bed had not been slept in.

Negative scenarios flashed through her mind as she paced through the house. She circled the telephone and wrung her hands. She became weak and nauseated. Needed to talk to someone. *HAD* to talk to someone!

For the briefest moment she considered calling her family friend and confidant Angus Green, then rejected the idea. That would get Cassidy in trouble with the law for fooling around with a minor, for which her headstrong daughter would not forgive her. She settled on Tina's Aunt Celia, knowing even before she picked up the phone that it was a bad mistake. Celia would most likely tell her brother Padro, causing all hell to break loose.

At Cassidy's garage/studio Tina Tosca woke slowly, anxious though she couldn't say why. Her coal-black hair covered the pillow and reached all the way down to her waistline in back. Her eyes blinked away the tiredness, the burning. The eyes, beautiful and rare (one green, one blue), moved across Cassidy's form as they lay together on the bed, Cassidy still in his party costume, her own slender body dressed in the burgundy wool evening gown.

The light coming in the window was bright, not the usual halfdark of dawn. She held her breath and listened attentively, with Cassidy's arm resting heavily across the small of her back. There! There it was again! A light static coming from the clock/radio. THE ALARM! She disengaged herself from Cassidy and bounded to the floor, standing akimbo as she frowned at the clock.

"What's wrong babe?" he rasped, startled out of a sound sleep by her quick movement.

"It's almost seven-thirty! Mom's gonna kill me!"

"I set the thing for six like you said. What happened?" he asked, adjusting the twist out of his New Year's costume.

"It just didn't go off, I guess. Boy am I gonna get it!"

"She won't like me any better either. Sorry about that."

She straightened her gown. Slipped into her shoes, cape, and pulled Cassidy along as she headed for the door. "Come on. Maybe we can still beat her home. Maybe she's late."

Running scared, she tripped several times as they headed for the Morris Minor. "Take it easy, Tina. It's too late to do anything about it now."

"Listen, we could say we were checking out the boats in the harbor," she began, then shook her head, knowing her mother would never buy it. "I'm busted. Let's get it over with."

As they approached her house on APS she craned her neck hopefully but was crestfallen as she spotted her mother's car in the carport. "We could say we went to Eller's for coffee and doughnuts. I go there a lot to do my homework."

"Probably closed for New Year's eve."

"Rats!" she answered, despair etched on her face. She hesitated at her mother's car and listened carefully; it was still making the CLICK noises of a warm motor. She placed her hand on the car's hood. "Still warm. She just got home."

Energized at the coming confrontation, Mrs. Tosca sat at the kitchen table and continued to stuff her hair with curlers. As Tina and Cassidy entered she gave them a look that was mild considering the imagined offense. But it was the way she glanced at her daughter, hurt, trust undone, that touched Cassidy. No words at first, just near-tears and the biting of the lips.

"I didn't expect you to pull something like this, Tina. What's the matter with you anyway?"

"We didn't do anything, Mom, honest. You weren't home. We just went to his place to wait for you and we fell asleep."

"That doesn't explain it. You're a minor. Only seventeen years old. You should be at home at night."

"Mom, I'm the same person I was last night. Please believe me, nothing happened. But even if it did, I'm a person just like you. You stay all night at Chuck's and I don't think any less of you for it."

Feeling somewhat responsible Cassidy sought to ease the situation. "Mrs. Tosca, it wasn't her fault. We got home early enough but I didn't want to leave her up here all alone. But we didn't…"

"My God, Alexander! At your age! You had no right!"

"Ma'am, please listen to me. We went to the KYLIX. We danced then came straight here to wait for you. I give you my word. Nothing else happened."

"Don't you two people understand? It's seven-thirty in the morning!" Mrs. Tosca answered, then tensed as she heard a familiar sound in the distance. "I called your Aunt Celia. I think I hear the Jeep coming."

"Oh Mom, how could you!"

"I needed someone to talk to and she's the only other family we've got."

Tina jumped to her feet and pulled Cassidy toward the door. "Come on, we've got to get out of here! My father's coming!"

"Christ, what am I getting into here. You're terrified of your own father."

"He's a violent person. I know he'll try to…Oh darn! Celia did call him! Quick, this way," she said, and steered Cassidy to a hiding place as the Jeep powered up the driveway.

Reuben 'Padro' Tosca's face worked into an ugly scowl as he approached the Tosca house. Watching his own father, the Sergeant-Major, all those years, he had learned his lesson well. 'Scowl first', the Sergeant-Major had told him, lowering his head, staring malevolently. Padro remembered those macho eyes, the eyes of a harsh powerful man. 'Make them fear you. Let them know that in fucking with you they have done the wrong thing. Then strike if you must,' he hissed, holding the boy Reuben with his cruel stare, chuckling as he tousled the hair of his ten year old son.

"You're gonna be one sorry *gringo*," Padro mumbled to himself as he drew near the house. "No old man is gonna fool around with my little girl and get away with it."

Some thirty minutes had passed since the phone call had ruined his breakfast. A frantic call from his sister Celia. Family trouble. Time to close ranks.

The camouflaged Jeep screamed its way up and came to a stop bare inches from the big picture window. Another lesson from the Sergeant-Major; worry them to death and then tell them what they must do to retain your affection. Padro pursed his lips as Mrs. Tosca sat open-mouthed, expecting the window to shatter. She watched him bound energetically from the Jeep and swagger through the kitchen door, his large shaved head glistening with sweat.

"I'd prefer you to ring the doorbell or at least knock," she scolded, dreading the defiant reaction she knew would follow, yet determined to defend her rights.

"I built this god-damn house, woman! You like bells all that much have at it. Now, what's all this bullshit about my daughter?" he demanded, thick black moustache thrust forth in a brazen stare.

"I've already taken care of it. Sorry Celia bothered you," she answered, hoping to defuse the situation.

"No shit. Tina's sleeping with a guy who's older than I am and you're sorry Celia mentioned it? Boy, you are one beaut, Marta."

"She did not sleep with him! Anyway, I spoke to them and it won't happen again."

"Better believe it, Toots. Why you tryin' to protect this jerk? You doin' him too?"

"How dare you talk to me that way! Get out of my house!" she shouted, face ashen, body stiff as she tried to block his way into the other rooms.

He brushed by her. Opened closet doors. Looked behind and under furniture. "I don't want my little girl out with any old man! Where you hiding this guy?" he demanded, head tilted back, mean black eyes insisting on an answer.

"He's not here. They went to breakfast with friends. I want you to leave, Padro. Go away, please."

"No way, girl. If that *puta* is here I'm gonna find him," he answered, scattering the contents of a closet on the floor. "That girl is vulnerable and somebody's got to look out for her. Frankly, you're not doin' too good a job."

"Reuben Tosca, that's ridiculous! If it wasn't for you…"

"That's what you say, bitch!" he shouted, and continued to tear his way through the house. "You and that jerk Green have been loadin' off on me for too long! Fuck you and the horse you rode in on!"

She realized it was a useless argument; he had refused to accept any blame before. Her calm returned. She went to the kitchen and sat down. "I'm not going to discuss it with you again, Padro," she said, feigning indifference.

A mocking sneer spread across his face and his voice was singsong as he imitated her last statement. "Okay, don't. But you tell this guy to move on, Marta, or I'm gonna fix his ass. I ain't kiddin' Marta and you know it."

"Will you leave now?" she asked, weary of him.

"Sure. Goin' right now, sweetheart," he chuckled. "But don't be callin' me up every time your plumbing gets stopped up, unless of course you want me to do your pipes."

"I don't need you anymore! Get out!" she shouted, and he threw up his arms in mock fear and backed away. "And don't come back or I'll tell Mr. Green!"

"You and Green can both kiss my ass," he flung over his shoulder, and peered around the corner of the house one last time, hoping to catch sight of Cassidy. Then he got into the Jeep and started the motor. "See you later, Toots."

She was completely unglued now and the tears came freely as she ran to the door. "You're an animal, just like your father! Just an animal!" she screamed as the Jeep started down the driveway, his laughter mocking her over the sound of the motor.

She sobbed and wiped her nose. She realized the danger of the incident. She went to the telephone and dialed Green's number.

Over in the neighbor's yard Cassidy and Tina heard the Jeep's departure with relief. The Thompsons, due back from Vegas on Tuesday, would never know that their humble tool shed had maybe saved a life. As they entered the house Mrs. Tosca was in the midst of cleaning up the mess Padro had made.

"Oh, Mom, what did he do this time?"

"Gave me a lot of abuse. The usual."

"Did he hit you, Ma'am?" Cassidy enquired.

"No," she answered, and fixed him with an accusatory stare that made him hesitate.

"We'll finish up, Mom. Why don't you lie down and rest."

"All right," she agreed, and sobbed as she left the room.

"Ohhhh! He's such an awful person!" Tosca said, gritting her teeth.

"Does that happen very often? Your father, I mean."

"Oh God no. He only comes when we ask him to fix the roof, or the electric or plumbing, something we can't afford to get fixed. Couldn't you tell? Mom's terrified of him."

"Don't call him anymore. I'll help out."

"We'll see what happens," she answered, then excused herself as her mother called her.

Cassidy continued to put things in order as Tosca talked with her mother. He knew the talk was about him. He wasn't pleased by this. Since the divorce his life had been simple, low-keyed. He wondered what he might be getting into with this troubled family.

"Mom called Angus Green," Tina informed him on her return. "He wants to talk to you."

"Who is Angus Green? Why should I talk to him?"

"He's my father's parole officer. That is, he was."

"Parole officer? Jesus Christ, Tosca. Well I don't know. What do you think?"

"I think it's a good idea. If you're interested…"

"Okay. Walk me to the car?"

She approached and wrapped her arms around his waist. "*Niña*. Call me N*iña*."

"Okay, N*iña*. What does it mean?"

"Little girl. Little lady."

"Mmmmm, I like it. *Niña* Tosca. So, how do I find this Angus Green?"

"Here. Mom wrote the directions."

Cassidy took the sheet of paper and checked it out. Then he asked what were her plans for the rest of the day.

"Tradition. New Year's day dinner with mom and Aunt Celia. Want to come along?" she asked jokingly.

"I've had enough hassle from the Tosca family for one day, thank you. But you could go for a boat ride with me if you like. Back before dinner time."

"That might be a trip. Whose boat?"

"The abalone boat I work on. Belongs to my friend Bair."

"Why do you call him Bear?"

"He looks like one. Walks like one. And that's his real name. B-A-I-R. Funny old guy. Still dives in one of those huge bronze helmets that bolt to a rubber suit."

"Are you a diver too?"

"No way. Bair keeps threatening to retire and give me the business but I just want to write stories." He started the motor then looked back up to her house. "You gonna be all right up there?"

"Oh sure. Mom's usually very mellow. Padro is about as upset as she ever gets."

"Okay, I'll pick you up at nine-thirty. Bring a jacket. It really gets chilly out there," he advised, and gave her a casual kiss. But for her the kiss was super-charged. Her eyes reeled as she tried to focus on him.

"Some date, huh. I hate to let you go, Alexander. I'm not finished with you yet."

"Me neither." He withdrew his hand from her and put the car in gear. "Take care, *Niña*. I'll see you at nine-thirty."

After a short drive Cassidy eased into the carport at #140. The cantilevered house was supported on tinker toy struts anchored into the steep hillside, and it made him queasy as he eased the Morris Minor out over what was a dead drop to the canyon below. He set the emergency brake, made sure the gear was in reverse, then opened the car door and got out carefully.

He made his way to the front door, pausing to check out the neighborhood. All middle class structures, each different than its neighbor and newly built. A wildfire had ravaged the area recently and some of the houses had not yet been rebuilt, their ruined fireplace and blackened metal appliances still standing upright.

Angus Green was a Scotsman with quick blue eyes, busy hands, red hair and pink skin to match. There was no mistaking the athlete in him as he moved to welcome Cassidy; chin high, chest out, one of those thick-legged roosters who confront rather than greet. He extended a handshake while still ten feet distant. "I like the red hat, Mr. Cassidy. Come in."

"A pleasure to meet you, Mr. Green. The Toscas talk a lot about you."

"Yeah, they're good people, and that's why I wanted to talk to you. Sit," he said, and fell into an easy chair.

Cassidy could see that he was a physical powerhouse. His face was thick and sat on a solid wide neck, the jaw massive. His blue eyes bored into Cassidy with purpose. "Do you have any idea what you're getting into? Have they told you about Padro Tosca?"

"No, this was my first date with Tina. I mean, I knew her before at the Greek restaurant but this is the first time we got one on one."

"Do you intend to see her again?"

"Probably. We like each other pretty well."

"Be careful Mr. Cassidy, she's still a minor. I advise you to back off."

"How come? Hey, we didn't do anything. Her mother never came home last night but we played it cool. Nothing happened."

"I believe you. Okay, here's our problem. Padro is…let's just call it over-protective of his daughter. Also he has killed men. He's not a person you want to get roiled needlessly."

Cassidy was shocked by what Green had just told him matter-of-factly. It occurred to him that this killer had been looking for him less than an hour ago, and not to shake his hand in friendship either. "Well who'd he kill, and why?"

"Padro was a client of mine in the California penal system. I was his parole officer and I'm not going to talk about that. But what you need to know is that he was a soldier in Brigade #2506 when he was only 13 years old. At the Bay of Pigs he was credited with killing some 100 of Castro's soldiers, Mr. Cassidy."

Green waited for a reaction but Cassidy found it difficult to absorb what he had just been told. He wondered if it was all right for patriots to do wholesale slaughter. But for Padro the Bay of Pigs had not been a noble cause, Green continued. It had been vengeance pure and simple. Padro's users (the CIA and the Cuban Revolutionary Council) were glad to have him aboard despite his tender age. The call to arms had not been embraced eagerly by the bulk of the refugees in Miami so each one was valuable, especially the teenage boys who made the best soldiers. Sergeant-Major Felix Amado Tosca, Padro's father, had been a much decorated soldier in Fulgencio Battista's army; a soldier who had switched sides to fight for Fidel Castro and liberacion. A national hero. He was also a fascist who got very pissed off when Fidel finally admitted that he was a communist. Disillusioned, he was shot and killed when he tried to escape from Cuba. In those early days of fever-pitch nationalism his corpse was spit on, pissed on, then dragged behind an army truck to the Zapata Swamp (the future site of the Bay of Pigs), where it was left for the wild animals and insects. Though the boy Padro had little love for his father the manner of his death had damaged his pride and traumatized him for all time. The event had made him his father's son.

"Hey, Mr. Green, I don't know about all that stuff. I mean, the girl and I just went folk dancing! That was it! Just dancing! And here you are tryin' to scare the hell out of me with this Rambo shit and dying! What's that got to do with me and this girl?"

"Everything, Mr. Cassidy. This man is very abnormal and still super-angry. So much so that the CIA shipped him out here to keep him away from the volatile Cuban community in Florida. He's like one of those stupid pit bulls that don't know when to quit. That makes him very dangerous and he's not just full of hot air either."

"What are you really saying? What do you want me to do?"

"Give her up. You're too old for her anyway."

Cassidy thought about it. He realized that the man who sat there trying to stare him down was just trying to resolve a dicey situation, both for him and the Tosca family. He got to his feet abruptly and stuck out his hand. "Good to meet you, Mr. Green."

"Likewise. Call me if the need arises."

Green watched as Cassidy backed the car out into the street and took off down the hill. "Rambo indeed," he mumbled to himself and looked over the deck handrail, down to the peaceful canyon of chapparal and pine trees. He hadn't even mentioned the good part. The part where the boy Padro had grabbed several abandoned AK47 rifles and bandoliers, then fled from the surrender at Giron Beach. To die fighting. To harass Fidel Castro from the very swamp where the militia had previously dumped the Sergeant-Major's body.

Alone, Padro had struck out through the snake-infested swamp and had paralleled the Playa Larga Road, the only road through that part of the swamp. After several hours of fighting the insects and his own fears he came to a bend in the road and ducked for cover. The victorious Castro forces (vehicle after vehicle) were strung out on the road, resting, savoring the end of hostilities. Brigade #2506 had fought them savagely, killing and wounding 3650 while only 500 of their own number fell. It was the perfect time and place for Padro's revenge of his father.

He crept along in the muck for the exact spot from which to attack. He went sprawling as he tripped over something large and metallic. He felt around until his hands closed on a mortar which had been abandoned in the final retreat of Oliva's Second Battalion. Alongside were a half-dozen phosphorous shells which he laid beside the AK47 rifles and bandoliers.

His attack took the resting Castro soldiers by surprise. An ammunition truck blew up. Scores of soldiers ran from the white hot mortar bursts and fell in agony by the roadside, their bodies smoking from the phosphorescent shrapnel. Soldiers and foliage were chopped to pieces by the rifle fire, the chaotic scene a smoking hell. The thirteen year old son of the Sergeant-Major had gotten his revenge. He had slaughtered more than a hundred before falling himself with multiple wounds.

"Angus, should I start breakfast now?" his wife called to him.

"Yeah, I'm ready," he answered, and spit over the deck rail, watching the spittle drift and plunge in the slipstream of the deep canyon.

CHAPTER 2

▼

Cassidy drove to the marina to prepare the boat for diving. Other than the trouble with Tosca's father this had the makings of a perfect day, sunny and warm, the distant foothills of the Los Padres National Forest half-shrouded in the hazy morning colour of an impressionist painting.

He recounted the unbelievable happenings of the last 21 hours as he drove. All in 21 wonderful hours! It had started at his writing table.

He had been feeling good about things though he was working on New Year's Eve day, and it was a typical southern California day outside; 'where the sun shines like a fool every day and each blue wave lisps', Edmund Wilson had once griped while trying to write a novel in the Santa Barbara environment. Pretty tough place for a down-and-out writer to get anything done, amid such luxury.

Rising early, Cassidy had spent the quiet hours powering away on his most recent novel, the true life adventures of the famous smuggler, Simon Lindero. He had become fond of Simon, admiring him despite his illegal activities. This in turn made the work easier, made it fun.

At half past the noon hour he moved away from the big table and toward the electric hotplate; time for his noon fix. He poured from the discoloured glass coffee pot then sipped loudly to avoid burning his lips. He removed the gold wire glasses and hung them on the lamp of his writing table, then sat on the bed and slipped into white cotton pants and blouse-shirt, the loose fitting east-India type that some mellow people still wear on the west coast (though the renaissance of the sixties and early seventies was past history as far as Cassidy could tell).

He began his daily vigil for the postman; possibly some news from his publisher or an interested agent, all too silent of late. He sipped from the coffee again and stretched out to gaze up the street.

"Okay," he mumbled, and moved to curbside as the red white and blue vehicle approached, a mailbox at a time. He was the only one on the street, the only anxious one, it seemed. But the postman just waved in passing, and shouted, "Nothing, Alexander. Hey, maybe in the new year, huh."

"Have a goodun, Paul," Cassidy replied, and started back to his studio to continue dressing. "So it goes. So it goes."

Ordinarily Cassidy did most of his research in the library at University of California Santa Barbara, but today he could get by with the town library. He just wasn't in the mood to drive ten miles to Isla Vista where the university was located. The young clerk at the periodical desk looked up as Cassidy inquired, "PUBLISHER'S WEEKLY...it's not on the rack."

"No sir, we don't have it here yet. Staff gets it first. Try the upstairs desk."

As he moved through the building Cassidy couldn't help being aware of the fabled beauties of Santa Barbara. Six females for every male, he had heard the figure quoted, and he believed it. The beaches, Stearns Wharf, the harbor, the bike path across West and East beaches, all were crowded with the lovely joggers, bicycle riders, skaters, lovers, mothers with their baby strollers and other children. Many of the beauties were from Los Angeles it was said; overflow from the film industry. He approached the reference desk which was being attended by one of those rejects at the moment. "PUBLISHER'S WEEKLY?"

"Just a moment," the librarian answered, and slid off the stool.

He watched her move gracefully away until she was out of sight, then switched his attention elsewhere. Lovely ladies everywhere he looked. It had been five months since Dominique; a long five months since he had last rolled a nipple between tooth and tongue. "Jesus! They just keep comin' on!" he whispered.

"Here it is, Sir. But stay close if you will. Staff hasn't finished with it yet."

"Right," Cassidy answered, and moved toward one of the table ensembles, the type equipped with headphone jacks for listening to tapes and records. He began to page through the magazine.

At the same time he scanned the area furtively, hoping to see a familiar female face. 'It's got to be the weather', he thought, concerned about his lack of concentration.

"Hey! That girl from the KYLIX," he whispered excitedly, straining to look down through the balusters at Tina Tosca, a very young dancing acquaintance of his. Clutching an LP and a portable turntable, she walked up the stair but did not see him wave to her.

"Oh my God," he sighed. "To be so encunted I can't even imagine. Damn, she is handsome."

But on this girl it was the eyes which were outstanding. Large, unguarded, one green and one blue. A bewildering experience, like being hypnotized, looking from one eye to the other and back again, unable to stop staring and being embarrassed by it.

He stared at her figure as she passed, eyes intent on the LP jacket. He heard the swish of her dress, toes pointed slightly inward, knees held chastely together as though trustee for something precious. She seemed almost innocent though she surely must have had some experience; a handsome California girl in her prime, how could one expect innocence.

His mind remained fixed on her even as she disappeared from view. He had watched that graceful body in motion hundreds of times as she danced at KYLIX, the Greek taberna where they were both habitués. Something special always seemed to pass between them but he had managed to keep himself in check thus far, considerate of the sizable age difference between them.

Oh well. He redirected his attention to the book reviews. His sister had called yesterday to alert him to a new book, one which had as its protagonist a smuggler much like his Simon Lindero. He read the review then relaxed when assured that Simon was still fresh material. At the same time he felt a slight sensation at his left shoulder. He used his peripheral sight, expecting to see a moth, a fly perhaps. Maybe it was only a sound. Nothing there. He continued to read. There it was again, definite this time and accompanied by a 'psssttt'.

Tina Tosca had recognized him and had taken the listening chair three feet in back of his own. The headphones were plugged in and her disparate eyes were aglow. She gestured to the spinning record and leaned forward. "Hey, want to hear something profound?" she said softly.

Cassidy swivelled his chair around, stopped the turntable and read the label, Beethoven's magnificent Ninth, music he had heard many times before and was fond of. "Sure," he answered, and shoved his chair back against her own. "Don't believe I know this one," he lied, placing the headphones on. He nodded a signal to her. She flipped the switch and leaned back to watch, a smile of expectation on her face. Alexander Cassidy was in for a mind-blow and she, Tina Tosca, was the discoverer, the giver. How perfect!

They shared the first movement of the piece. She watched his face for the emotional signs. He gave them to her on schedule. The awe, the swelling passion of the first movement, the sweetness and joy of the second, almost too much for him to bear along with the closeness and the sensuality of her watching eyes. It was the most delicious game he could remember ever having played with anyone. *Christ, what a face,* he thought as she responded with a range of emotion to match his own. He would enjoy all four movements of this performance, he was certain.

Midway through the adagio she began to leaf through the notebook on her lap. The immediacy of her discovery had dissipated. Periodically she glanced up to make sure he was still enraptured, then satisfied, continued to read from her notebook. That was fine with him, sitting close enough to touch knees and smell her, closer than he had ever been except in the line of dancers at KYLIX. But that was always impersonal what with thirty or forty dancers, the music and crowd noise. Here now, singly, he felt the heat of her body, smelled the earthiness she exuded in close quarters.

She was different than the others of the California melting pot. Not pale and stick-like as were the models of VOGUE and COSMO, but handsome and strong like the peasant girls of Raphael's paintings. Yet, thankfully due to her young age and inexperience she had not yet developed the haughty indifference for which those ladies had been famous. She was slender and small breasted, had long black hair, prominent cheekbones and straight white teeth. A sensual girl, he thought as he removed the headset and handed it back to her. "Wheeew, Jesus!" he thanked her, then basked in her gaze.

"Nice, huh?"

"Yeah. Thanks for sharing it with me."

"Sure," she replied, and squinted at the several magazines on his lap. "What are you reading?"

"Trade magazines. I came to research an article," he said, and showed her the cover of the top magazine.

"UNDERWATER? I never heard of it."

"It's a monthly. Travel glossy with photos," Cassidy explained.

"Are you a writer or a photographer?"

"Writer."

"Ever published anything?" she pushed on.

"Yeah. Poetry, a few articles. A novel which lost money."

"I'd like to read the novel sometime."

"Okay, if I can find it. It's in storage somewhere."

"Hmmm. Well, I better go."

She seemed to turn shy now that the incident had bottomed out. She gathered her notebook and purse and slid the recording back into its jacket. Cassidy wanted to prolong the encounter but only if it could be accomplished gracefully. He was conscious of the age difference and didn't want to scare her away. "I've missed you at KYLIX lately," he offered.

"Yeah, I've been jamming. I want to keep focused so I can get into UCSB when the time comes."

"Great. Just so you don't quit dancing. I enjoy watching you. A lot of people dance like truck drivers. You're very good."

"People are all different, you know," she answered, then changed the subject. "You're a boat person, aren't you? I mean, I've heard you live on a boat."

"Not at the moment. My boat's in storage down at Newport. But maybe I can treat you to a sail if I ever bring it up here."

"I'd like that. My mom likes boat people. We were talking about you once."

"Oh? I'd like to meet her. Invite me up sometime."

"I don't know about that. She's already got a boyfriend," she answered somewhat testily.

"Sorry, I didn't mean it that way."

A faint smile returned to her face. "Are you going to KYLIX tonight?" she enquired.

"Absolutely. How about you?"

The question brought a change in her mood. She glanced down at her feet and answered dejectedly. "I haven't got the twenty-five dollars. Neither has mom."

"How about your boyfriend? What's his name?"

"Oh, you mean Mark. No, we broke up a month ago. He's got a new girl-friend now."

Cassidy felt sorry for her. He got an idea but it stuck in his throat as he tried to give it voice. "I…uh…You could be my guest if you like. You know, no strings attached."

"Really? You don't have a date?"

"No, and I'd like to share with you. Pay you back for Beethoven."

"Aaallll right!" She reacted beautifully. Her smile, her eyes, everything radiated pleasure. "What time do you want to pick me up?" she asked, writing her address down, handing it to him.

"Seven-thirty," he winked at her. See how clever I am. I'll get to meet your mother after all."

"That's okay by me." She seemed embarrassed now that they had concluded. Palms turned upward, she shrugged. "Hey, I really appreciate this, you know.' My New Year's was gonna be pretty miserable."

"Great. Your turn next time," he said as she turned and walked away. But that had all happened yesterday and Cassidy tried to focus on the present as he drove past the marina parking attendant and exchanged New Year greetings. It was time to go to work.

He snapped a look at his watch, then approached the SANDSPIT CAFE and ordered a takeout coffee. He had missed his usual what with he and Tosca oversleeping and the ruckus with Padro. He sat on the concrete breakwater and sipped from the plastic cup. 'Damn, that hits the spot', he thought, and watched the early risers and late party people stroll along the breakwater. He tried to get his mind on Bair and abalone but his thoughts kept returning to Tosca and their New Year's eve date. He could think of nothing else.

Having had the fantastic experience at the library there was no way that Cassidy could get back to Simon Lindero and the story though he had spent the rest of the day trying. As party time approached he stood before the mirror in a shirt-frock and tights of renaissance design, cinched it at the waist with a leather thong, and topped it off with the ever present cap of red velvet. This night was special so he made an extra careful appraisal of what he saw. Five-ten, 165 pounds, healthy, strong; prominent nose, high cheekbones, long jaw framed by the shoulder length sun-bleached hair. No loose ends. He smiled at his mirror image, slipped on the gold wire glasses and Macedonian dancing shoes. He had then turned out the light and left to pick up Tina Tosca.

New Year's eve, like the day, had been clear if colder. Not knowing the layout of her house he parked on the street down below and began to walk the many steps upward as he pondered just what her parents' reaction might be to him. The firing squad probably, although he had no experience on which to base the premise. But he sighed away that troublesome spectre as he gripped the brass lion door knocker and rapped it stoutly.

The woman who opened the door was surprised by his costume and startled by his apparent age. It seemed that Tina hadn't mentioned it to her.

"Hi, I'm Alexander Cassidy."

"Yes, I'm Marta Tosca, Tina's mother. Come in." She paused to look him over, then said, "What a great costume."

"Thank you. My daughter helped me make it."

She observed him closely. Checked out his open pores and crow's feet, her slackened jaw hanging open till, embarrassed, she closed it with a silent chomp.

She watched him move into the room, hoping for a limp, a lump, any sign of approaching infirmity. Mother had not felt good about his health and surety. "She'll be ready in a minute. Have a seat."

He had settled on the sofa and glanced around for the signs which revealed something of the people who lived there. The stucco house was ranch style with large windows and deep overhangs. The combination of limpid pastel colours, wall-to-wall carpet and bland furnishings told him they were not style oriented people. He had somehow expected brilliant colour and wild undisciplined pattern from California Cubans. "Nice house," he offered.

"Thank you. We're comfortable here. So, you and Tina are going to the KYLIX?"

"Yes Ma'am. I haven't missed a New Year's eve since the place opened." Cassidy noticed she was still in housecoat and curlers so he gave in to a sympathetic impulse. "You and Mr. Tosca are welcome to go along if you like."

"Mr. Tosca and I are divorced, but thank you anyway. I'll be going out later."

As the conversation lagged Cassidy picked up a young Siamese cat which had been sniffing at his ankles. It nosed into the crook of his arm and began to suck hungrily at the skin, causing him to squirm, scratch, and draw the arm out of reach.

"Behave, Sam!" Mrs. Tosca had scolded, then offered an explanation. "She was weaned too early. The veterinarian says she'll need that all her life. Poor Sam."

Cassidy continued to pet 'poor Sam' until Tina Tosca entered the room. She looked breathtaking in a long evening gown of featherweight wool, burgundy in colour. The scalloped neckline accentuated her olive skin, and the long black hair was gathered in a tiered topknot and tethered by circlets of faux pearls. Draped over her shoulders was a cape of black silk, fastened at the neck with a brooch of jet and silver.

"Hi, Alexander," she flirted, savoring his reaction. Then she became aware of his costume. "WOW!" she exclaimed, curtsying. "My prince!"

"I have to say," Mrs. Tosca joined in, "you guys look pretty darn impressive."

"Thank you, Mom. Well, are we ready?"

"Let's go," Cassidy said, and followed the two of them to the door.

"Be good now. Have a nice time and a Happy New Year."

Outside, walking to the car, Cassidy had not been able to take his eyes off her. She was totally the boss. The fragrance, the presence. He knew he would have to restrain himself with her.

"Tina, I have to tell you…I've never in my life seen a more handsome girl."

"Yeah? *Te gusta?*"

"What does that mean?"

"It means...You like?"

"*Te gusta?* Yes! And that gown, it looks so expensive."

"I got it at STELLA'S THRIFT STORE. We're pretty broke, mom and I both."

"Hey, everything I own right now comes from a thrift store. Speaking of which...now don't laugh," Cassidy said, and bowing to the waist with a mocking flair before his old OLD British car (a mustard yellow Morris Minor) he walked around to the driver's side and reached across to open the door on the passenger's side. "The lock doesn't work," he apologized, and took pleasure from her amused appraisal of the car, a basket case.

"I think I gave your mom quite a shock" he said, as they drove away.

"The costume, or what?"

"No, my age. She really checked me out while I was waiting for you."

"She wasn't rude or anything?"

"Oh no. She seems to be a very pleasant person."

"Good. That would have been an awful way to start the new year."

The KYLIX was a genuine Greek taberna patterned after those in the PLAKA, the night club section of Athens which caters to the tourists. For this celebration the KYLIX was decked out with a huge Christmas tree, ceiling swags of crepe paper, strings of blinking coloured lights and a hundred gay baloons.

Tall moustachioed and charismatic, Satyri Papanikolas, the owner of KYLIX, was at the head of a line of dancers. For this celebration he had dressed in a *fustonello*, the white wool tights and blouse-shirt of the Greek soldier. The *fustonello* was topped off by a magnificent red velvet jacket embroidered in gold. Worn as a cape, the winged sleeves of this garment flew behind him like an array of pennants as he danced. A red fez-like hat perched on his head and his red dancing shoes had a black wool tuft fastened at the toes. He was a happy Greek, whirling in tight circles, leaping high in the air to slap at his shoe and holler OPA!, the Greek equivalent of OLÉ or YAHOO.

Tina and Cassidy had been assigned places at the big table by the dance floor, the one always reserved for regular dancers. Also there was Satyri Papanikolas II, a beautiful blond boy of eight who was the only child of his father.

Tina had just returned from the ladies room when Satyri got his first look at her. "Tosca! *Agape mou*!," he had moaned, at the same time twirling at a furious pace the worry beads that Greek men twirl around their index finger to emphasize certain emotional feelings. He backed off and stared at her in approval while duplicating the shape of her body with his hands and mumbling unmistakable eroticisms in the Greek language.

"Hey, Alexandros, sonofabitch! Now you're gettin' smart! I approve," the Greek had responded and walked away.

"I didn't know he was that stuck on you," Cassidy chided her.

"Greek men don't get stuck on any one girl. They want us all."

"Looking the way you do tonight I can't blame him. Hey, I like the way he calls you *Tosca*. It's got style. Tina is too light for you."

She agreed with the comment. Tosca was her favorite opera. It had been easy for the troubled young Tina to suspend belief and identify with the tragic heroine. "Call me Tosca", she had invited him.

Her directness, the red fire of the votive candle reflecting on her face, and their special intimacy had been interrupted by Satyri from the dance floor, his voice booming into the microphone.

"Folks, I need to say a few things about tonight's program. In a few minutes our belly dancer will come out to entertain you. Her name is Yasmina, she's the best in town. I guarantee you'll love this girl. Then my son," he gestured toward little Satyri, "will do us a table dance. It's his first try. He's just starting."

The crowd had applauded as the boy hid his head under his arms, terribly embarrassed. "Okay, then I'm going to do my world-famous table dance for you. That should take us up to midnight. Now you see that handsome guy standing by the plates at the bar? That's my younger brother. Take a bow, Yorgos! OPA!"

Yorgos waved his hands at the customers then unleashed a spirited exchange in the Greek language with his brother which amused the crowd.

"Okay. Yorgos will see that everybody gets a plate. Everybody gets to throw a plate at midnight. It's included in the cover charge so don't be shy. It's a Greek custom, a KYLIX custom. You'll have good luck in the new year if you smash all the old plates at midnight and buy new ones next day. So we'll blow a siren at midnight and you throw the plates out on the dance floor. For all you timid guys who never smashed a thing in your life I'll show you how we do it in Athens."

He instructed them in the art of plate smashing then it was time for Yasmina. Dressed in exotic costume, driven by wild discordant music, she whirled, shimmied and glided from one table to the next to accept a gratuity from the patrons seated there. Perhaps a dollar bill tucked into bra or waistband, sometimes ten or twenty singles scattered like confetti over her head and shoulders.

But even as Yasmina concluded her dance and was still acknowledging the tumultuous applause little Satyri could no longer wait. He came up behind his father and tugged sheepishly at the tail of his *fustonello*, causing the patrons to roar their approval and his father to grin with pride as he took hold of the microphone.

"He wants the table! He wants to dance! OPA Satyri, here we go!"

The band started to play and father and son approached a tiny table all decked out in its own checkered tablecloth. The boy bent low and chewed around for a good bite on the corner of the table while his father gripped one of the table legs to assist him in the lift. The patrons were supportive as father and son walked the perimeter of the dance floor together, the table sinking lower and lower until it finally scraped against the floor. But the boy heard the applause, smiled bashfully then clapped his own hands in response to their's.

"Too heavy for the first time. You have to build the neck muscles, you know. We'll get it the next time," the Greek promised, and the patrons quieted expectantly.

"Okay, time for the big event. I'm gonna do my table dance for you. Hey, you know how lucky you are? I mean, over at the BILTMORE or FESS PARKER's you know what they do for New Year's? They get these stupid little paper horns and hats, you know, and they go toot toot and throw paper confetti up in the air, right. You guys get to throw plates. Smash stuff. (looks at watch) Okay, I'm gonna do the table dance, then in five minutes you can smash the plates. But give me a chance to get off the dance floor first. Last year I got seven stitches in my arm. Aaaalllll right! Here we go! OPA!"

He snapped his fingers in cadence as the bouzouki and clarinet began their wail. The patrons clapped in unison and he danced a circle around the dance floor before stopping at an unoccupied table. He dropped to his knees, gripped a corner of the table in his teeth and rose with it held firmly in place, arms outstretched to each side for balance, then whirled in a tight spin at the center of the dance floor. He danced several more turns around the perimeter of the dance floor then dropped to his knees and relinquished his bite on the corner of the table.

Now he danced away to a second table piled high with dinner plates, wine bottles and glasses. He picked this table up as he had done the first one, danced it over and deposited it on top of the first one. Straining, ever so careful, he had then lifted both tables as one and repeated the dance routine. The patrons went wild over Satyri Papanikolas, 'the greatest table dancer in the world' as he circled the dance floor with two tables and contents clamped in his jaws, barely brushing against the ceiling light shades with the tables, pushing his luck to the limit at all times.

The music stopped and Satyri eased down to his knees to disgorge the load. And not a moment too soon. The siren blasted out its New Year greeting, forcing Satyri to duck to one side, barely averting with his upraised hand the first of a hundred or so dinner plates which rained down on the two dinner tables left standing in the middle of the dance floor.

It took ten minutes for the plate smashing, noise makers, kissing, groping, and auld lang syne to subside. Tosca and Cassidy were barely aware of the chaos: they had turned inward to each other. He helped her up from the chair and held her close. At first hesitant, she then eased up as her shyness and inexperience melted away.

"Happy New Year, Tosca."

"You too," she had answered.

Their lips came together in a searching, eager kiss, and the background noises faded away as the power of the kiss mushroomed. And then someone was tugging at her, drawing her away from Cassidy. It was the Greek, come for his New Year kiss. He smothered her with it. Her arms flailed helplessly as she tried to catch her breath. "Happy New Year, kid," Satyri offered.

"You too," she grinned, happy about all the attention coming her way tonight.

"Alexandros..." With the single word Satyri embraced him in a bear hug. "Hey, Mr. Writer, this is going to be the year for you, eh. Some movie producer to give you a million, huh?"

"I hope you're right, Greco. And may this be a year of even greater prosperity for you. If you can keep from getting married again, that is."

"No way. Four times is enough for Satyri, better believe it. Hey, gotta find my kid. It's his bedtime. Gotta be on the plane for Philly at seven a.m.".

"You'd think Erica'd let you have him a day longer, it being the holiday season."

"Naw, she loves to put the screws to me. But that's all right. I get to see my parents while I'm back there."

"When you coming back?" Tosca enquired.

"Three, four days. Hey, don't you worry, Tosca. They don't make 'em like you back there. I'll be back," he said, and gave her a big hug.

"Have a good trip, Boss, and give my regards to your folks," Cassidy added.

After Satyri left them Alexander led her to the dance floor where the musicians, set up in the middle with all the broken plates around them, played romantic couples music. Their bodies were warm and intimate as they danced, or rather, swayed from side to side to avoid stepping on the broken plates. Her slimness, her silent yielding, felt wonderful to him. They looked deeply into each other and Cassidy was enthralled by her half-closed eyes of green and blue.

On leaving KYLIX they had parked in the turnaround on APS, overlooking the old mission grounds where a goodly number of revelers had gathered to celebrate the New Year.

Tosca learned of his boyhood home in old Newport Beach (before the upwardly mobile hogged it down with one rapacious contraction of the uvula). He told her of the sailing trophies he and his father had won on Beer Can Thursdays, and later on his acceptance in the Travelling Classics Program at UC Santa Barbara, with diplomatic passport and field trips to such places as Thira, Mycenae and Knossos. He in turn applauded her work in the Junior Theater Project working with underprivileged talented children, and he relished her copping the coveted role of Juliet at Santa Barbara High in her senior year there.

Though the turnaround was fairly secluded they had sat apart at first but soon reached that magic stage of touch, kiss, fantasy, where their undergarments became warmly moist. But they decided to play it cool, so Cassidy fired up the Morris Minor and drove the short distance to her house.

By the time they parked in the carport it was after 2a.m. and the house was dark. "I guess your mom's already in bed. I hope she won't be mad because of the time'."

"Her car's not here. She won't come home till morning."

"How do you know that?"

"She's got a boyfriend. If she's not home by 1:30 she always stays till morning."

"Well Jesus, I can't just dump you here all alone. What if something should happen to you. Hey, let's go down to my place. I promise I'll behave."

"Okay. As long as I get home before she does."

As they drove to his studio they used the time to get better acquainted. "So what do you want to do when you graduate, Tosca?"

"Interpreter, I guess, though what I truly love is mime theater," she answered, then enquired of him, "You and Satyri are such great friends. How did you meet him?"

"I used to freelance for the NEWS PRESS. I was going down to the harbor one day to interview a famous sailor, a circumnavigator. As I passed by the KYLIX those murals on the windows blew me away so I stopped. I pressed my face against the glass, curious as to what was inside. I heard some wild music and caught a glimpse of something big and fast moving around so I went inside."

In the telling, Cassidy's face reflected the excitement he felt at first glimpse of Satyri Papanikolas. Thinking himself alone, long arms outstretched like the wings of a giant bird, the dancing Greek literally sprang from one spot to another on the dance floor, driven along by the wild Macedonian music which blared forth from a recording. Unnoticed, Cassidy had settled back into the muralled background, eyes fixed on the bounding dancer, but Satyri spotted him eventually and moved in his direction.

"Hey, we're not open, okay. Come back at six o'clock," Satyri had said, annoyed, and pushed the coal black hair out of his eyes.

"I didn't mean to intrude. What kind of a place is this? How long have you been open?"

"It's Greek, Mister. A restaurant, a coffee house, a taberna. Wine, beer, ouzo, folk dancing. Come back at six o'clock", he said, and went to the bar for a drink.

"Got menus?"

"End of the bar. Help yourself."

While Cassidy took several minutes to study the menu and the cover picture the Greek sipped wine and watched Cassidy impatiently. "Pretty exotic fare. That you on the cover?"

"Better believe it. Nobody but Papanikolas can do the table like that. Two tables! Come back at six o'clock I'll show you two tables!"

"Interesting place, Mr. Papanikolas. I'd like to write you up."

"What you mean, write me up?"

"I'm a writer. I do feature articles for the local newspaper. You've got an interesting thing going here. A little publicity might help business."

"Yeah? Well it is a little slow right now. Yeah, I could use a little help. Everybody eats Italian or Chinese. Nobody knows about *souvlaki*, or *moussaka*. All they know about Greeks is that Zorba thing, the movie. They never even heard about my table dance. They think I'm nuts when they first see it. Yeah, come back at six. I'll do the table and you can write me up."

"So there you have it, Tosca, one of the luckiest days of my life. I went back with a photographer. I got hooked on Satyri and KYLIX. He got rich, bought up half the block, and hasn't let me spend a nickel there since. A good story, huh?"

"A great story."

"Any more questions while I'm in the mood?"

"Uh huh. Why the red hat and white cotton clothes? You wear them all the time."

He told her the hat was a reaction against the conservative person he had been before the divorce; a badge of his subsequent change. The whites were another badge, a holdover from that time of hope and exuberance when the now-mean-ingless phrase 'Have a nice day' was first used universally, in the jubilance of the nineteen-sixties. Also the whites represented simplicity to him, an innocence of sorts, and he hoped she didn't think that was silly.

As they walked down the stairs in unison she stopped, looked up to him and wished him Happy New Year again. He stooped to brush a kiss against her cheek and as he did so the moment was broken by the shrill song of a mockingbird. Tosca turned away and pointed up toward her house. "That's Bo Diddley. He rats on me. Sings louder to let mom know when I'm coming in or going out."

"Where is he? I can't place the sound."

"The big oak tree. It's his home. He loves it up there."

It was a short drive to his garage/apartment behind KYLIX. The lights were out as they drove up. He unlocked the door, hit the light switch and watched her as she smiled and looked around. "Oh Alexander, I love this place!"

"I knew you would. We're pretty together in our tastes, I think."

"It's wonderful! Kind of like a museum."

"That's no accident, I guess. In my other life art was my passion as well as my profession. These few things are all I have left from that time."

The lights threw eerie shadows on the beamed ceiling and the garage resem-bled a hunting lodge with its hidden corners and clerestory windows. A fireplace, cement floors painted char-brown and accented by oriental rugs; a Brussels tapes-try of deep blue and green colours, gothic in style, gave the place distinction as a sanctum where intimate thought might mature from seed to form.

In front of the tapestry stood a bed of four black spiral columns, each topped by a guardant lion. There was the large work table, disarrayed by reference books and work in progress. Also on the table were a word processor and a janus-headed wig stand painted with familiar likenesses and labelled in gothic letters...RICH-ARD MILLHOUSE BORGIA on the one side, and a neandertal-like cartoon YORGI BOOSH on the other. Cassidy removed his hat and from five feet away threw a ringer onto the wigstand, rocking it precariously for a few moments.

"Whoa!" Tosca said as the wigstand stopped swaying and settled. She studied it for a moment then approached it, rubbing her fingertips against the famous Nixon jowels. "It's been a long time. Shouldn't you forgive him?"

"Oh sure. Hitler and J. Edgar Hoover too. No way Tosca. They're all icons of darkness and we've got to remember what they look like."

"You a Democrat?"

"No."

"Republican?"

"Nope. I'm not innocent enough to be either. I try not to think of anything as ugly as politics and its whores. Change of subject, Tosca. How do you feel about our age difference?"

"I don't think of us as being different, Alexander. We feel the same, you and I. Yeah, like it kinda surprised me."

"I 'm glad you like us together. Isn't it curious, seeing each other a lot at KYLIX but just now coming together as much closer friends."

"Yeah," she had agreed, and edged closer to the writing table to pick up several pages and scan them. Apprehensive, he moved closer.

"Please don't move anything or they'll have to put me in with the loonies."

"Do you like what you're doing here?"

"Love it. It's the one thing in the world I feel special about."

"What are you writing now?"

"A love story."

"Can I be in it?" she asked mischeviously.

Cassidy had grinned as he contemplated his answer. Oh my...could she ever be in his love story! He would give anything to seduce her and maybe discover new material for Simon Lindero. He had been ready with a double-entendre, one she might have taken exception to, so he opted for subtlety instead. "Maybe the next time. This one is too complicated already."

"When can I read the novel? You promised."

"Yeah, I laid it aside for you," he said, rummaging around until he found it. "But it's my only copy and it's out of print so don't lose it."

"I'll protect it with my life."

She remained at the table, preoccupied by the half-dozen B.C.'s grouped together on one corner; an ancient terra cotta statue, several pieces of irridescent Roman glass, a faience vessel from the 18th dynasty in Egypt. "What are these things?"

"Artifacts. I used to have an ancient art gallery. These are the leftovers from when I was that other person."

"Why do you refer to yourself as that other person? Are you not still the same?"

"No I'm not. I had a family, a home, a career. Far different from what you see here. Speaking of which...Anyone ever tell you that you don't talk like other people?"

"Yeah, it's the theater thing. Does it bother you?"

"Yes it does, in a good way. Don't change a thing."

Cassidy stood beside the stereo and put an LP on the spindle. With the soft music as background he took off his shoes and edged up on the bed. Fluffing the pillows he apologized to Tosca who stood by hesitantly. "Sorry, no chairs. It's a basic work studio," he said, offering his hand.

"Will you take it easy?"

He was at first put off by her fear of him, though there were those times in the past when he had been guilty of a subtle seduction. "I promise, Tosca, I'll be cool."

Secure with his promise she had then faced the bed and, feeling the exhilaration of her young years she took several quick steps and hurled herself up onto the bed next to him. As the bed oscillated wildly then settled down she giggled and looked up to him for a reaction. It came as quiet adoration as Cassidy worshipped her with his eyes. Her smile faded as he guided her mouth up to his own. Her body flexed and she moaned as he tickled her lips with his tongue. She had not been kissed with that sensuality for three long years now. Not since…In remembering, her gaze faltered, away from Cassidy, safely away to the other side of the bed.

"How old are you, Tosca?"

"I'll be eighteen in a few months. And you?"

His face serene, distant, Cassidy had stared hard at the beams overhead. He felt like an actor who had been asked the same question before, on some bed or other. His mouth twitched as he continued to watch the ceiling, then he answered in a flat voice. "Thirty-nine."

The only indication that she had heard him was a slight breath sucked in. After a few seconds of silence he turned to look at her. "Well, what do you think?"

"I think…I think you're handsome in your red hat," she replied, managing a mischievious grin.

"I feel handsome in my red hat, Tosca, but that isn't what I asked you."

"I think you're considerate. With you I feel special, not just like another dumb kid. I think…"

"Tosca, what I really want to know…I've never had a friend as young as you before. After New Year's can we still be friends?"

"Yes, I like being with you, Alexander," she said, yawning, rubbing at her eyes.

The yawn caused him to look at the clock; five minutes after 4 a.m. "Jesus, time flies when you're enjoying yourself, doesn't it? Want to take a nap?"

"Yes," she had yawned again and turned over on her side, "but I have to get home before mom does. Set the alarm for six, okay."

"I'll join you. I'm pretty whacked out myself."

He turned down the fireplace a notch and set the alarm. Propped up on one elbow he admired her face as she drifted off to sleep. "Tosca, I really do love to be with you," he said softly, aware that she was barely, if at all, still conscious. But there was another thing he wanted to say. An important thing. Something he hadn't felt since his divorce. "Tosca, I trust you, somehow."

There was no answer. She was asleep, having had too much New Year's celebration. "Tosca?" he made one last try. His hand reached out to touch her cheek but stopped in the middle of its arc. "So it goes," he whispered, and bent close to inhale her scent though careful to not wake her. This was going to be his best New Year in a long time, he thought, and closed his eyes in satisfaction. There wasn't a doubt in his mind about that.

CHAPTER 3

▼

Tosca watched as Bair and Cassidy prepared for diving. It was a strange ritual to her though she had been to sea before with family friends who owned boats. She had never been aboard a working boat.

New Year's day at sea was sparkling bright, the water clear and flat with no wind or ground swell to complicate the diving. That was unusual for the waters around the Channel Islands, a natural trough which contained some of the wildest water on the California coast. This unseasonal weather was the reason Bair had decided to work on New Year's day. He would have to go deep for the fine abalone bed he had saved for just such a forecast. The other divers would be nursing giant headaches from last night's parties and he would be able to work the site in peace, without all the new divers following him around. Paranoid? Maybe, maybe not. But most important were the elements, never passive in this channel for too long. One could wait as much as six months for another such opportunity.

MABEL & ME was a Radon boat, specially designed for abalone fishing. Twenty-nine feet on deck, she was one of the first Radons, built when abalone was still plentiful, when a diver of Bair's savvy and strength could harvest three times the number he could take today. Abalone was nearly an endangered species now.

The fiberglass surfaces of MABEL & ME were scarred by the hundreds of dings she had taken in service, plus the continual deterioration from salt and sun. She wasn't a pretty thing. A big Chevy engine and hydraulic lifting boom were her prime features, plus the hot water shower just recently installed. There were some at the harbor who claimed Bair used the shower too seldom but they whispered it safely beyond his gargantuan arms and gnarly fingers, fingers which seemed to be locked in a permanent clawlike mode. But Bair insisted (with a glint in his eye) that Quackenbush the Gander had caused it by attacking him almost daily at the boyhood farm in Michigan. Bair said he took many a thrashing on the run from the huge bony wings before he found out one day (while locked in a death struggle with the foul-tempered old bird) that he could win by simply wrapping his hands around the neck and choking Quackenbush till he became faint.

Tosca had little to say as she watched, fascinated by the ritual of Bair suiting up. The boat wallowed listlessly while Cassidy helped Bair with the components of the dive suit, the largest ever made by YOKOHAMA DIVING, a #4. It weighed more than a hundred pounds and stood 7 ½ feet tall, though part of that weight was simply counter-balance to the bouyancy of water and material. The suit had numerous patches on shoulder, forearm, hip and thigh, wear spots from the thousands of ladder rungs and ab baskets he had handled.

"Okay, get me a jigger of soap," Bair bellowed over the clatter of the air compressor, raking a hand towel across his deeply pockmarked face. Cassidy approached with the bottle of detergent and lubricated both cuffs, standing by until the huge fists popped through for an airtight fit.

"Weights!" Bair demanded, eyeing Cassidy curiously.

Cassidy lifted the 30 pound lead bib and draped it over Bair's shoulders, half to the front and half to the back. "Got it on straight?" Bair goaded him, and shifted left foot to right, adjusting his feet inside the weighted boots. Cassidy checked the rubber flap and corselet over which the big bronze helmet would fasten. "You see that wind pickin' up, or ground swell, gimme a call pronto, you hear."

"Hey, would I let you die like a dog down there?" Cassidy joked, and turned to grin at Tosca who watched from the opposite gunwale.

"Never know about you pretty boys, gittin' in love. If I didn't keep an eye on you you'd fall into the ocean and croak," Bair said, winking at Tosca. He then pointed to the belt with decompression guage and kelp knife attached. Cassidy strung it around his waist and buckled it.

The weighted boots thumped heavily on the fiberglass deck as Bair walked across to the ladder, reminding Tosca of the Frankenstein monster. He reached out to grab an abalone basket and sat down on the gunwale to wait impatiently for the helmet to be clamped on. "Final adjustment?" Cassidy offered, giving Bair the option.

"I did it while you were makin' cow eyes at her. Drop it on, pretty boy."

Cassidy eased the helmet down over Bair's head, and once it was seated gave it a sharp twist to lock it in place on the neck ring. He snapped the catch and tapped Bair on the helmet. Bair sat for several moments longer then eased down the ladder and below the surface, trailing the air bubbles which marked his descent.

"Well there you have it, babe. What do you think?" Cassidy asked.

"Wow! Amazing!"

"What you just saw is a disappearing act. He's iron age. The only guy on the south coast still picking abs in a hard hat."

"Why does he do it then?"

"Hard-headed. Eccentric. And he swears it's more comfortable. Besides, he's about to quit so there's no point in spending a lot of dough for scuba gear. Look! Thirty feet down and he's still visible."

"How deep will he have to go?"

"Seventy-five feet. Maybe eighty."

"Will he…"

She was interrupted by Bair on the phone, highly excited. "Hey, it looks like we hit the jackpot. They're thick as fleas down here."

"Great. So quit talking and make us some money," Cassidy answered.

The original rush over, Tosca began to ease off. She came close to where Cassidy was watching the air compressor and leaned close to him. "Glad you came?" he asked her.

"Uh huh, though I'm awfully hungry."

"Yeah, it drives you nuts out here. We've got snacks in the cabin. Why don't you fetch us some."

Alone on the deck for the first time Cassidy continued with his discipline. Extra baskets for collecting the abs, ab irons for prying the abs loose from the rocks, kelp knife at hand and ready for use. He snapped a look at the air hoses; clear and functioning. He ducked back to fine tune the compressor; purring precisely. And then he heard Bair on the line again. "My hoses feel heavy. Got kelp?"

"No Sir, clean as a whistle."

"Okay, uphaul."

"Boy, you're workin' fast today."

"Got to. Runnin' outta steam already. Listen, me and Mabel were talkin' it over again last night. We figure New Year, new life, so this really is my last shot. I know I been talkin' it up but this time I mean it. Truth is I just don't wanna do this shit anymore. I had a good run, it's time to go. You gotta find another meal ticket, okay?"

Cassidy was stunned but then he realized the inevitability of Bair's decision. He didn't need the money. He and Mabel owned several rental units and 20 acres near the Sequoia Forest. She was pensioned from the old Hughes Aircraft.

"You sound serious this time, Cap. You're not just jiving me?"

"I'm damn serious. Hey, you're sure there's no kelp? No wind suckin' up?"

"Positive, Cap."

They put in a hard day at the abalone bed, and an unforseen incident complicated the program despite Bair's assiduous planning. By mid-afternoon they had taken enough abs to call it quits and still make it back to Santa Barbara in daylight.

Tosca sat in the cabin reading while Cassidy worked topside, lashing the equipment down for what looked like a rough ride home. The prevailing winds had begun to blow and the ground swell had started to roll.

In his swim trunks, Bair emerged from the tube-like compartment which served as fresh water shower, towelling his red hair as he entered the cabin.

"Damn that feels good! Always itch like crazy after a couple hours in that suit," he said to Tosca, then suggested she go topside while he dressed. He was alone when he heard Cassidy's urgent knock on the cabin roof.

"Hey Skipper, we've got company."

Bair bent over and squinted through a porthole. A 50 foot schooner had approached to within several yards of MABEL & ME. There were three men and an attractive young girl standing at the schooner's life rail. One of the men held a towel up to his head.

"Ahoy, MABEL & ME! I'm Joe Morgan, the schooner ACHILLEAS, out of Half Moon Bay."

"Yeah," Bair answered as he emerged from below deck. "What's goin' on?"

"Looks like you're about ready to head in to port, right?"

"All trimmed and ready. What's on your mind?"

"This is Frank," Morgan answered, and pointed to the crewman holding the towel up to his head. "He's bleeding and in a lot of pain. Gotta get him to a hospital. Can you take him in with you? You're much faster. That's a seven hour trip for my schooner."

"Sure Mate, glad to help," Bair agreed and kicked a couple of fenders over the side to cushion ACHILLEAS as she drew closer. "What happened?"

"Broken eardrum. Maybe concussion. We can't stop the bleeding. Okay, Frank," Morgan continued, handing him a credit card, "go straight to the hospital and have 'em check it out. And don't lose the card, huh."

"You're coming back for me, right Joe?"

"In a few days. I've got business to do in LA then I'll be back. Get yourself a motel and relax."

"I really appreciate this," Morgan said, and squinted down at Bair. "I didn't get your name."

"I'm Bair. That's my tender, Cassidy, and she's Tosca."

"A pleasure, folks," Morgan answered, appraising Tosca pointedly before nodding to Cassidy. "Okay Frank, see you in a couple of days. Let the harbormaster know where you are. *Mucho gracias*, Bair."

As the ACHILLEAS pulled away Bair led Frank to the cabin. "How'd that happen?" he asked after Frank had relaxed on the bunk.

"Scuba diving. It popped just like that," Frank moaned, gripping the towel closer to his ear. "Fifty feet down."

"Okay, you just hang out below here. We'll be gittin' up speed and the wind'll hit you like a sore tooth."

Bair took the first watch on the trip back to port. It had turned colder, the sun's warmth diminished by the approaching dusk. The heavily-laden boat laboured against wind and ground swell, and Bair knew the fog bank was close out there somewhere. He could smell the dankness in the dimming light.

"Coffee, Skip?" Cassidy asked, poking his head out of the hatch.

"Does a bear shit in the woods?" Bair grinned in answer. "And while you're at it bring me a handful of them cookies Tosca brought along."

Cassidy lit the gimballed stove and started the water to boil. "Stand some coffee?" Cassidy asked Frank.

"Huh uh. Hurts when I swallow."

"How did it happen?"

"Scuba. Morgan assumed I knew how so he never gave me instructions. Hell, I only used snorkel before."

Frank told the story to him and Tosca. The first few minutes of the dive had been fun, and easy. The four of them had descended into a mature kelp bed, Frank bringing up the rear. Though there had been bright sunlight topside the water darkened as they penetrated deeper into the kelp bed. Like a thicket of closely planted trees the giant columns and foliage of the kelp shut out all light from above. Frank became concerned. It was hard for him to keep up with the experienced others; the exotic discipline of swimming and breathing with unfamiliar equipment and doing it with a regulated rhythm. He was falling back in the darkness, barely catching a glimpse of an arm here and a leg there. Alone at this point, anxious, he chased hard after them and it depleted him. His breathing became irregular and laboured, the mouthpiece annoying.

He was down to 20 feet when he caught sight of the others working their way down a sheer rock face. He followed along but became alarmed at the increasing pain in his head and ears. The water pressure was oppressive and his strength was fading fast. No one had told him about *clearing*, the process of expelling air from lungs and ears every eight or nine feet as one descends; a thing necessary to equalize the difference between water on the surface and below. The alternative could be a painful case of the bends, perhaps even death.

Frank was down to 35 feet now and had still not cleared. The pain was unbearable. His mind began to drift as he fought it off. He knew he had to keep control and make them aware of his predicament. Struggling, he made his way down to the ocean floor, fifty feet, despite the agony. He hallucinated, a stream of consciousness without order or detail. He lost the ability to breathe, too disoriented and exhausted to work the mouthpiece. He drifted aimlessly.

The others were taking abalone from the rocks, unaware that he was in trouble. He fell close in to Morgan and touched him on the shoulder, pointing to the surface. Not understanding the urgency of the signal, Morgan rebuffed him with a wag of the head and kept working.

Frank hung there in the gloom, not breathing, almost unconscious. The last thing he remembered was activating the CO_2 life vest. The ominous hiss of the released gas got their attention. As Frank shot up to a probable case of the bends Morgan lunged, caught him by the foot and slowed his ascent to a safe rate. Though he was at the present time in a lot of pain Frank knew how fortunate he had been.

On arriving in port Cassidy and Tosca drove Frank to the emergency room at Cottage Hospital, then returned to the waterfront.

The marina was nearly deserted. MABEL & ME lay dripping wet under the glow of the dock light, freshly scrubbed after transferring her catch to the processor's waiting truck. Bair and Tosca sat in the dingy cabin, sipped hot drinks and waited for Cassidy to return from the bathhouse. "So, from the looks of things you two have got pretty close, huh?" Bair enquired, gauging her with his deepset ice-blue eyes.

"Yeah, pretty tight for one day," she answered. *He's watching me too intently,* she thought. *Something's on his mind.* Bair's eyes narrowed as he slurped his coffee, then he looked away from her. "How long have you known him, Bair?"

"Fifteen years. Kinda like my own kid, you know."

"That's a long time. He's got a lot of respect for you."

"Yep."

Awkward silence followed, then his penetrating scrutiny again. "How old are you, Tosca?"

"Eighteen, almost. Why?"

"No say," he shrugged it off, having got the answer he expected. Simply put, he was worried about his friend who had had several affairs since his divorce though none was serious.

But there had been a special excitement on Cassidy's face this morning as he raved on about Tosca. Only once before had he been somewhat high on a woman, and though she was near Cassidy's own age Bair considered Dominique a bush leaguer. For Cassidy's own sake Bair decided he would discourage the affair with Tosca whenever a discreet opportunity presented itself.

To Tosca his question had been calculated to intimidate her, to put her down, if gently. Upset, doing a slow burn, she glared across the four feet of cabin space which seperated them and stuck out her chin defiantly. "It's none of your business, Bair," she said curtly, and swivelled around to give him the finality of her back.

Caught off balance, unsure just how to respond, Bair laughed sheepishly, revealing his two missing front teeth. "Spunky little beaner, ain't you."

"I am not a beaner. I'm Cuban."

"I didn't say what kinda beaner," he grinned at this half size person who had just stuck it back into his own ear. "But you got it right, lady. He's free, white, and twenty-one. Not my business."

"We like each other a lot, Bair."

"I can tell. But hey, you're awful young. Like the man says, 'Here today, gone to Maui'. Maybe you oughta leave him alone, Tosca."

"Why? He's old enough to take care of himself. Bair, I'm not out to cause him any grief. I really like him."

"Sure, you might not hurt him on purpose but you're kinda young, and sooner or later you're gonna hurt the man. Especially him. He's too vulnerable."

The last comments were given in a hushed manner as Cassidy approached on the wooden dock and boarded MABEL & ME. He was aware that he had been the topic of a discussion. "Okay, what are you two guys whispering about?"

"Difference of opinion," Bair grinned. "She thinks you're a good lookin' dude, and I think you look like a Portugee Man O' War with all that long hair hangin' down to your bum."

"My bum, my hair. I'd rather talk about supper. I promised I'd get Tosca to her Aunt's house by six o'clock. We've got ten minutes."

"Time's awaistin'. Let's go," Bair said, gathering his jacket and a few choice abs for Mabel's evening meal.

CHAPTER 4

▼

By the time Mrs. Tosca buried the hatchet with Alexander he and Tosca had become inseperable friends. Bumming together in the boatyard and harbor, biking, dancing together at KYLIX, hikes together in the mountains and creek beds, scrounging at thrift shops and swap meets, doing her homework together (most always at his studio/garage). And there had been no direct confrontations with Padro though he had been seen parked nearby, observing the area. Inevitably that respite came to an end on the Tosca patio.

Tosca and her mother were taking breakfast on the patio, in the early sunshine. Tosca, still in housecoat, was reading Cassidy's out-of-print novel while her mother scanned the morning paper, trimmed her toenails and fussed with her hair curlers.

"Be right back, Mom. Gotta go," Tosca said, laying the novel down and withdrawing quickly to the bathroom.

As Mrs. Tosca worked on her nails her gaze fell on the novel lying face down on the breakfast table. She became curious though she had never been what you could call a reader. Tosca had said she liked the work but seemed reluctant to discuss it with her mother. Mrs. Tosca turned the book upright and read a few pages then stopped abruptly when she heard the Jeep wind its way up to the house.

"Well, look what we have here. The Tosca family at Sunday morning breakfast," Padro taunted, and alighting from the Jeep he dropped heavily into Tosca's empty chair. "Hey, kid, you know how I like mine. Heavy on the cream and sugar."

"You were not invited, Padro. Why don't you just go home."

"Because I don't feel like it, Marta. I was hoping I might catch you-know-who around here so I could kick his head in."

"Sorry to disappoint you."

"No hurry. What you reading there?" he asked, seemingly subdued.

"It's Tina's book," she answered, and scooted the book away from him. He feigned indifference, then moved quickly to seize the book. He looked at the cover and then read a few sentences while she watched him closely.

"So, this is the guy, right? Cassidy...Never heard of him." He continued to read as she held her breath. He lowered the book to the table and got a strange and distant look on his face. "I used to write when I was a kid. Poetry. Stories."

This was a surprise to her, and embarrassing as well because it was obvious he was waiting for a comment from her. She fidgeted some then responded. "Really?"

"Uh huh. Elementary school. Maybe ten, eleven years old."

She waited for the other shoe to fall. After all he had put her through she had a difficult time trusting him, or even talking to him.

"You don't believe me, do you," he said, and looked away, shrugging his shoulders as she watched him closely. "The nuns said it was pretty good. Even asked me to read in class."

She remained silent but expected him to react angrily at her reticence. She felt the pressure building. His attention was fixed on the ivy patch near the patio, then he turned to gaze down at Santa Barbara in the distance. "My mother liked it too," he said, barely audible.

He got to his feet, put the book down, and without a word he walked to the Jeep and drove away. Mrs. Tosca was stunned by his behavior. It was so unlike him. She thought about it, the nuns praising him, and his mother as well. But he had said nothing about the Sergeant-Major, an ominous omission.

In the following weeks things appeared to mellow out for all of them. No unpleasant incidents. Mrs. Tosca seemed to accept the status quo. Then one evening as they were getting ready for bed she suggested that her daughter call Cassidy and invite him to breakfast.

It was a Saturday morning. Fog billowed in from the Pacific and overspread Santa Barbara, obscuring the Los Padres National Forest in the distance. It put one in the mind of the antique paintings of China, the bulk of Le Cumbre and Gibraltar peaks piercing the white blanket of fog, along with the tops of pine trees poking through here and there.

On such a morning there was little to do. The fog hypnotized with its bland-ness and sapped one's vitality. Mother and daughter lounged at the big window, drank coffee and watched Cassidy come up the hill. It was Tosca's not-yet-awake voice which broke the silence. "Be nice to him, huh Mom?"

She stared at her daughter. The idea that she might be abusive to him, or anyone, was unthinkable. "Why of course I'll be nice to him! He's our guest."

"You won't ask him questions, or..." her voice trailed off as Cassidy's wraith-like form appeared at the door. "All right, Mom, remember I was nice to Chuck."

"Okay, honey! Okay."

Tosca went to the door and held it open for Cassidy and the gray swirl which sucked in behind him. "Good morning, Mr. Cassidy."

"OPA! Tosca, and Mrs. Tosca."

The casual peck on the cheek they exchanged was observed by Mrs. Tosca and it upset her. It was a corroboration of the continuing closeness between them.

"Did you guys order this fog?" he kidded, handing a white paper bag to Mrs. Tosca.

"Not me. I'm a sunshine person," she answered, and headed for the kitchen. "Coffee? Tea?"

"Coffee, thank you. There's a dozen doughnuts in that bag."

"Great. Any jellies?"

"Of course. Everybody likes jellies."

Tosca took his hand and pulled him toward the big windows in the living room. "Eerie out there, isn't it."

"Yeah, but I love it with you," he said, and brushed close.

"Have you noticed, mom's trying to be nice to you."

"That's the jelly doughnuts. It always works on older women," he said just as Mrs. Tosca entered the room with coffee and one doughnut. She sensed their disappointment. "You'll spoil your breakfast. You can have more for dessert if you're still hungry. It's all ready except the biscuits. Just a few minutes more," she added, and disappeared into the kitchen.

Tosca and Alexander sat down to share the doughnut. His eyes fluttered to the top of his head when she licked the icing off his fingers one by one. "Tosca, you're just too much."

"But the icing is the best part," she grinned, then kissed his cheek. "Come on, quick. Help me pick a costume for KYLIX tonight."

"You're kidding me. You're better at that than I am."

"Not today. My mind's all bogged down by the fog. Come on."

She took his hand and led him into her room. It stood on one corner of the house, with great views of both ocean and the town. Her bed was still unmade. A low chest squatted at the foot of the bed with half-open drawers of socks, under-garments and other small items. In one corner were shelves supported on stone blocks which held her books and school supplies. Also there was an aquarium of fish, and next to that a large bird cage which was littered with confetti. This was the home of her family of pet black mice which varied in number from a dozen to three dozen. In another corner Tosca kept her collection of bizarre hats, tophat to coonskin, displayed on a bentwood costumier with as many as seven hats stacked on a single peg.

The fourth corner was dominated by *the pile*. Coats, dresses, jeans, blouses and shirts, all tangled indiscriminately to a depth of two feet and a diameter of seven, with no regard as to newly washed, partly clean, or unclean. When Tosca took 'em off, onto the pile they went. "Well, what do you think?" she asked as he stared, intimidated by the pile.

"Well what do you feel like today? A carpenter, an Arab slave? What?"

"I'm not sure. It's kinda hazy right now. How about…Mmmm! Yeah! Yan-kee!" she shouted, and attacked the pile happily. "See if you can find the black knickers."

He bent over and dug into the interlocked arms and legs of material, eventu-ally coming up with the pants she wanted. His mouth hung open as she held up one of her prize thrift store finds; an old Yankee baseball shirt ten sizes too big for her, the number 34 covering her entire upper torso. A chuckle escaped him as they stood staring at each other, then a chuckle of her own, then resounding laughter from them both. "I'm tellin' you, Tosca, I'll never understand you and that pile."

"Me either. Like, I just do it," she said, and turned to the chest at the head of the bed. "I've got blue striped socks somewhere if I can find them."

"Boy, you're off the wall, Tosca."

"I know," she answered. "And beautiful too?"

"Beautiful too you little shit."

Mrs. Tosca interrupted them, holding grapefruit that was bound for the table. "Tina, get me a new jelly from storage. The biscuits are ready."

"Sure," Tosca said, and jumped up to get the jelly. She was barely out the door when the phone began to ring. Mrs. Tosca regarded the ringing phone helplessly, her fingers messed with breakfast drippings. "Darn, it never fails. Would you mind getting that, Alexander."

As she went to clean her hands Cassidy picked up the receiver. "Yes, the Tosca residence. Who would you like to…" he began, but was interrupted by the caller. "Me? I'm Alexander Cassidy, a friend of the family. Who do you want to talk to?"

Mrs. Tosca watched from the kitchen as he tried to make a connection but a growing apprehension filled her as she listened in on the conversation. "Well, I was invited to breakfast, Ma'am," he continued. Catching Mrs. Tosca's eye he pointed urgently to the receiver as the voice on the line became increasingly more audible, "But I'm not out to hurt her, Ma'am," he tried to defend himself against the caller. "She's my good friend…" Again he was interrupted. "Hey now, profanity isn't called for, Ma'am."

More angry than he would have thought possible for her, Mrs. Tosca seized the phone. A deep pink coloured her face as she listened. "Celia! You oughta be ashamed of yourself! How dare you!"

Tosca returned from storage just in time to hear this last statement. She stood motionless and monitored the conversation. She understood at once and her eyes shifted from her mother to Alexander. She shrugged her shoulders helplessly.

"Maybe so, but don't ever do this again!" Mrs. Tosca continued. "And another thing…It's a little early to be at the bottle, isn't it?"

Hurt and humiliation mirrored on her face, Tosca approached Cassidy and laid a hand on his shoulder. "Sorry."

"Me too. Nothing we can do about it."

"I know you're of a legal age, Celia. We'll talk about it when you sober up," Mrs. Tosca concluded and hung up the phone.

Tosca spoke first, feeling her mother had broken a trust. "Mom, how could you do that. It's none of her business."

"Well she's your aunt, isn't she. The only relative you've got out here besides me and your father. Some things just need to be discussed," she said, gesturing at the breakfast table. "Come to breakfast now."

Tosca turned angrily and marched to her room and slammed the door. Cassidy started after her but Mrs. Tosca held up a restraining hand, "Let her go. She'll be all right."

"Mrs. Tosca, I understand. I've got kids of my own."

"How is it possible for you to understand this? Has any of your children ever brought somebody home who is twice as old as they are?"

"Or maybe even a three-legged geek, or a murderer", he answered testily. "Aw, sorry I said that, okay?"

"For God's sake let her go! It can't possibly work out!"

He started to respond but backed down. It wouldn't have mattered what he said. But it was the hands of Tosca, pressing on his shoulders as she stood behind his chair, tearful and defiant of all, that made it all right again. Even Mrs. Tosca felt the nuance and shook her head in resignation.

"Let's have some breakfast, Tosca, then we'll pile on the clothes and walk out on Stearns Wharf," he proposed, holding her chair out for her. "It's so nice in the fog."

CHAPTER 5

▼

It was the deep of night, that time when most of man's machines and noise had ceased for the day, but not the incessant hum of traffic on the 101 Freeway. Tosca had read somewhere that taxes and death were the only constants of modern life but the ubiquitous internal combustion engine had now joined that club.

Tonight there was also another sound as she slipped quietly out of the house; Bo Diddley. She frowned up at the oak tree, pursed her lips and shushed him quiet. Things had not been too smooth between her, Cassidy and her mother. This was not a good time to get busted for sneaking out. Also, the last few days had seemed strange, almost surreal for her and Alexander; something was not quite right.

Unable to sleep, she had put on her dress and sandals, slipped into her cape and made the short ride to his studio though she had not long before left him. She leaned her bike against his studio wall and took a small coach lantern from her saddlebag. As she lit the lamp it occurred to her that anyone who might chance upon her, dressed in cape and slippers as she was and carrying a coach lamp at three in the morning might mistake her for a thief and call down the law on her. She looked witchy hunched over his door stoop, tapping softly with her knuckles, long black hair and strong face lit dramatically by the candle. "OPA, Alejandro," she called musically, using the Spanish form of his name.

She heard him scramble out of bed, groan, then a light went on inside. Blanket draped loosely around, he peered sleepily through the open door at her face which was fixed with a smile. "It is I, the *Senorita del cabo y linterna*," she announced importantly, pleased with the improbability of the moment and savoring his reaction to it.

"You just left an hour ago."

"An hour and a half, Sir," she corrected, and placed the lantern on his writing table. She took off the cape, turned out his night light, darkening the room further. "See how it dances, my flame," she said theatrically, then turned serious. "What's wrong with us, Alexander?"

"What are you talking about? Nothing's wrong."

"You're holding back from me. What the heck did she do to you, anyway?"

"What did who do?"

"Your ex-wife. What happened?"

"I'd rather not get into that if you don't mind."

"It would help me a lot if you did. I need to know."

Her comment disturbed him but he thought it might be better to clear it up. "Okay. Just this once. I get angry and depressed when I think about that and it accomplishes nothing. Put simply, I always wanted a family more than anything else in the world and when I got it she fucked it up."

"Well, what did she do?"

"She got bored and took on a lover. Then another."

"How many kids did you have?"

"Three. Two in high school. One in Junior High."

"Did you beat her up?"

"Huh?" he replied, startled. "That's not my style, Tosca."

"Do you ever see her? Talk to her?"

"Only when I go to see the kids. We tolerate each other."

"But you've never forgiven her?"

"Jesus! How do you forgive something like that. Look, that's all I want to say about it, okay."

"All right. Do you trust me, Alexander?"

"Most of the time. But like the other day, you mentioned that guy Mark again. What's going on there?"

"Nothing. He's an old boyfriend, we have a coke now and then. I'll cut him off if you want me too," she offered, and ran her fingers through his hair.

"No, that's okay. You need friends your own age."

"Alexander, mom says that girls who get it on, you know, make love…mom says they're loose, like sluts. But I can't handle that anymore. Will you make love with me?"

Cassidy smiled at her then and his hands raced over her pliant form, quickening the beat with frantic kisses as his body pressed against her own. Then, edging off the bed she stood in the lantern's glow and disrobed, proudly offering her young body to him in a rush of passionate giving.

They fell asleep after that burst of passion and it was the faint music of bird-song outside that aroused him finally. Satisfaction spread across his face as he remembered what had happened a few hours earlier; his first complete loving with Tosca. The clock/radio was the second thing he remembered. Already 8 a.m.! He closed his eyes and reproached himself inwardly. 'You've done it again, dummy.'

He observed her sleeping form beside him. Long black hair spread out on the pillow like Spanish lace, the rest of her cradled to his torso, her skin luminescent in its tightness as skin is firm until gravity starts it sagging. A few dark moles here and there to accent her olive beauty. He sniffled uncertainly at the fragrance, unsure if it was her or the honeysuckle trellis outside his door. He began to gently disentangle their limbs and the movements woke her.

"Good mornin', darlin'," he whispered in her ear.

She stretched out like a cat, cracked her eyes open and mumbled, "Morning."

He slipped out from under the sheets and opened the door to let in the sun's warmth. "We overslept again."

"She'll kill me this time for sure," Tosca moaned, her voice gravelly but without fear.

"Hey, we'll face her together from now on," Cassidy said, and massaged her back with sweeping circular motions from shoulder to shapely backside.

"That'll be nice. Gracias, *amante*."

"You're welcome. *Amante*?"

"It's Spanish for lover. *Amante…amante…amante*", she purred softly.

"So beautiful. Teach me more."

"Si *amante*, much much more."

"Great. And now my little peanut, let's go talk to your mom. Come on."

"I'm the peanut *shell*," she said, and slowly traced a circle around her navel as he watched, fascinated. "You fit inside so you are the peanut," she smiled seductively and rolled over on her back to watch him through heavy-lidded eyes.

"You were delicious last night, peanut shell."

"You too. Do you realize that a year ago, even a month ago, this couldn't have happened. I wasn't ready for you. I couldn't have done it."

He kissed her hotly, the underarms, groin, the thighs and other places as she watched, enthralled. "Shouldn't we be going?" she teased him, pretending to wriggle free.

"She can only hang us once, luv. Let's do it again."

And not being a very resolute person where passion was concerned she acquiesed, moaning as Cassidy spread then entered her body. But it wasn't that easy for Mrs. Tosca. She had nothing to take the edge off her anger, no balm for her disappointment. Imagine her alarm, her anger, when she called Tina to breakfast only to find that she wasn't in her room. The black cape was not in sight. The bicycle was not in its usual place. It was obvious that she had slipped out sometime during the night to be with Cassidy.

There was no way she could have known that last night had been a first for Cassidy and her daughter. She could only assume they had duped her all along. She was humiliated.

Four cups of coffee later and after much agonizing she took the newspaper out on the patio and sat to wait for them. Arm in arm they finally approached, seemingly unconcerned.

"You haven't paid a bit of attention to anything I've said, Tina," Mrs. Tosca began the confrontation.

"I'm sorry, Mom. I didn't plan it this way."

"I'm deeply disturbed, Tina. I don't know what's happened to your sense of propriety."

Cassidy stepped forward to say what a really fine daughter Tosca was, but Tosca beat him to it, anxious to keep him out of it if she could. "I'm the same person I always was, Mom. Just like you and Chuck and everybody else I've got a body too and it has feelings just like yours." Then as if to prove a point she grabbed Cassidy's arm and put it around her waist. "We love too, Mom."

"Listen to me, I've known Chuck for six months now. You've only known this man, who is twice your age, for about six weeks. Six weeks, Tina! Now tell me about love. Go ahead."

"Begging your pardon Ma'am, but your daughter is one of the most principled girls I ever met. A lot of mothers I know would trade you places in a second."

"Alexander, I'm not trying to be cruel or insensitive when I ask you this, but how old were your other girlfriends before Tina? Were they young too?"

"No they were near my own age. What's that got to do with us?"

"Then why didn't you stay with your own generation? Why did you pick on my daughter?"

"Pick? I didn't pick on her. This stuff just happens or it doesn't. You know that." Cassidy took a deep breath but there seemed no way out of the unpleasantness. "Look Ma'am, Tina is the first young woman I've dated and I find that I like it. With folks my own age the music is always too loud, the walk too far, the weather too threatening. I mean, just compare that to Tina. We talk art, literature and history, we dance, rummage in thrift shops and chum around together, walk the creeks and mountains and experience stuff. And as long as we're at it let's throw in aesthetics. Now that I'm almost forty I'm supposed to redefine my sense of beauty? Not prefer her grace and quality? Hey, I ain't blind yet."

Taken aback by his tirade Mrs. Tosca could only watch as he moved to stand beside Tosca.

"Sorry Ma'am. I wouldn't have said that stuff voluntarily but you know damn well that I'm not talking trash. What I'm seeing and feeling for her is as natural and honest as life itself."

"It wasn't my intention to be mean about this, Alexander, but I have to do what I think is right for my daughter and lovely or not, you're just too old for her. It won't work."

"We've got a chance, Mom. He's the most considerate friend I've ever had. I mean, some of the guys I've been out with…Dan Wilson for instance. He snorts coke like you wouldn't believe. And your favorite, Bud Weiser…Boy does he ever take his name seriously. You let me go out with them. Are they more preferrable because they're my own age?"

"No, and I wouldn't have let you go out with them if I had known that," her mother added heatedly. Then she threw up her hands in vexation and stalked through the kitchen door. "I've gotta go. I have an appointment with Dr. Dorbin."

Finally alone with her, Cassidy put his arm around Tosca and kissed her forehead. "Jesus, I get tired of this shit. Sometimes I just feel like sailin' down to Mexico and leave all this bad kharma behind."

"I don't want you to go down there. Those federalles will put you in jail," she said, looking worried. "You were kidding around weren't you, I mean about the boat?"

"Well it is cheaper. And I bought an old scow in marina 4 just for the dock space, so if I can somehow just get the junk up here from Newport I'll be sitting pretty."

"But I don't want you to give up the studio. It's such a happy place for us."

"I know, darlin', but let's just be cool and see what happens, okay. Hey, want to bum on lower State? Maybe get some pie and coffee at ESAU's?"

"I'll come down later. Mom's pretty upset."

"You don't mind if I split?"

"Actually better if you do. Let things cool down. Anyway a couple of the baby mice got loose. You might step on 'em, if Sam doesn't get 'em first."

CHAPTER 6

▼

The sky was bright and the weather unusually hot for this day, one that would always be remembered by the both of them. It was Monday, her eighteenth birthday. They were in the Los Padres National Forest, trudging ever upward into the rocky canyon that contained the spring-fed creek; the *secret* place she had told him about.

Because of the heat (and their own sensuality) they were naked, carrying their clothes in a poke slung over his shoulder. The brilliant sun highlighted their physical differences as they walked side by side. Her body slender, the hip flaring from a tight waist, the thighs long and shapely. His body firm and well-muscled, the skin showing the coarseness and large pores associated with middle age. Her face was an olive beauty, smooth and seamless; his ridged, lined, accentuated by long sun-bleached hair, almost patrician if that elegant term could be applied to a man whose only cover was the rock boots on his feet.

"Tosca, it's wonderful up here! Thanks for sharing it with me."

"Yeah. It's called Hot Springs Creek. No one ever comes up here. We'll make it one of our secret places."

The area was one of gentle foothills which rose to a craggy ridge about a mile distant, the creek cascading down through dense green chaparral. Large sand-coloured boulders studded the panorama, adding a touch of ruggedness to the green order of the area.

"Pretty remote up here," Cassidy remarked.

He couldn't say exactly why he was disturbed but somehow he wanted to have been the first to share this with her. He would like to have known her in that first brilliant awareness.

"Come on. We're getting near the ruins."

"Ruins? Like what?"

"An old lodge. It used to be a spa in Victorian times. The rich people came from all over to get the kinks out. Belongs to the Montecito Water Company now." They were rounding a curve in the path when she bolted ahead and pointed excitedly, "See! The old walls. The foundations."

Though Tosca seemed to have a more romantic attitude toward the place it appeared like any other old ruins to Cassidy. The foundation walls were made of smooth stones taken from the creek bed and were still in place, but the rest of the building had lost its fight with changing cultural styles and forest growth a long time ago and was now covered by a heap of vines and chaparral.

"Keep an eye out for rattlers," she warned, and pulled him through what had been a small basement doorway. The darkness unnerved him at first. As he adjusted to the darkness he could make out the shapes of fallen timbers, black mounds of rubble, and old water pipes. But it was the frantic scurrying in a far corner which gave him the worst scare. They had disturbed the solitude of some wild creature.

"Boy, this is scary, Tosca. But great background for a gothic, or maybe even a love story."

She reached out and caressed his chest, wet with perspiration. She slid her arms around his neck and pressed her body close. Cradled him hungrily between her legs, straining for maximum contact. "How fortunate I am to have my own pornographer," she commented between slow sinuous thrusts.

"Now look here, lady, I don't write trashy stuff," he joked, his hands touching her everywhere. She responded with hot hydrous kisses and yet more fervent body movements.

"Alejandro, will you write about us making love?"

"I will write about this passionate young latina who is driven to make love to this older guy, see. She can't help herself. She has got to have what he's got," Cassidy said, and with a firm passion lifted her bodily, teasing her with his penis, then penetrating her suddenly and deeply. But at the last possible moment and with superhuman effort, she loosened herself from his grasp and stood silhouetted in the bright doorway. "Come on, there's a better place," she said, and arm in arm she steered him toward the creek which flowed beside the ruins.

"Smell it?" she said, and crinkled up her nose at the vague sulphuric odor. "Feel the pipe," she suggested, pointing to the culvert where it came out of the mountainside.

Cassidy laid his hand on the culvert then instinctively drew his hand away. The metal was warm to his touch and had surprised him. "It's the chemicals. Weird, huh?" she said. Cassidy placed his hand back on the pipe and smiled at the warmness. She took hold of his hand and together they negotiated the stones and rivulets to a point where the creek formed a small pool. She pointed at it and watched him expectantly. It was a small oasis; two banana trees and a thicket of bamboo so overgrown and dense that it excluded most all the sunlight. It more resembled a private room in the great outdoors, so thick were its sidewalls and ceiling of interlocked bamboo stalks.

"There!" she said, and pointed at a large boulder in the thicket. "I call it Coupling Rock," she announced and crawled out onto it, reaching back a helping hand to him.

"Hard on the knees, I bet," he said, and opened the poke to spread his clothes for a pad.

Appraising this pastoral beauty they dangled their feet and listened to the moving water as the humidity raised beads of sweat on their skins. Cassidy bent low and licked the salt from her nipples. "Mmmmm. Tastes like sunflower seeds," he murmured. And then, overcome by the perfection of the place, the isolation and their own body juices, they were in and around each other making such passionate love as he could not remember with any of his former lovers. "Happy Birthday, darlin'," he said, as they writhed together in the half-dark of Coupling Rock.

"Mmmmm, Mmmm," she mumbled in response, her face turned away from him, contorted. She seemed to be in another place, another time. But Cassidy, who had all his adult life been in awe of a woman's fantasies during the love act...Cassidy had taken no special note of it. At the same time he had been puzzled that Tosca (with whom he had so far enjoyed tantalizing orgasms) could not come on despite cunnilingus or any other touching he devised for her pleasure.

Later, as they drove down Hot Springs Road toward Santa Barbara neither seemed to notice the landscape zipping by, their minds still on Coupling Rock. Then finally responding to their surroundings she snuggled up to him, close and communicative once more.

"*Alejandro*, hurry with the story. Here I am eighteen already and I've never been out of Santa Barbara County."

"I'm doing the best I can, sweetheart. Meanwhile, why don't you go up to Chico with me tomorrow. My mother had another stroke and my sister says it's pretty iffy this time. I'll introduce you to my family. The kids'll eat you up."

Tosca said her mother wouldn't let her go at this time. Perhaps in a few more months when she got to know him better. She stretched out on the seat beside him, suddenly tired. It had been an eventful birthday for her, a busy one.

"Can we spend the night together, do you think?"

"Oh yes. With my cape and lantern I'll come, after mom goes to sleep. But first, you promised me a birthday dinner."

"Hey, that's prostitution, pure and simple."

"I know. Let's go get ready, huh."

It was dark by the time they managed a shower and change of clothes. As they entered KYLIX they were confronted by a boisterous capacity crowd. Satyri spotted them and moved to welcome them.

"*Kalispera*, Alexandros! *Yasou*, Tosca! Hey…" he stopped short to stare at her old leather flying helmet, jodhpurs, boots and white silk neck scarf. "What's this? Who you supposed to be this time?"

"Waldo Pepper, Sir, if you please!" she said, grinning audaciously, snapping to attention and saluting the dumbfounded Greek.

"Crazy woman! Hey, go have a seat. Jim Kern brought a birthday cake for his niece. You can help us celebrate."

"You betcha, Boss," Cassidy answered. "Tosca's birthday too, you know. Eighteen today. What do you think of that?"

"Eighteen years old? *Mana mou*! You lucky stiff, Cassidy. Aaaallll right! We're gonna celebrate! Gonna drink some retsina, gonna dance!" he said, and snapped his fingers at the waitress.

"Hey, take an order here! The flier, it's her birthday! Anything she wants."

Satyri toasted the birthday girls. Clinked his wine glass against all at the big table, then against the beer bottles, wine carafes, votive candles and ash trays. He lifted the glass to his lips and yelled, *YAMAS!*, drained the glass dry, then snapped the stem off with his fingers. All at the table applauded his *savoir vivre* as he next turned toward the musicians. "Hey, all right, we're gonna dance! Play the new hisapiko!"

The musicians stood there plucking strings, doing riffs on the clarinet, in no apparent hurry; talking it over in the Greek tongue while they passed a cigarette around liesurely. Satyri lost patience, throwing his hands in the air, bellowing, "A HEAVY SILENCE FELL! Hisapiko!! Don't you understand English!"

They settled down after his tirade, played the music beautifully. As they danced a glazed look came over Satyri and Cassidy, the music affecting them greatly. "Only eighteen, eh? You lucky *gahmeesoo*, Cassidy.! Eighteen! OPA!"

"Can't help it, Boss. They just keep on keepin' on."

"Love that farkleing! Yasou! Keep 'em comin'," Satyri added.

The response to the dance was spirited as they returned to the table. Satyri poured and downed another glass of retsina then turned back to the dance floor as the music for his table dance commenced. "OPA! folks, here we go! OPA!"

He began the dance with usual stuff but instead of putting a second table on top of the first one he placed the birthday girl up there. "*Khronya pala!*" he wished her a happy birthday, but she was frightened and looked to her uncle for reassurance.

"Nothin' to worry about kid, Uncle Jimmy's watchin'! Jimmy not gonna let anything happen to you!" her uncle shouted.

But Cassidy was troubled. Trying to appear nonchalant he passed close by as Satyri positioned the birthday girl for balance on the table, centering her weight, tucking the left leg closer to the middle. "She too heavy, Boss?" he mumbled covertly.

Satyri glanced at him, then looked carefully at the girl, until his face broke into a wide grin. "Nah, she's only sixty, seventy pounds. Tonight I can do ninety easy."

"You sure?"

"Go sit down, old lady. You worry too much."

"Your funeral, man," Cassidy answered, and made his way back to the big table.

Satyri lifted the table and occupant slowly, first one side up then the other, very carefully. The girl sensed how iffy the whole thing might be and held on tensely, eyes bulging and pale lips drawn back in a frightened line across her teeth. Tosca leaned close as Satyri circled the dance floor, table and girl supported by his strong faultless teeth. "What was that all about?" she asked Cassidy.

"He's got bad legs. I'll tell you about it later."

After the dance ended Satyri helped the girl down from the table and the band segued into a rendition of the birthday song.

"Hey, what a night, eh!" Satyri hugged her. "You go to school tomorrow you tell the other kids to come here for their birthdays and I'll give 'em all a ride! OPA! Hey!" he called over his shoulder to a waitress, "bring me a glass so I can drink with my…" He left the sentence unfinished as he stared over his shoulder at the front doorway. "Holy shit. Who's that?"

Bair stood there, massive, stunned, holding onto the door frame for support. The drinks tonight at Rocky's had been the best in a long time. Bama Ford, Bobby Zwieg, J. Gill, the Mahl brothers, all the oldtime divers were there, all drunk on their ass. Nothing special. The Mahl brothers had taken a 16 foot

Great White today, and, what was scary, only a half-mile offshore. No big deal though their boat, the MAUL'EM, wasn't a whole lot bigger than the shark. With a cry of 'LET'S HEAR IT FOR THE FISH', they had toasted to each hundred weight of the frightening monster, successfully gulping down the first 23 drinks, but leaving the other 4 to a future time.

Bair was shit-faced good. He fanned the air with one unmanageable hand, motioning Cassidy to come near. He had decided that tonight was the right time to get rid of the diving suit. A twenty-seven hundred pound maneater only a half-mile offshore was a damn good time.

He was aware that Cassidy wanted the suit as a remembrance of the affection and years of comradeship between the two of them. Well he was welcome to it. Brrr, that was one scary fish, though the Encyclopedia Britannica had modern day 40 footers and claimed 90 footers for pre-historic times.

Bair said nothing to Cassidy; simply turned and waved him toward the van parked at curbside. Bair fumbled helplessly with the side door until Cassidy slid it open for him. Bair pointed wordlessly at the suit, laid out neatly there. "Take it. You earned it."

"Right now?"

"Want it or don't you?" Bair answered aggressively, but his gaze wavered. "You want it…" again Bair fanned the air with his floppy arm and his body teetered as he tried to stand tall.

Cassidy gathered up the suit piece by piece and took it into the back room of KYLIX, the room used by the belly dancers for costume change. "I don't see the helmet, Bair," he said, peering into the corners of the van.

"It's still at my house. Still polishing," he answered, slouching behind the wheel, almost asleep.

"Okay. You know how much I appreciate it."

"Yeah, me too." Bair reached out to touch the starter. "See you around."

"Wait a minute. Let me drive you home."

"You're pissin' upwind, boy! I'm in charge of this ship!"

"Sure Captain, and you're gonna end up with a DUI. Be cool. I'll be right back."

Cassidy returned to the dressing room where a crowd of dancers were examining the dive suit. He said his goodbyes and returned to the van but it was gone. He glanced up the street and saw tail lights moving away in the distance. He shook his head. Somehow it had turned out to be a sad night for him. He returned to KYLIX. Tosca would help him assemble the dive suit. They talked it over with Satyri. It would be perfect in the corner by the mural of boats and fishermen.

After leaving KYLIX they parked outside the big kitchen window, whispered and stroked while keeping an eye out for her mother who was washing dishes. "She'll probably be angry," Tosca said. "We usually give presents at the dinner table."

"Just tell her you got a special treat from Satyri and all the dancers who love you."

"She's still gonna be upset. So what was that about Satyri's legs."

Cassidy told her the story. How the boy Satyri had been wounded in the Greek civil war, his legs to remain a questionable pastiche of muscle bone and artery; how the veins had once ruptured while he was dancing at ZORBA's in Reseda, his life saved by a young intern in the audience who stanched the flow of blood.

"Is that why you never see him with a woman at KYLIX?"

"Oh no. He just thinks women are too possessive and that's bad for business. Don't worry, he gets his share. Just never at KYLIX."

She opened the car door to leave but nestled close, not yet ready to call it a night, enjoying one last bit of contact. "God, I'm exhausted."

"Rather forget about later, peanut?"

"Nope. Peanut shell will take a nap then come down about two-thirty."

"I'll leave the light on."

"No need. I'll bring my *linterna*. See you later."

He watched her enter. Mrs. Tosca engaged her in a terse conversation for a moment, but whatever the exchange was her mother's face softened and broke into a grin. She hugged her daughter then resumed washing the dishes while Tosca removed the flier's helmet and sat down at the kitchen table to discuss the day's events. Sketchily, Cassidy hoped.

CHAPTER 7

▼

In the gentle even climate of southern California the relationship of the lovers matured. They were almost always together. Tosca no longer bothered with extra-curricular activities at school, even giving up her beloved mime theater. Her entire energy was given over to the relationship, her intention to make it last forever.

But it wasn't that simple for Cassidy. It was time for the writer. Where before he had been content to pass idyllic moments reading to her, grooming her hair, massaging her back and listening to soft music, he now became impatient when he could not get on with Simon Lindero. At the same time he was only too aware that this pattern had caused him big problems in his previous relationships. No woman he ever knew could tolerate such competition for his time and attention.

Meanwhile his relationship with Mrs. Tosca had improved tremendously. She watched through the side window as the two of them ranged the badminton court in pursuit of the shuttlecock, both sometimes clumsy and sometimes graceful, zestful, eager to enjoy, until a long drive from Tosca's racquet hit Cassidy between the eyes as it floated erratically to earth.

Tosca doubled over in laughter and fell in a heap to the ground. He rushed to where she lay and tickled her wildly while she tried to escape. Mrs. Tosca's grin froze there. She experienced a twinge of melancholy at the memory of picnics of her own, the adolescence, the exhilaration. She jumped suddenly, startled from her reverie as Tosca, still giggling, poked her head through the side door.

"Mother, we're going down to his place for a while. "I'll take my homework," she said, and hurried to get her books.

Dusk had arrived by the time they got to his studio. The bougainvillaea cascaded darkly beside the walkway. Crickets had begun their evening lament and the delicate yellow sourgrass had already closed its bloom against the coming darkness. Arm-in-arm they entered the studio. Their retreat.

She walked across the room and dumped her backpack on the floor, then flung herself up on the bunk and fluffed the pillows. Cassidy went to the hotplate and put on a pan. "Pita and hot milk?"

"Hmmm, sounds good."

She watched him light the fireplace and then take his position at the work table. "Would you mind buttering the pita, Tosca?" he asked absent-mindedly, arranging his writing paraphernalia in order. Tosca smoldered, then found the courage to confront him. "Alexander..."

The tone of her voice told him what was on her mind. She was posed on the bunk with arms circled up behind the head in that gesture of acquiescence that is irrisistible to men.

"Make love with me, *amante*," she said, teeth glistening through parted lips, torso flexed to hardness as she stretched to her full length.

"Darlin', I really do need to get on with my work. I've got an acute case of 1-1-logorrhea coming on," he joked guiltily. "Okay?"

"No, not okay. You worked late last night. Why can't we have tonight for ourselves."

"Because I've got a rush coming on, Tosca. I've got to take it as it happens."

Rebuffed momentarily, she tried a new approach. "Alexander, still love your Tosca?"

"Well I don't know. You do have funny eyes."

"Alexander! I'm serious!"

"Yes, I love you. More than myself, more than god," he swore, raising his hand to oath. "Darlin', have patience. When I sell this story we're going to Athens to live. Maybe even Rome and Paris."

"You're serious? You'll take me with you?"

"Dead serious. You go where I go."

"Well in that case...Back to the French, I guess," she answered, and turned back to her books. He watched her struggle with it for ten minutes or so. The book eased lower to her chest until, with a sigh, she gave it up and closed her eyes. She slept soundly as he went about his business, or rather, tried to. He became frustrated. The anticipated rush had somehow disappeared. He tried time and again but with each new failing he became even more anxious and ineffective. In a burst of temper he crushed the unsatisfactory page and hurled it to the floor. She awoke and watched him covertly for a few moments before raising up in the bunk.

"Alexander, come over here by me," she offered, and scooted over to make room for him.

"Couldn't you sleep?"

"A little. Couldn't you write?"

"Nothing. Come on, let's go get some supper. Change the mood of the…He stopped in the middle of the sentence as a sharp knock rattled the door. "Wonder who that is?"

"Mom's the only one who knows we're down here. I think."

They waited anxiously until the knock became more insistent. "Padro?" Cassidy suggested, rising sharply from the bunk.

"Alexandros, you home?"

They were relieved to hear Satyri's voice. Cassidy cracked the door open and peered out into the perspiring face of the Greek who stood there in his apron and fisherman's cap, twirling his worry beads. He made a move to come in but Alexander held the door rigidly. "I've got company," he said, and nodded over his shoulder.

"Lucky stiff, eh. I'm killing myself over there in a hot kitchen and you're over here farkleing around. Look I got a madhouse over there. Two birthdays, an anniversary, and no candles for the cakes. Go to Long's and get me a box, huh, and a couple of gallons of vanilla ice cream too."

"You betcha, Boss. We were on our way over for supper anyway."

"Aaalll right! I need some dancers too. I'll hold 'em off until you get there. *Efkhareesto.*"

Tosca was already dressed when Cassidy closed the door. She felt a small triumph as she watched him slip into the white cottons. She had gotten him away from the newly troublesome Simon Lindero. For the rest of the night he would be her's alone.

CHAPTER 8

▼

Who was it said 'All comes to he who waits'? Well that's just what Tosca and Alexander did. Waited. Played it cool. Mrs. Tosca finally realized she would have to deal with them as a single entity. She even began to feel a certain fondness for Cassidy. This disturbed her as she still had her defenses set against him, still somewhat resentful of his continued closeness to her daughter. And yet, just several days before, they had shared their first personal conversation as Cassidy waited for Tosca to finish dressing.

"I don't mean to be nosey, Ma'am, but I can't help wondering how you and Padro got together in the first place. You're so pleasant and easy-going. So different than he is."

"Yes. Well he was nice at first. At least he was to me. Celia and I went to high school together in Miami. Padro never had any friends. He was a very strange young boy. A lot had happened to him, the war and politics. He was a hero, not like the rest of us."

"How'd you get together?"

"After I graduated he suddenly became interested in me and we started seeing each other. Uh...why don't you call me Marta. Ma'am makes me feel so old."

"Sure. It was just a respect thing. Marta...Marta...How about Marty?"

"I like that. Marty's fine."

It was lunch time at Tosca's house. They had spent the morning working in their garden of zucchini, corn and tomatoes, a hit-and-miss affair with Cassidy doing the spade work, Tosca the gathering of rocks and seeding. They loved the sharing. Something their's, together. At the moment Cassidy was cooling off in the shower while Tosca and her mother prepared the food.

"You two did a good job out there," Mrs. Tosca lauded as Tosca set the table. "That soil hasn't been turned in years. Not since..." her voice trailed off weakly.

"Oh Mom, don't. He isn't worth the thought."

"He's your father, Tina, and he wasn't always this bad," she said, remembering her thoughts of a few moments ago as she watched them work the garden. She and Padro had once worked the garden and shared the fruit. Despite his presently jaded attitude he had once adored her. But after Tina's unwelcome birth he had reverted to his old bachelor behavior. Booze and whores were plentiful and cheap in Miami. Whereas before he had treated her with respect and affection he now tried to control every facet of her life with his macho behavior. Their relationship became one of mutual loathing, spousal rape and alienation.

Tosca was pained that her mother thought of Padro at all, but she was pleased by the friendly remark about Alexander. She sidled up, put an arm around her mother's waist and stood head to head. "I'm glad you and Chuck have each other. I don't worry about you so much now."

"He's a real find. I lucked out."

"So did he. Are you going to marry?"

"He hasn't asked. I hope you and Alexander haven't thought about marriage."

"We've discussed it. But he thinks all marriages are doomed from the start."

"How come?"

"The divorce. His ex did a job on him."

"A lot of people do jobs on each other but they get over it. I want to say something Tina, but I hope you won't get mad at me. Please don't consider marriage with him."

"I don't know how to answer that, Mom."

"I just wanted you to know how I feel about it, that's all. By the same token there's something else I want to say and you can repeat it to him if you like. He's a good person. I've come to like him. I haven't seen you this content since before..." Mrs. Tosca hesitated..."for sometime now." She reached to untangle the strands of Tosca's hair, an act of love and caring. They continued in this frame of mind until Cassidy, fresh from the shower, entered the kitchen, licking his lips in anticipation.

"Boy you've got radar," Mrs. Tosca joked. "It's just now ready. I meant to ask, Alexander, how's the new job coming along?"

"Perfect. Two hours a day for the man. The rest for writing."

"Cleaning floors and toilets isn't my idea of proper work for a writer," Tosca answered curtly, "I don't care what Steinbeck recommended."

"Yeah, I know, but I've got to keep my head clear of all that stress a regular job puts on you. And it buys enough food and there's still enough left for child support."

"I don't call tuna and crackers food."

"It won't be forever, babe. Have faith."

The lunch continued pleasantly, the conversation alternating between politics, Tosca's planned transfer to UCSB after next semester, and Alexander's tribulations with editors and publisher. Out of a reason to put it off any longer Cassidy excused himself from the table. "Back to work. I can only give it a couple more hours today."

"Okay, let's do it," Tosca replied, and got up to join him. But her mother touched her shoulder and winked conspiritorially. "Help me clear the table first, honey. I have to be downtown in an hour."

It was only when they were out of Cassidy's earshot that Mrs. Tosca broached the subject. "I wasn't gonna mention it but your father came up here last night, drunk, looking for Alexander. Wanted to beat him up."

"Mother, you tell him if he even touches Alexander I'll have him arrested. I'll tell Mr. Green."

"That's what I said and I called Mr. Green this morning, so he knows what's going on. By the way, I'm going to Chuck's tonight for dinner so lock up if you go out."

"I'm grounded tonight. A Theater Arts assignment. THE MERCHANT OF VENICE is on TV."

"Okay, I'll be home about midnight. Oh yeah, there's another mouse on the loose. I saw him over by the sofa."

Tosca decided to watch THE MERCHANT OF VENICE in her mother's bedroom. It had the biggest colour TV in the house. The room was one of those middle-class auditoriums which serve as bedroom, beauty parlor, bathroom, ski and tennis storage, and TV room. Just like in the cartoons he and Tosca sat side by side, propped against the king-size upholstered headboard, four legs and feet pointed toward the TV set, TV trays with the remains of the TV dinners still resting on their laps.

They were nude, skins pink and aromatic from a hot bath, appetites sated by the light meal. They were successful at watching Olivier at first, the best Shylock ever. But only for the first 15 minutes, until the commercial breaks started.

"Alexander, turn off the dresser lamp. It's causing a glare on the TV."

Cassidy got out of bed and crossed over in front of the TV to kill the light, and as he started back to the bed he heard her moan sensually. "Back up a little, Alexander. Please."

"Why? What's goin' on?" he asked, and stood waiting.

It became obvious what was on her mind; to see, with the TV screen as back-light, the outline of his body where the thigh joins the groin, genitalia projecting downward like a bouquet of dark flowers.

"Oh that's nice," she whispered, then patted the adjacent bedside. He slid in beside her. Her hands were on his body, sampling, squeezing. His mouth came down hard on hers, pushing the lips aside until their teeth ground together passionately. He licked her nipples and navel, drove her up the wall, then stopped and asked facetiously, "But what about Shakespeare?"

"Who's he?" she asked, and jumped off the bed to turn down the sound. She pressed him backwards and straddled him in the dominant position. Her body was outlined by the light from the TV as she gyrated, head thrown back, eyes closed to all around. Roughly his hands traced her nipples, calves, thighs, feet, and the hidden places that only lovers dare search out. Pressing her backwards and down he assumed the dominant position and reentered her body. As the tempo of their passion increased he felt a tickling sensation on his leg, as though from one of her mice, and drew away sharply. But it was only Sam. Drawn by the sounds of their urgency and her own need for affection, Sam made her way along their intertwined bodies and curled around Tosca's neck.

"Come on cat, go get your own," Cassidy urged, and started to ease Sam off the bed.

But Tosca, eyes closed, placed a protective hand on Sam and stroked her fur. "Mmmm, soft. Feels good," she whispered, barely audible. "Do it, *amante*. Keep going."

"Okay darlin', whatever's good for you."

Cassidy bent backwards away from Sam and continued to stroke Tosca who was in deep passion. But it was Sam who was responsible. Sam was licking at one of Tosca's nipples! Too early weaned, the cat was nursing at her breast!

"Ohhh, sandpaper! I can't stand it!" she said, her hands covering her face, gripping at her head. But it was an acceptable torture; she couldn't bring herself to push Sam away.

Cassidy watched in fascination as Sam kneaded Tosca's breast with paw and claw, Tosca's head rolling from side to side in exaggerated ecstacy. Cassidy withdrew and eased down along her body, kissing navel, thigh and groin until finally cunnilingus. "Oh my God, baby! Yes, yes, YES!" the frantic energy came over her in a surge and the thrashing climax frightened Sam who sprang from the bed and skittered away. Cassidy inched upward along her body and reentered once more. "Do it, Alejandro! Do it, do it" she urged, totally out of it now.

It was only in the rapturous afterplace where exhausted lovers lie stunned from the chaos of a climax that either of them grasped the rarity, the purity of what had just happened.

"Incredible!" Cassidy whispered in her ear. "My editor would swear I made this one up."

"Unless she's got a Sam too. Jesus, I couldn't handle the two of you like that everyday. Burn out," she said, shuddering deeply. "One thing for sure…I better treat Sam a little better from now on, right."

"Hey, you forget about Sam. I'll give you what you need."

He felt ridiculous for having shared her with a cat, yet, perversely, it had been a beautiful experience. He began the ritual of resting lovers; the massage of strained calf muscles, thighs and feet. He nibbled playfully at her groin, where shapely thigh linked to faultless hip. "I'm surprised they don't just pop out of their sockets, as wide as you open," he said, and kissed each hip tenderly.

Eyes closed, she lay contented while he continued the indulgence. Then suddenly he stopped and studied her face. "Has Sam ever done that to you before?"

Her eyes fluttered open, the gaze faltered, she nodded her head. "Are you mad at me?"

"Mad? That's not possible with someone so natural and honest. Tosca, how do you say 'beautiful soul'?"

"*Alma hermosa.*"

"You, *alma hermosa*, are too much for me."

"Yeah? *Te gusta?*"

"*Si, mi gusta mucho, amante,*" he answered, and jumped out of bed to turn up the TV volume. "What if your mom asks about Shylock? Do you know the story well enough to fake it?"

"Oh sure, we do a lot of Shakespeare in school. She won't ask, don't worry."

"Good. Hey, this has been a real mind-blow. I need coffee. Are you game?"

"Yeah, and pecan pie! Let's go down to MUDDY WATERS', huh?

They got up and went to 'the pile'. Fished around until she found one of those granny gowns that the girls of the 60s and 70s used to wear without bra and panties. Tosca still did.

"Amazing! Has that pile ever failed you?"

"Nope. It's just the right size. I had to experiment, you know, get it just right."

It shocked their senses, going from warmth out into the damp night air. A dense fog had rolled in and reduced visibility to 15 feet, and the deep-throated fog horn sounded its warning from Stearns Wharf. As they strolled arm-in-arm to the Morris Minor she teased him mischeviously. "Rather go to your place, *amante*? I could handle some more of that."

"Jesus! Haven't you had enough for one night? Let me squeeze in the coffee break, huh."

"Si. Coffee break first, then the garage."

"Okay, peanut, the garage it is."

"*Peanut shell*," she corrected him, and took a tighter hold on his arm. They approached the Morris Minor and walked around to the passenger's side. As he passed the radiator he noticed a puddle of liquid under the front wheels. "Damn! I'm losing water!"

He took a flashlight from the glove box and flashed it around. "I can't believe this! Look, my radiator is full of holes, like from a screwdriver or something!"

Tosca was silent as she thought it over. "Don't you get it?" she asked.

"No, I can't understand how..." he stopped as the realization took hold. "Do you really think so?"

"It was him all right."

"Christ, what a radical fucking thing to do!" he said, shining the flashlight into the nearby bushes. "Come on, let's get outta here. Feel like walking or you want to go back?"

"Walking, *amante*. Pecan pie then the garage."

"Christ, Tosca, you're trying to do me in."

"Yeah, I'm gonna wear you out," she grinned, and held on tighter as they headed for Haley Street, and MUDDY WATERS' coffee house and deli.

CHAPTER 9

▼

Wrapped snugly in Cassidy's bathrobe Tosca sat propped up on his bed, reading yesterday's production on Simon Lindero. She sipped at a cup of tea and now and then observed him covertly, bent over the writing table with his head resting on his forearms, creaking the chair absent-mindedly. Ever since his mother's death several weeks before his discipline had suffered and he was just now getting back to normal. Tosca finally dropped the pretense and pushed the manuscript aside.

"Alexander, lie down beside me."

He looked at her there, arms outstretched, abundant sympathy showing on her face. He moved to the bed and flopped face down next to her. She ran her fingers through his hair and massaged his back lightly. "It'll be okay, *corazon*. Hang in there."

Sure, he knew that. Time would take care of it same as with his grandmother, who, except for the age difference, was a perfect twin to his own mother. Weathered, handsome and peppery, this grandmother had been the nearest thing to a perfect woman that Cassidy had ever seen. Hollywood had duplicated her general character in dozens of movies. She even resembled those pioneer women with her sharp jaw, piercing eyes and hair worn in a bun. She had died of grief the doctor said. Small, pasty, drawn up in a fetuslike gnome, unaware of all around her. His own wonderful mother had gone the same way, but from the effects of her 8th stroke rather than the death of a favorite son as Granny had done.

"Mom was so gentle and loving. Not a mean bone in her whole body. Couldn't even focus her eyes at the end. Just stared into space and grinned like an unfocused newborn."

A long silence followed as she rocked the bed and patted his shoulder rhythmically. Ruthful, healing moments.

"Ssshhhh, ssshhh, it's all right...all right," Tosca tried to soothe him. But it all seemed so futile to Cassidy; birth, life and death. Always finally death. An austere word, aesthetically flat, as emotionless as the condition itself. The word filled him with dread and a strong need for relevance. He stirred and moved to the foot of the bed, and with a look that begged of understanding, he took hold of her feet and spread her legs apart. "Take off the robe, sweetheart. Please?"

She watched as he untied the robe, opened it and removed her panties. Lying face down he moved upward between her legs until the top of his head was pressed tightly against her vagina. His head and face were warm against her legs. She felt the tingle start, the juices begin. *Incredible*, she thought, and hugging her legs tightly around him she rocked the bed again.

Cassidy remained silent, his arms locked around her thighs. She reached up and turned off the reading lamp, masking the studio in darkness. They shared quiet intuitive moments as the bed rocked with a hypnotic squeak. She broke the silence finally.

"*Pobrecito*, what are you thinking about?"

"Birth, death, the line is broken and I'm next on the list."

She gripped his head tightly and pressed it closer to her groin.

"I wish I could crawl up in there, Tosca, and be your own new baby. I don't want to be parted from you, not ever."

They layed that way for several minutes, dozing, secure in this cocoon of her making. Then she felt him move off the bed, leaving her suddenly empty, a feeling she didn't like.

"Thank you, darlin'," he said, and turned the light back on. "I don't know anyone else who would have understood that."

Still in a trance of sorts she took hold of his hand and whistled softly. "My God, what an experience."

"Yeah, weird huh. You won't tell anybody will you?"

"Who'd believe it. Alexander, you talk about your mother but never talk about your father. What kind of man was he?"

"Two words...a drunk and a fighter. Died when I was two, thankfully. So, what's the verdict? Like it so far?"

"Like what?" she asked, confused.

"Simon Lindero. Last night's stuff. Is it okay'""

"Jesus! Give me a minute to come down, will you," she complained, frustrated by the sudden change in him. Reluctantly she took up the manuscript and read the last page again.

"Well, it's pretty heavy stuff, boats and dope."

"I know you're not high on the topic but do you like it? The style, quality of writing?"

"Sure. It's well done. It's just that I'd like to see you write more like you are. Your experience, your values and sense of humor."

"But it's a caper, an action story. Strictly commercial. Something to take us to Greece and Rome."

"Couldn't Simon be a carpenter or an executive? Why does he have to be a dope smuggler?"

"Because the story is based on a real person, Babe. It gives him a strong character, see. Bad boy goes straight for the love of an angel. Besides, I can't buy into a wimpy accounts executive rescuing his best friend from a Mexican dungeon, then carrying off the warden's 15 year old daughter. My Simon is the only one who could have managed something that audacious."

Indeed Cassidy had originally written Simon bigger than life but soon realized he was too partial to the character. He got to liking Simon too much, identified with him too closely. They were both sailors. Both had a strong preference for smart women. Both were articulate and had similar dislike for the society in general, loved the fine arts etc. etc. Though he had cut Simon back somewhat he was still pleased with him as drawn and felt a strong kinship to him.

"But do you like it?" he persisted. "Yes? No?"

"I like it. When will you be finished?"

"A couple of months."

"That's a long time away from me."

"I'll make it up to you in Athens and Paris."

"I'm gonna hold you to that," she said, and started to hum in the silence that followed. "This guy Simon…Have you ever known such a man?"

"Aha! You do like him!" Cassidy answered, and was thoughtful before continuing. "Several close, but no, never one such a guy. Simon is a true composite. A collage of sorts."

"A shame he's not real. I have to admit he is sort of fascinating."

"Hey, maybe I better not let you read anymore. You might get hooked on him and blow me off."

Almost ritually Tosca put her hand to his forehead and touched first the eyes then the nose and mouth. "But you've got the life, Alejandro," she whispered, and put her hand to his heart. "You've got the power."

"And I've got love for you, *niña*, a boundless love. Remember that in the next few weeks," he said, and turned away as though to avoid her eyes.

"Something wrong?" she asked, sensing the negative.

"Awww nothing. I was just thinking about tomorrow. Satyri's gonna bring me a list of stuff he wants us to pick up when we go to Ventura. I don't really want to go."

"It's something else, isn't it. Come on, out with it."

"Can't fool you, eh kid. Yeah, I was just thinking about my work."

"Why be sad. You're so lucky to have that."

"Remembering the past. My values get turned around at this stage. The writing takes me over."

"I don't understand. How can something take you over?"

"I get hyped up and irrational. Withdraw into myself. And when the energy comes on I might even reject us temporarily. I've done it in the past."

"Reject me? Reject your Tosca?" she was dumbfounded, the blue/green eyes wide and staring. Unable to stand the hurt in her eyes and on her face he took her in his arms. "I'll do my best darlin', but it happened before."

"I'll be all right," she assured him. "I'll just do my homework, make love to you, and just be glad to be there."

"I didn't even allow for making love the other times."

"No love? No sex?" she said, searching his face for a sign of uncertainty. "I bet your Simon would never do without sex."

"I'm serious, Tosca. And besides, Simon is only a flash in my gut, he's not a writer."

Still she did not take him seriously and began to disrobe. "Better not," Cassidy reminded her. "Satyri's due any minute now."

"Let him come. We don't have to answer the door." Hypnotized by her deliberate movements he watched her disrobe and lower herself down onto him, inhaling sharply as he penetrated her. "I am eighteen and beautiful, Señor, and I will make you forget Satyri and Simon Lindero too," she moaned, her face aglow with passion, her body squirming.

"I swear…I know…them not…" he framed his words to match the cadence of her deliberate thrusts. But passions were quickly forgotten as the door rattled violently and they heard her father shouting obscenities outside.

"He found us! He knows we're in here," she panicked and jumped off the bed to begin dressing as Padro continued to pound the door.

"It had to happen, Tosca. We might as well get it over with," Cassidy said, putting on his clothes.

"Don't open it! Call the police!"

"And tell 'em what. That I'm in here seducing his daughter while he's pounding on the door and cussing me out? Let's just deal with it, okay."

She jumped up and tried to block his path. "He's tried to catch up with you several times! Don't do it!"

"It can't go on like this," Cassidy said, brushing by her. "I'll try to reason with him."

But the sight of him only infuriated Padro more. "You son of a bitch!" he shouted, and made a lunge for Cassidy as the door opened.

"Get the heck outta here, Padro! Leave us alone!" Tosca screamed angrily, and dashed between them to push and flail at her father. But it was Satyri's timely arrival which kept the worst from happening.

"Hey man, what you doin' here?" Satyri demanded, towering over the smaller man.

"None of your god-damn business! Out of the way!"

"Forget it! You ain't goin' in there!"

"He's got my daughter in there! Who are you anyway?"

"I don't care who he's got! You ain't goin' in there and bust up my property! Now simmer down!"

"Listen, there's nothing wrong here," Cassidy interjected. "We're both adults. She's my guest."

"Guest you call it! You old bastard!" Padro shouted and made another jump at Cassidy. But the move was anticipated by Satyri who blocked his way.

"You wouldn't like it if that was your daughter in there!" Padro insisted. "Out of my way!"

"Hey, want the cops, Mister! It's okay by me. Tosca, get inside!" Satyri shouted, and tried to hustle them back into the studio. But Padro charged, scattering all three of them. Satyri lost control, jamming Padro against the wall, side-stepping as Padro aimed a kick at his groin. "Listen to me!" Satyri screamed, tightening his choke hold until Padro gave it up. "I don't take this shit off nobody, understand! I'll break your fucking head! You want it? You want it?"

Eye to eye with the Greek, Padro got the message; primitive against primitive, the animal with teeth bared.

Satyri released his hold and turned to Tosca and Alexander. "Enough of this crap, you guys. Inside," he said, and slammed the door on them before turning back to Padro.

"Listen, don't come down here like this and shit on my head, okay. I got enough problems already."

Padro glared at him a moment then got into the Jeep and started the motor. "Hey man, you were a shithead before I ever met you!" he shouted and drove away, leaving Satyri to shake his head and stare after him.

As the sounds of anger receded Cassidy wanted to discuss Padro further though he felt she wouldn't be receptive to it. "Darlin', can we talk about it?"

"Like what?"

"Your father and your hatred of him."

She looked at him sharply and paged through the manuscript with a vengeance, doing her best to ignore the question, but Cassidy just crossed his legs and stared at her until she finally gave in.

"He broke up the family, that's what. We weren't important to him anymore. We ran into him downtown once with a whore. He called mom a *vaca de leche*, and told her to get home. Do you have any idea what *vaca de leche* means, Alexander? MILK COW, for god's sake! He called my mother a milk cow right in the middle of Macy's, in front of a bunch of strangers!"

Cassidy went to her and put his arms around her, felt her shudder. The tears were minimal and slow in coming. The sorrow was an old one, bone deep.

"He didn't want me, Alexander. He wanted a son. He ignored me because I was a girl and said it was all mom's fault." She stopped to blow her nose. Casssidy waited. "I don't want to talk about it anymore, Alexander. It really pisses me off."

"It's okay, darlin'. You don't have to," Cassidy replied, realizing that this was truly plenty of reason for her loathing of her father.

CHAPTER 10

▼

Despite all their wily tricks and pleas Cassidy would not tell Tosca and her mother why today was such a special day. Only that he would pick them up for breakfast and have a fine surprise for them. Something they would like; something for all three of them.

In thinking it all out Tosca whittled it down to three possibilities. #1—he had received good news from either his publisher or his agent, Rome and Athens now imminent. Or, #2—he would ask her to marry him, or perhaps just to live with him, either one acceptable. Or maybe, #3—he had been talking about the boat a lot lately. YUK! for #3.

Mrs. Tosca had worried right along with her daughter and did not sleep well either. She feared it was going to be #2, a choice she would oppose outright. But then, why get overwrought until it was for sure. That would be the right time to assert herself and try to dissuade them.

As her mother moved to let Cassidy in the door Tosca caught herself wishing her mother would wear a babushka, a hat, a bucket, anything to cover up the head full of curlers in perpetual sprout there. The old frayed housecoat she could handle but the curlers were definitely ugly. Cassidy was in a buoyant spirit as he entered and kissed Tosca on the cheek. "Morning, *niña*, and Marty. Did you guys sleep well?"

"Yes, once I finally dozed off," Mrs. Tosca answered.

"Well I'm glad it's morning. I didn't close my eyes all night long. Ready for a good breakfast?" he asked energetically, rubbing his hands together in anticipation.

"Been ready for half an hour," Tosca answered, slipping into her fur hat and coat.

"Why don't we just have breakfast here and save the money?"

"Thanks, Marty, but I think I'll take her out for a change. She's been throwing Simon and his dough up to me a lot lately. I just might lose her if I'm not careful."

"Oh?" Mrs. Tosca's interest took a quantum leap at the mention of Simon's name. "Who is he?"

"A rich guy. The hero in my story."

"What's so great about him?"

"Oh not much," Tosca interrupted. "Just he's rich, handsome, generous. Got a degree in architecture. A big boat. He travels when he feels like it. Other than that…" she stopped and shrugged her shoulders in jest.

"Yeah, tell her the rest. He smuggles dope on this big schooner and he's on the make for this sweet innocent Mexican virgin who is barely 15 years old. That's the kind of guy her Simon is."

Once finished with his description Cassidy realized the small difference in age between the Mexican virgin and Mrs. Tosca's daughter. His eyesbrows arched involuntarily as he and Mrs. Tosca locked onto each other, embarrassed. Finally she shrugged and looked away. "You better take her out for breakfast maybe."

"Preposterous what people will believe as long as it's between book covers. Okay, we're going to the SANDSPIT CAFE, Marty. Are you ready?"

"Not quite. I've got some business to take care of first. You go on ahead and I'll meet you there."

It was 11 o'clock by the time they finished breakfast and Mrs. Tosca never did show up. They sat on the seawall and watched the parade of tourists go by, and urchin divers and day sailors, until they spotted Mrs. Tosca hurrying toward them. "What a morning! Sorry, I just couldn't make it in time," she apologized.

"We held off as long as we could, Mom."

"I'll get something at home. But I should tell you…I had an appointment with Mr. Green."

"Oh? About what?" Tosca was apprehensive.

"You two and Padro. I thought he should know what's going on."

"What did he say, Mom?"

"He said to tell Alexander about Marcel. We should have told you before, I guess. Marcel was a football player at City College, a nice young man who had a crush on Tina. Padro found out about it and beat Marcel so bad he almost died.

Padro went to prison and Mr. Green was his parole officer when he got out. He was the only one ever able to deal with Padro."

"Why did he hurt the guy?"

"He was nineteen, already in college. I was sixteen and still in high school."

"Jesus! Well what did Green have to say about us?" Cassidy asked.

"He said he'd talk to Padro, let him know he's aware of what's happening. But he said Padro's off parole so that's all he can do. But enough of that. What's this fantastic surprise you promised us?"

"Come on, I'll show you," Cassidy said, and led them to the gate for Marina #4.

"Alexander, you got the boat!" Tosca faked the excitement.

"Yeah, she's been bleeding me dry for storage down there and rent up here so I talked to Bair about it. He fronted the dough, had her trucked up from Newport. Come on. You're not gonna believe this one."

Inserting his key card he opened the gate, took Tosca by the shoulders and pointed her toward the nearest dock. "There she is! MARCO POLO!"

They were looking at an old Chinese junk, three masts, a black hull, the freeboard painted with red and yellow dragons. Low in the water, wide of beam with a poop deck abaft the cabin, she measured 32 feet long on deck. Her olive-drab cabin and ecru-coloured sails gave her the character of a craft that might have been built for an old China hand or other far-east salt.

"Well what do you think Marty?", he asked as she eyed the teak pile as if it was a UFO.

"Well...it's a...interesting."

He was disappointed by her reaction; that of a matron checking out a radical Picasso. But her's was the normal reaction to a Chinese junk. He should have anticipated it.

"How about you, Tosca? *Te gusta*?"

"*Te gustaaaa*! It's got character. Similar to a boat I've dreamt about for years."

"Oh? Like what?"

"Phoenician sailors. A big black boat comes in from the sea and a dark mysterious man carries me away on the boat. Wierd, huh?"

"Hmmmmm. Come on, you'll love it below deck. It's got handcarved fretwork, pastoral scenes painted on the bulkheads, and a modern galley I'm still not sure I like. Yeah, and the bunks are made of bamboo poles and canvas."

MARCO POLO was heavy underfoot as they boarded her. She had solidity, that feeling of substance one should get from a craft that is to be taken to sea. A musty odor greeted them as he opened the hatch to go below. "Wheeew!" Mrs. Tosca pinched her nose against the smell and followed them below.

"She's been closed up a long time but she'll freshen up."

"Smells haunted," Tosca observed.

"Strange you should say that. The former owner swore it is."

"You're not really going to live on it then?"

"Yes I am, Marty. It'll help the ambience of my story which is about boats," he answered, then opened several portholes for ventilation. "I think it'll be a great work space."

"Will it be safe to go out on?"

"Sure. Junks this size can cruise blue water, no problem."

Tosca took sightings from several of the portholes, her point of reference the adobe bluffs of Santa Barbara City College which overlooked the harbor. "Hey, I can pop right down the bluff from school and study between classes and it won't be so boring."

"Right. And I'll make you decent lunches. No more peanut butter and junk food, pardon the pun," Cassidy added.

"And you can have the pick of the harbor for your Freehand Drawing classes," Mrs. Tosca noted.

"It's gonna be great. I want you to feel welcome here too, Marty. Anytime."

"Thanks, that's very nice of you. Well I've got a lot of chores to do so I'll see you kids back at the house. Congratulations, Mr. Cassidy," she smiled at him as he helped her up onto the dock.

He turned back and watched as Tosca poked at the battens of the mainsail. "This bamboo feels real spongy," she said. "We'll have to go to the hot springs to cut some new stuff."

"We will eventually. But for right now let's go pay the dock rent (he shook a handful of greenbacks in her face) before I spend it foolishly."

He turned off the cabin light and locked the hatch before going ashore. "Did you notice? Your mom called us kids before she left." Cassidy pulled her close and kissed her cheek. "It took a while, *niña*, but god-damn you're sure worth it."

"Speaking of worth…I never dreamed you had enough money to own a boat like that. It looks expensive."

Cassidy told her it was the only thing he took in the divorce. Everything else went to his wife, the artifacts, the money. But he had made the adjustment and seldom gave it any thought. He also told her he would be more bothered by moving further away from her. He would miss her cape and lantern in the middle of

the night and her soft voice calling out OPA! on entering the studio. And Bo
Diddley. He looked at her sadly, the beginnings of a blue funk all too obvious.

"I've got a feeling MARCO POLO isn't going to be a happy experience for us,
Alexander. Can't we keep the studio too?"

"I'd love that, darlin', but huh uh, I can't afford both of them. Damn! I've got
to click with Simon Lindero. Got to!"

"I'm afraid for you to be so far away. You might forget me."

"How could anyone ever forget such a sweet peanut."

"Peanut *shell*. You're the peanut."

He paid the harbormaster. They took pizza down to the junk. They sat quietly, ate, absorbed the movement of the water. They checked the boat out from
stem to stern, storage lockers and clothes lockers, the head, the bilges and book-
shelves. They poked everywhere.

"Let's go to STELLA's and rummage," she suggested. "Maybe find something
for MARCO POLO."

"Good idea. Remember that whale oil lamp? We should get that to make love
by."

At STELLA's the whale oil lamp was gone but they found a wicker bookshelf,
a spice rack for the galley, and a Kelim rug remnant for the aisle of the cabin.
Tosca was poking into a cardboard box of fur fragments, when Stella approached.
"It gets cold down in the harbor, child. A fur throw could come in mighty
handy."

"Good idea, Stella, for his birthday. How much for all of it?" she whispered as
Cassidy passed close by.

"Good customers like you guys…seven-fifty."

"I'm busted. Can I owe it to you?"

"Don't worry about it," Stella said, patting her on the arm.

"*Gracias*. I'll pick it up tomorrow."

The harbor was socked in with fog by the time they returned to MARCO
POLO, and Cassidy's mental state had improved considerably. This was the
environment he liked best; boats, fog, the sea. And now MARCO POLO again.
He thought of her as fine architecture, like Frank Lloyd Wright or the Green
brothers, maybe a black 1940 Lincoln convertible or the Wainwright Tomb. She
satisfied his addiction to the ideal, a pleasure he might not experience again if he
did not connect with Simon Lindero.

He was nudged back to reality by the huge foghorn out on the end of Stearns
Wharf as it commenced its reassuring sound to all within earshot, a sound so
penetrating that it could be heard clear up on Alameda Padre Serra.

The adobe bluffs, dense fog and sea were not the elements of Tosca's choice however. She was more structured for mountain canyon and forest. The harbor was too exotic for her, too foreboding, and a symbol of the change which was overtaking them.

"God, babe, isn't it great down here," he said, attempting to lift her spirits, but she was just plain down and wanted none of it. She said she was afraid she wouldn't get to see him as often, and wouldn't know where to find the little yellow car.

"Want to stay at the studio tonight?"

"Yeah, after mom goes to sleep."

By the time they reached her house the fog was as thick as down in the harbor. The foghorn sounded so powerfully to where the three of them sat on the patio, grouped around smoldering logs in a metal wash tub, listening and staring at the crackling fire.

"I'll miss you, Alexander. You've been a big help around here," Mrs. Tosca finally broke the silence.

"Hey, I'll still be around. It's like family, you know. I don't get much chance at it these days."

"Can we talk about something else, please."

"Sorry, honey," Mrs. Tosca said, and leaned over to kiss her cheek. "Past my bedtime. Be sure to put out the fire."

"Okay, Mom."

"And Tina, please…that mobile…take it out of my study. You know how it depresses me."

"All right, Mom. Sorry."

"Goodnight, Marty," Cassidy called after her as she headed for the door. "What was that about a mobile?" he asked Tosca.

"A class project I did in junior high. Mom hates it."

"I'd like to see it sometime. Hey, your mom is really coming on to us. I think she…" He stopped to listen as a single sniffle sounded in the darkness. "Are you crying, Tosca?"

"I'm just tired of things changing all the time. Things always seem to mess up just when they're going best."

"What things? What are you talking about?"

"Well like giving up the studio. Didn't you like it there with me? Did you have to get the boat?"

"For Christ's sake, I love that setup and you know it! But it's not the end of the world, Tosca. You have to roll with the punches."

"And you've begun to write all the time. I've noticed the difference."

Her complaint struck a vital nerve. Alarmed, he bent over and peered upward into her downcast face. "No, darlin', I'm not gonna let that happen again."

"But just the other night you said you might reject me."

Ashamed, Cassidy turned away to the fire tub to avoid her accusing eyes. "I couldn't handle that, Alexander. I'll kill myself."

"Hey! Don't ever say that, Tosca. Just keep in touch and we'll work it out. Promise?" She nodded in acquiescence and he slid an arm around her waist. "Want to go down to the four-poster?"

"Yeah, we don't have much time left."

He turned the Morris Minor around while she smothered the fire with ashes, and her spirit had improved by the time she scrambled into the car. "I'm ready. Let's go."

"That's better. I like to see you happy. I want to make you happy," he said, and eased the car down to the fogbound street. They had driven less than 100 feet when she grabbed at his arm suddenly.

"Do a U-ie at the corner and go back."

"What for?"

"You'll see."

He hit the brake. Made the U-turn back toward her house. She eased the window down on her side and pointed. "Real slow now. See it?"

"Yeah," he answered, surprised to see the Jeep outlined in his headlights, parked at the curb, Padro hunched up in his peacoat against the fog.

"Find what you're looking for?" she shouted, thrusting the upper part of her body through the open window. She leaned close to the Jeep as they passed, gave him the finger, and shouted angrily, "Go home! You don't belong here anymore! Go away!"

Cassidy winced, certain this would get them immediate retribution. He watched in the rearview mirror for Padro's headlights, for the Jeep to come screaming after them. Nothing happened.

Padro lit a cigarillo calmly and watched the tail lights of the Morris recede in the distance. A rare moment of regret passed over him as he thought of the trouble and ugliness he had brought to his little girl, perhaps the only human being he had ever really truly loved.

He started the Jeep and turned on the radio. He changed the dial until he found a news station. Most people did this to find out what was going on in the outside world but Padro did it for bile. Politics and politicians. Scum which never failed to restore him to his stable center of contempt and cynicism.

"Fuck you, Bush, you stupid moron! Go tell it to the poor Iraqis!" he shouted, and his mind shifted back to his favorite theme, the event that more than any other had shaped him; the bloody beach at Giron. The Bay of Pigs. Back to his beloved commanding officers, San Roman, Erneido Oliva, Ruiz-Williams. Men of stature with huge *cojones*, not the pussy Cuban Revolutionary Council or the CIA which had planned the fiasco. The CIA which had packed all their ammo gasoline medical supplies and communication gear on one ship which was immediately sunk by Fidel's ridiculous air force of two or three old fighter planes. The fucking bunglers! And it was the CIA who had trained the Cuban underground fighters to rise up bravely at the moment of invasion to strike hard at Fidel's rearguard, but then failed to signal them until 7 hours too late. Forewarned, Fidel arrested 200,000 of them, tortured some, killed others including Rogelio Corso, the heroic underground leader. Also in for a measure of hate were the Kennedy brothers whose officials had promised air cover then reneged on their promise, insuring defeat. And not to forget the American destroyers which steamed in close to evacuate the survivors of Giron Beach, only to turn tail when Fidel lobbed a few shells in their direction. Brigade #2506 hadn't lost the battle. It was the Americans! Big time warriors! Putahs one and all!

Yes, he felt better now with the thoughts on governments, cops, the military men and women. As for Cassidy…Padro wasn't in a hurry. He could wait for a better time. One of his own choosing.

CHAPTER 11

▼

Tosca responded well to MARCO POLO, much better than expected. It was due partly to the environment of the harbor. Not the fogbound melancholy she had dreaded, but pleasant days which were warm and clear before giving way to the nightly fog.

Lying bikini-clad on the dock beside MARCO POLO with her books coke and sandwich she felt privileged, like a member of a special club.

It was October 1st, their nine-month anniversary, and it was dazzling under a hot sun. Not a good sailing day but one of those flip sides that are equally fine when properly spent. Usually out of the northwest at anywhere from 6 to 18 knots, the wind had not come up at all today. Not a whisper. With Satyri and the dancers aboard to help them celebrate, MARCO POLO wallowed in the languid blue swells with lovely Santa Barbara a half-mile off the starboard beam. Flying fish were abundant, jellyfish floating nearby, and several sharks appeared somewhat inquisitive.

Attempting to catch the fickle wind Cassidy had repeatedly steered toward the telltale ripples on the surface only to have them disappear as MARCO POLO lumbered, motor-driven, among them. Finally giving up after a dozen such chases he had shut down the diesel and committed the junk to serve as a party boat for the rest of the day. The beer and retsina was plentiful. The junk drifted aimlessly, her decks crowded with healthy tan bodies in dazzling bikinis, her sails flapping uselessly as she wallowed. But Cassidy could not indulge, and remained alert for the daily fog bank which was driven down from Point Conception by the prevailing wind. However, the pressure front held up and they were given a clear warm night to match their perfect day.

By the time the party wound down Cassidy was exhausted. His discipline while at sea had excluded him from the fun and games. His boat, his responsibility. With the junk safely at dockside, the party had, at his suggestion, moved to a nearby apartment. Without further word he had relaxed on the cabin roof and had fallen asleep immediately.

It was after dusk when she woke him. The night sky had turned to indigo and the palm trees which ringed the harbor were swaying in a gentle breeze. She closed her eyes and inhaled the faint eucalyptus pungence that had wafted down from the foothills to blanket the harbor.

"Alejandro," she whispered, touching his elbow which dangled over the edge of the cabin roof. No answer. "Alexander, wake up please."

He turned his head away from her and didn't answer. She was at a loss, wanting him awake but not enough to risk irritating him. She bent down, licked between his fingers and waited for a reaction. The fingers twitched but he did not otherwise acknowledge her presence. She licked again. He withdrew the hand and stuffed it protectively under his body, then finally turned to squint at her. "You pervert," he rasped sleepily.

"Are you awake?"

"No dummy. I'm still asleep."

"Like me *amante*?"

"No. Love you," he answered, and pulled her atop the cabin where he traced the outline of her body with his hands. "Don't, Alexander. You know how hot I get."

"Since when did getting hot terrify you."

"Since my period started. Maybe a cold shower, huh, and shish-kebab?"

"You're on. That is if Satyri has recovered from the party. He must have downed a gallon of retsina out there."

Indeed Satyri had recovered; child's play for a Greek who loved his cups. The apartment above KYLIX was spartan in design, classic white black and gold the colours, Biedermeier and Italianate the furniture most favored. He sat cross-legged at the desk, strummed his thigh with a pencil and listened to his mother on the telephone. Since his father became a semi-invalid she had assumed the entire burden of keeping their lives in Philadelphia on a healthy, functioning level. Satyri was certain it was taking a toll on her, if slow and deliberate.

He reached over and turned on the desk lamp. His gaze moved across the family photos before him; relatives still in the old country; wizened, wasted ancients in the traditional black garb of the peasant, macho young men and shy girls posed stiffly with smiles of innocence. He lingered at the photo of himself as a child of nine, standing between proud father and mother, his beautiful face, blond hair and pageboy haircut belieing his male gender. A nubile delicacy that got him spat on by the jealous, less fortunate mothers of the village, and many a whispered hex conjured meanly against his soul, a village response to beauty in its midst.

Beside his own photo stood a picture of the Papanikolas cottage in a picturesque village outside Athens where his widowed Aunt Soula and her 3 daughters had come to live under the protection of his father. That is until the communists came to take the girls for indoctrination in Albania, Roumania or Yugoslavia, some said even beyond the Urals, never to be seen again.

Fortunately, young Satyri had not been in the first groups taken, and this gave the family time to plan and execute what proved to be a hair-raising escape. Unfortunately both of Satyri's legs were seriously damaged in the escape, the left one nearly amputated by machinegun fire. Though he recovered the army doctor assured his parents they would have to be forever vigilant. It would always be touch-and-go as far as the legs were concerned.

As if that weren't enough the retreating communists set fire to their ancestral home and outbuildings, then slaughtered the livestock. Marcos and Anastasia Papanikolas decided enough was enough. They took themselves to America where they would not have to suffer Greek killing Greek.

"*Mana*…Listen please, *Mana*. You and papou should be here with me and Yorgos. It's a beautiful town, warm all the time like the Mediterranean. I got plenty room, or you can have the house next door. I own that one too. Market's half a block down the street. We got a Greek church, hospitals, anything you need right here."

He fumbled with a Byzantine icon as he listened patiently to her familiar objections. He turned the icon over and blew away the dust accumulated there, then returned it to its place.

"No no, that's not a problem either. I told you before, Erica agreed I could have the boy more often in that case. And you can fly back to Philly anytime to see him. I got plenty money."

"Yeah," he continued to drum with the pencil as he listened and began to fidget some.

"Yeah," he got to his feet and stretched. "Listen, *Mana*, my customers are waiting for me downstairs. You think it over. Talk to papou and let me know, okay?"

He listened to her final goodbyes. Stretched the phone cord to the hall mirror where he squiggled up his moustache and examined his pride and joy, the strong white teeth. "*Adheeo, Mana,*" he said finally and hung up the phone. Humming at the mirror he hitched up his trousers and tugged at his crotch. Fluffed it up. Descending the stairs to KYLIX a smile formed on his face when he heard the faint strains of the Greek music and crowd noise. This was his game, his life blood. He took hold of the taberna door knob, opened, and clapped his hands loudly as he went through the door shouting a spirited OPA! to all.

KYLIX was jammed with diners and dancers, all driven outdoors and away from the TV by the unusual warmth of the night. They had abandoned their conservative clothes for such as safari shorts, loud Hawaiian shirts and sandals for the feet. The air in KYLIX was sultry and charged.

As Tosca and Alexander came through the front door she hesitated and drew a pensive breath. He had learned to appreciate this sensory talent of hers, usually confirmed by some oddball happening or other. "Want to go somewhere else?" he asked.

"Yes I would, but we're stuck with it if we want good shishkebab. Nobody makes it like he does."

"Let me know if you can't handle it," Cassidy offered, and they made their way through the crowd to stand beside Satyri at the bar.

"*Yasou*, Alexandros! *Tekanis?*" Satyri asked, grinning broadly.

"Not much, boss. How about you? Recovered from this afternoon?"

"Hey, no problem. *Ela*, Tosca! *Agape mou...*" he ogled her, put one arm around her and one around Cassidy's shoulders. "Hey, you're the best dancer I got, you know that?" he said (for the thousandth time) and then added, "I taught you everything you know, right Tosca."

"Not everything," she answered, and hugged him back.

"Hey, watch it now," he protested, wriggling up his thick black moustache in mock indignation. "You young girls better not farkle around with Satyri. I'm not one of those cold-blooded north Europeans. I got passions, know what I mean."

Tosca worked up a stern expression on her face and wriggled her own imaginary moustache in a perfect mime of his haughty Greek expression. "Hey, I'm not one of those north Europeans either, know what I mean," she retorted, and winked slyly at him.

"Jesus Christ, Tosca. Alexandros, you gotta teach this girl her place."

"Oh sure. Why don't you try it."

Satyri looked out over the crowd then snapped his fingers at a waitress. "Hey, give my friends table 9 and a litre of retsina. We gotta dance Alexandros. Get 'em worked up for the belly dancer."

"You haven't done the table dance yet?"

"Naw, I pulled a muscle swimming today. I'm gonna have to go get cranked by the chiro. But I got a new belly dancer that'll blow your mind away. She makes me talk to myself," he said, then reached for Tosca's hand and said softly, "*Mana mou*, Tosca, dance with your Satyri."

Tosca was busy stuffing hors d'oeuvres. She wanted to eat not dance, and objected with a whimper. This did not please him. "What's this? You eat my food then refuse to dance with me! Hey!" he complained, and dragged her out onto the dance floor.

She settled down, they danced, losing themselves in the music. But once back at the table Cassidy noticed that Satyri was unusually edgy. Perhaps he was responsible for the ominous energy they had experienced on entering KYLIX.

"Something wrong, boss?"

"What you mean?"

"You're hyper. I just wondered."

"Hey, it's cool," he answered, but continued to fuss, flashing nervous glances around that always seemed to end up at the front door. He hollered excessively at his brother Yorgos. Lit cigarettes one from the other, hassled the waitresses. "Guess I better tell you…Tosca's old man came by earlier looking for you. Called you a communist hippie. Said you were trying to make a whore out of his daughter."

"Well did he wait around or what?"

"Naw, I threw him out. He called us a bunch of faggots. Said you wouldn't find men dancing with men down at the Club Latino. American guys just don't understand dancing. The Indians do but the rest of 'em are stupid."

"Damn, I hate that man so much," Tosca said, exasperated.

"You shouldn't say that about your father, Tosca," Satyri said, perking up. "How can you hate him like that. He gave you life."

"You should see how he treats mom and me."

"Well, we better watch out now that he knows about KYLIX. I wonder how he found out?"

"Probably figured it out from when he found us in the studio. Or maybe Celia told him or someone saw us together. He knows a lot of people," Tosca said. She picked up her sweater and backpack and got to her feet. "Can we go, Alexander. I don't feel so good."

"Hey, how about a bowl of my lemon soup. It's good for the stomach."

"I don't think so. Thanks anyway."

"Okay, let me use the restroom first," Cassidy said.

There was a tension between Satyri and Tosca as they waited for Cassidy to return from the bathroom. He was watching her closely and it made her nervous. "So you two guys are really into it, huh? Gonna get married?"

Tosca shrugged her shoulders and did not answer. "What do you think about his writing?"

"He's a good writer. Creative, lots of energy."

"Not what I mean. He's a workaholic. That all right with you?" She looked away from him and didn't answer.

"So it's already started, huh. Listen Tosca, I'm gonna give you some advice. I know this guy, right. He's hyper when he's working see, so give him some space. Know what I mean? He's one of them romantics, head in the clouds, feet dangling. Thinks the world is full of Greeks, virgins, and big beautiful schooners, and it ain't that way at all."

"What are you trying to tell me?"

"Just that he isn't all that easy to get along with when he's working. Remember that and you'll be all right."

As Cassidy returned to the table he reached for his billfold but Satyri would have none of it. Twirling his worry beads at a furious pace he walked them out to the Morris Minor and glanced around for a sign of Padro. "Tosca honey, I realize it isn't your fault, but tell your old man to stay away from KYLIX, okay."

"I can't make him. He doesn't live with us anymore. He's not part of the family."

"Well watch out anyway," he hugged her and clapped Cassidy on the back. "Boy I miss you guys out back in the studio. I got a guy out there who can't even speak the language. Oh well, long as he pays the rent, right? *Kaleeneekhta.*"

Satyri watched the Morris disappear down the street. He would make it his business to watch out more closely for Padro from now on. Harsh individual. Satyri purposely avoided mentioning part of the exchange with Padro; that part where he had grabbed his own genitals, grinned, and rasped between clenched teeth, '*Capar! Capar!*'.

Satyri winced at the thought of castration, his or anyone else's. "*Mana mou,*" he shivered, and brushed a sympathetic hand across his penetralia before returning to KYLIX. Back to the retsina and dancing.

CHAPTER 12

▼

"Beautiful day for a hike," Cassidy noted, lacing his rock boots to the ankle. "I'm glad you insisted."

Yes, she too was glad to get away. Away from Simon Lindero and the book. It was nearly a week since they had gone anywhere, done anything together. He was pressing hard, his natural easy manner giving way more often now to fits of cussing and temper. Satyri's warning helped her somewhat; at least she knew it wasn't her fault or his being interested in another woman. But that had not helped her deal with the lonliness.

"Where are we going, Tosca?"

"The hot springs."

"You mean Coupling Rock, don't you," he clicked his tongue at her in mock disapproval. "You baaadd girl."

"Well I like it up there. It's secret."

"What's in the lunch basket?"

"Egg salad sandwiches. Fruit and veggies."

Driving through the Los Padres National Forest they were fascinated by the exotic growth of chapparal, cactus, grasses and eucalyptus trees accentuated by rock outcroppings. Not as profuse as at Walden Pond perhaps but a more rugged, different kind of beauty. He pulled the Morris into the turnaround and they started to disembark but instead froze in place and listened, mouths agape; the nearby trees were alive with the electric hum of thousands of honey bees.

"Maybe we should leave," Tosca said, super alert and half afraid.

"You're not susceptible to bee stings, I hope. We'll split if you are."

"No, but what if they're killer bees like they found up at Bakersfield."

"We can go somewhere else, darlin'. Le Cumbre? Cachuma?"

"Aw they probably would have got us by now if they were interested. Let's just keep an eye out."

"Right," he agreed, and together they started up the trail. "The ruins, right?"

"The ruins," she grinned, and locked arms with him as they walked. The air was pure and warm, the soil a dry powder which vaporized as they scuffed it with their boots. Lizards and squirrels ran for cover, birds and dragonfly took to wing as they passed close by. Neither of them were what could be termed hardline environmentalists but such an intimate communication with the natural affected them deeply.

"This really upsets me, Tosca. All this beauty in my back yard and my head's stuck in a word processor all the time. Talk about wrong priorities."

"We'll do it more often from now on. We could pick one day a week and schedule it. That way nothing would interfere..." Tosca hesitated at the sound of a powerful engine which had just entered the turnaround. "Rats! We've got company," she groused, and turned around just as her father's Jeep slid to a halt on the gravel, blocking the exit of the Morris Minor. Padro kicked the door open, jumped down and stood with legs widespread, threatening, "Not here, Tina! I won't allow it!"

"Go away, Padro. Leave us alone. Please?"

Still hopeful to ease the situation Cassidy took several steps forward. "Mr. Tosca, I'm not looking for trouble. We just want to be together."

"You can't be with her, you red fucking hat freak!" Padro hissed and advanced on him. "After I'm through with you, you won't be with any young girl ever again!"

Tosca knew what was coming on. Padro had made up his mind long ago to savage Cassidy. His powerful body full of rage, he charged Cassidy head-on and flattened him. He sat astride Cassidy's chest, pounded his face over and over until he stopped moving, then slid sideways off him and slammed his fist into Cassidy's genitals. "Fool with my kid you'll never use it again," he snarled and drew his fist back to punish him again. But before he could strike Tosca slammed a large stone into the side of his head.

Stunned, blood oozing from the open gash, he turned to look at her. "I...I have to watch out for you, Tina," he mumbled in a dazed, broken fashion. "I have to take care of you."

And then a curious thing happened. Tosca...her hands clutched together at the thing she had just done...Tosca cradled her father's bloody head in her arms and sobbed brokenly. "Sorry. I'm sorry."

"You're my girl, Tina. My baby."

"I know," she answered, then knelt to administer to the unconscious Cassidy. "But I love Alexander and I want to be with him."

"Listen to me, Tina, I'm family! Don't do this anymore! Don't bring him here again."

Tosca got to her feet and faced him directly, seeming to have gained the power over him. "Padro," she said softly as Cassidy began to stir, "if you bother us again I'll tell Mr. Green. I'll press charges."

"But they might send me away again, baby."

"I'll do it to you, I swear I will! Now leave us alone, please," she said, and bent over Cassidy as Padro started for the Jeep.

"Tina, don't tell Green, huh."

Tosca ignored him which caused him to get arbitrary again. "All right, tell him, see if I care! But I'm tellin' you, this guy's gotta go. I ain't kidding!"

She ministered to Cassidy as Padro started the Jeep and turned it around. Moaning painfully, Cassidy clutched at his genitals and tried to sit upright. He glanced around in alarm and spotted the Jeep as it pulled away. He lurched to his feet, grabbed several stones and hurled them after the Jeep.

"You creepy bastard motherfucker!" he screamed, then hurled the remaining stones at a nearby tree. "MOTHERFUCKER!" he hollered one last time before lurching back to where Tosca huddled, crying copiously. "Take me to the hospital, Tosca, I don't feel so good."

She helped him to the car. She tried to comfort him as they drove along but she got no reaction from him. His eyes were blurred with tears. He saw nothing though his attention seemed to be on the passing terrain. His mind seethed with confusion. He had a bad BAD feeling about what had just happened but was loath to think further about it. Not the beating; he understood that. He felt there was something sinister going on here, something far more compelling. Unable to control it any longer he turned to face her. "Want to tell me about it?"

She acted as though she hadn't heard him but her quick breath and darting eyes betrayed her. She shook her head and remained silent.

"You don't think I have a right to know?" he continued, and touched a hand to her cheek. She refused to look at him. Kept driving.

"Tosca, your old man just tried to kill me and I don't think it was because we were out having a picnic. Now you can tell me or Angus Green can tell me. Take your pick."

The tension was unbearable. She broke down and told it to him in a sobbing voice. "He did it to me, Alexander. My own father did that to me."

"You mean sex, right?"

She brushed at the tears on her face. "At first I didn't realize what was happening. It was my birthday. I just turned 13. He said we were going on one of our picnics. It was a hot summer day. We swam in the creek. I never understood until it was too late."

Though he was shocked her admission didn't take him totally by surprise. Mrs. Tosca's bitterness, the curious inclusion of Angus Green in family affairs, Tosca's virulent hatred of her father. He knew it had to be major trauma but he wasn't quite ready to believe it was incest. That was something that happened to strangers not to anyone he ever knew. "Stop the car, Tosca."

"Why? What...?" she began, leery of his tone of voice.

"Just stop the goddamn car! Stop the fucking car!"

She did as he demanded. He threw open the door and got out. Like an enraged animal he released the pent-up anxiety in an explosive burst of tears and rage, pounding and kicking at the front fender. "Dirty sonofabitchin' bastard! I'll kill that fucker! I'll kill him!"

She sat and waited till the paroxysm passed. He massaged his bruised fists. Supporting his genitals he got back into the car, sat there and sobbed, unable to satisfy his desperate feeling. "What a shitty thing to do to your own kid. Just rotten. I can't believe it."

"I was just a dumb little kid, Alexander," she said, and taking him in her arms she rocked him gently, trying to console them both. "Just thirteen," she repeated, and began to cry along with him.

"It'll be all right, peanut, you couldn't help it. You were too young to know the difference."

She glanced at him like people do when they desperately need sympathy and understanding; the wiping of the nose, sniffling, the breath coming in spasms. Then the hint of a smile flickered across her face. "*Peanut shell,*" she corrected him.

"We'll work it out Tosca. Not to worry, okay?"

Cassidy had the luck of the Irish, as the saying goes. Despite the severe beating there were no broken bones, no permanent disfigurement. Tosca had saved him from that. "Some minor abrasions where your face hit the gravel, but nothing to frighten the kiddies," the young intern had joked.

"Ha ha ha," Cassidy mocked him, and waited to be released.

"Take it easy for a few days. Change the bandage or come back and we'll do it here. Any headache or dizziness come in to the emergency room right away. Possible concussion."

"Guess I won't be writing for a few days. She'll like that."

"You're a writer?"

"World famous," Cassidy answered cynically.

"Me too. Short stories, though no one has published me yet."

"I don't have insurance. How much is this going to cost?"

"They'll tell you out front," the doctor replied and got to his feet. "Uh, Mr. Cassidy, I'm curious. Why did he beat you up like that?"

"His daughter and I are lovers. He thinks I'm too old for her."

"How old is she?"

"Eighteen," Cassidy replied, and the intern whistled. "Would you like to take a poke at me too?" Cassidy offered his chin as target, then winced as the movement hurt.

"No, but I can understand a father wanting to."

Cassidy's eyes watered as he avoided the doctor's gaze. He didn't answer. Just turned and left the doctor standing there.

The following week was very strange for Tosca and Cassidy. Like a third presence (Padro's) was there with them, though the intensity of that had lessened in the last few days. Aaron Green had avoided saying 'I told you so', and had agreed to meet with Cassidy to discuss options.

Cassidy waited in the red leather chair but felt conspicuous because of its throne-like proportions. As a local he seldom visited this world-famous courthouse, its baronial spaces decorated with stained glass, old world tiles, majolica urns in tripod, walls emblazoned with armorial crests. Immense doors of baroque carving marked the entrances to courtrooms of rich leather, panelling, and murals of conquistador and Franciscan founders. Display cabinets lined the stucco walls and were crammed with swords, pistols, legal writs and documents, all signposts of the Spanish, Mexican and Yankee rape of the California natives. There was even a beautifully carved wagon once used to carry the product of a local vintner.

Cassidy sat beside this wagon and watched the citizens who passed by, their heels clicking smartly on the large red tiles as they hurried along to business and legal affairs in the building. He in turn was of some interest, the bumps and bruises still evident though less vivid and hurtful than in the previous week. "I've got an appointment in the building," Green had told him on the phone. "Meet me at the big wagon. Three sharp."

Cassidy didn't care for this building despite its luxury and beauty. Like government buildings everywhere it exuded threat; a feeling unsoftened by the skills of its craftsmen, some of whom might even have come out losers at law here. Cassidy had not had any dealings in the building since his divorce. It suddenly occurred to him that Tosca was of legal age now, and he felt more at ease with that fact.

"That shiner's a beauty, Mr. Cassidy," Green mused, checking out the abrasions on his face. "Padro's calling card all right. Gonna press charges?"

"No," Cassidy answered, and followed him out onto the lush south lawn. "We'll tough it out."

"It might be tougher than you think. Okay, tell me what happened."

Cassidy kept the details as brief as possible, describing the violence. He admitted to a sketchy knowledge of the incest. In turn Green told him some things about Padro's family background. Padro's mother had committed suicide while still in Cuba. She was a delicate girl from a good family. She had married the Sergeant-Major while still too young. For years he suppressed and brutalized her. Padro the boy was eleven when she took her life and he never came to terms with her death. He was 30 before he finally understood, but despised her memory for her weakness and his abandonment.

Fortunately for him but unfortunately for his sister Celia, she was forced into the role of mother to the young Padro, a role she relinquished gladly when he married Marta Freyre. But acting as mother to Padro had soured Celia's outlook. She became a drunk, too bitter to ever marry, alternately loving and hating her brother.

"Several years ago Padro almost killed a young boy here in Santa Barbara, and he was sent to prison. As you already know I was his parole officer. While he was under my control I discovered that he was abused by his father both physically and sexually. I tried to get him into a therapy program but he refused, denying what he had revealed to me in a moment of desperation. So this is the nature of your nightmare, Mr. Cassidy, and I don't envy you."

"Tell me about it," Cassidy said, managing a grin. "I really appreciate it, your discussing this with me."

"Mrs. Tosca and I are in agreement that this might help Tina, and she's the one we want to think about here."

"Mrs. Tosca knows about this meeting?"

"Hell yes. Incest isn't something you just talk about to everybody. So what is it you need to know Mr. Cassidy?"

"I'm not sure. Tosca told me about some of it. I could use some advice."

"My advice is one thing, my preference another. My preference would be for you to leave her alone. You're too old for her. But for Tina's good, I mean right now, today, I'm not talking future here, my preference is for you to stick around. I'm hearing good things about the relationship, and its effect on her."

"It has been wonderful to this point, yes."

"What has Tina told you about Padro?"

"Skipping school, the creek, the seduction."

Green seemed pleased that she had told that much to him. She had not been willing to face it before this. He agreed that she was marked by the experience though not as bad as some girls. She was going to make it all right. In the beginning it was minor, he said, the caresses of an ardent father. Slip of a hand here, a breast touched lightly there. Normal stuff almost, some say even healthy if kept within reason. But in puberty his interest in her increased markedly. She knew *something* was going on but was too inexperienced to feel alarmed. She was always a loner with few friends so she had little input to balance it against.

"Aw Christ…" Cassidy began to squirm. "Maybe I shouldn't listen to the rest of this."

Green said it was up to Cassidy but if he truly wanted to understand he might want to hear it out. "So that's how it got started," he continued. "Over a period of time slight familiarities, increasing in intensity and purpose. That's what seduces 'em, the gradualness. Tina stayed in her room at first. Cried a lot. She thought the other kids could tell just by looking at her body, certain they were all talking about her. She refused to take gym classes or any other that would attract attention to her, like oral recitation. Her classmates thought she had gone stuck-up but in truth she had nothing to share with them. The other girls her age were being taught about sex by each other while she was being taught by her father. She lost sleep. Started popping pills. Stopped going to church. No telling how far it might have gone if she hadn't seen that TV program and told her mother."

"God, that's awful. Yet, I can't help wondering…Wasn't she old enough to know the difference?"

"A typical reaction. Even her mother asked that question. But what's the fine line between that and familial affection, gradually done? I mean, how's a kid like her to know until it's too late. He was her father, for Christ's sake! Her buddy! At that point she thought maybe it was normal for all fathers."

"How did she get wise to him? What happened?"

"Remember the Bridges killing? The kid who blew her uncle away with a shotgun? It was all over the papers and television. The same day as 9/11. Her whole world collapsed. She confided in her mother and the divorce followed that. They've had a tough time but they're some of the lucky ones. The families always seem to blame each other. The girls frequently end up as prostitutes, frigid, junkies, suicides, you name it. Anything to deaden the hurt and guilt. That's why I say you're important to her right now."

"What can I expect from her? What can I do to help?"

"As far as I'm concerned she has never looked better, and I think it's a plus, her coming out into the open with you."

"What about her father? Can you help us with him?"

Green said it was unlikely and cited the fact that Padro was a citizen again. He (Green) could buy into a pile of legal trouble if he went too far. To Cassidy's request that he at least talk to Padro Green said it was about all he could do unless Padro came back into the system, though once, when younger, he had closed the door and had one hell of a fight with Padro, something the macho bastard understood but not something he, Green, wanted to do every day. But Tina was the one to worry about; not enough time had elapsed since the crime against her. She was still on shaky ground, the love/hate thing still marginally present. "She still remembers the security of the early years, needs it desperately, yet hates him for what he did to her. You want to help...give her back the security."

"I intend to."

Green nodded his approval but sat still, his eyes skipping over Cassidy with interest. "You know, I've always wondered about something. Why is it a girl her age gets involved with a guy your age? I mean, how many have you had? What do you know that I don't?"

Green's impetuous query caught Cassidy off guard. It was completely unexpected.

"I don't know the answer to that, but handsome and pretty has nothing to do with it. She's more intelligent and perceptive than other girls her age. She has an inner poise, a knowing beyond her years. She seems to be searching for something substantial, not just sex and a skateboard. Aw, I don't know. But I love it, whatever it is, and I'm gonna do my best to keep her happy. Did I answer your question?"

"Hmmm, you must be giving out vibes or something. I mean, no young girl has ever come on to me. Not ever."

"No, no vibes, just abracadabra. Something special happens."

"Think you two might end up gettin' married?"

"No way. That's a cultural fix. Unnatural."

"Hey, I don't agree with that. So, Tina's not just a piece of ass then?"

Cassidy's mouth dropped open in surprise. "Man how can you say a shitty thing like that! You think I'm having fun with this?"

Green shrugged at the reproach. "Jaded I guess. So much bad shit these days. Sorry."

Cassidy got to his feet, now anxious to leave Green. But Green pressed close and stuck out his hand, insisting on an apology. "My mistake. Don't be offended. I want you to know I take my work seriously, I'm on her side." He kept the hand extended until Cassidy took it. "Matter of fact I'm kinda glad you're with her. I got time for you and her whenever. Just pick up the phone."

CHAPTER 13

▼

"No, no, no, not yet!" Alexander complained, and reached out to shut off the radio/alarm clock. It was noon aboard MARCO POLO. His morning had been incredibly productive. His notes and accoutrement scattered around him on the bunk, he was even yet in the grip of a creative surge. Still, Tosca was waiting for him on the bluff. Reluctantly he laid the manuscript aside and eased himself off the bunk and into his sandals. "Simon, be cool and don't forget your lines till I get back."

He ran his fingers through his tangled hair, put on the red hat and went topside to scan the adobe bluffs of Santa Barbara City College. Yes, she was waiting just as she had been every day of the new semester. It was a tough discipline after being footloose for the entire summer, but taking lunch on campus every day helped ease them into the new regimen. And happily, Tosca had rejoined her beloved mime troop and was jazzed at the prospect of performing again. It had renewed her sense of purpose. Watching him scramble up the bluff toward her she called out his name and waved as he drew near. "OPA Alexander!"

"OPA *mi* Tosca! Hey, you should see the dynamite stuff I got today! Outrageous plot development."

"Kiss me. Tell me hello first," she said, jolting him with her somber manner.

Cassidy realized he was being a turd. He dropped to his knees on the blanket and hugged her to him. "Sorry, babe. Get carried away, don't I."

"I...I don't know. I can't even think straight anymore. All I ever hear is Simon Lindero...Simon Lindero."

"Well I do have to finish the thing. Just a little longer, huh?"

"That's what you said three weeks ago! I've got feelings, Alexander. I can't handle this."

"Come on, Tosca, you're overacting."

"Bullshit," she said testily, and sat on the blanket. "We've been invited to go camping at Cachuma for the weekend. How about it?"

While he thought it over a queasy feeling gnawed at her stomach. She knew the answer even before he opened his mouth but yet she hoped subliminally, *please God, make him go with me.*

Cassidy scratched his head and glanced up at the pine trees. "I don't think I can right now, Tosca. One day away right now might break my momentum. You know that."

"What about me? Am I just supposed to sit around and wait? I'm young, Alexander. We need to do things together."

He sat still and his chest heaved as he struggled for control.

"Tosca, I don't want you to get pissed off but I've tried to make this clear. I'm a writer and I have to take care of business. Nobody else can do it for me."

"And I've tried not to say this, but I'm fed up with Simon Lindero, his schooner, and Mexico too! I just don't care anymore! I don't want to go to Rome. I don't want the money. I want you!"

On the brink, he held his head in his hands and rocked back and forth. "Yeah, I guess you'd be happier if I was a fucking nine-to-fiver. All right, what do you want me to do? Who would you like me to be?"

She was surprised by this outburst. She remembered that both Satyri and Bair had hinted that he could get touchy sometimes. "Alexander, you okay?"

"Are you going camping without me, Tosca?"

"I'd rather you go with me."

"Darlin', don't you understand, I can't right now."

"Then I'm going. I've got to get away from this fixation of yours."

He calmed down somewhat. Perhaps she was right about getting away from MARCO POLO, and words and promises that never did materialize. "When do you leave?" he asked forlornly.

"Right after school." She glanced at her watch and got to her feet. "Shakespeare. I've got to go."

"But you haven't eaten a thing."

She said she'd get some chips and jello from the student cafeteria. But as she turned to leave she faltered and came back to embrace him. "My God, I don't want to go without you, Alexander."

"Come down to the junk after Shakespeare. We'll talk some more."

"Okay. Anyway, I've got a present for you. A surprise."

"My birthday! See how screwed up I am!" he said angrily, and kicked at the dirt, scattering it in the wind.

"Later, okay," she promised, and walked away.

Cassidy returned to MARCO POLO and continued with his work, but Tosca and the mountains were on his mind. He glanced at the clock/radio; she should have arrived by now. He went topside to check the adobe bluffs, noticed a large package tucked in by the gunwale. He picked it up and read the attached note. *Happy Birthday, Alejandro, from your lady who loves you very much*, the note said. *To keep you warm on the nights when I'm not with you.*

He went below and unwrapped the package. His face broke into a grin. It was the fur throw she had designed for him. "Oh man, great. Just what I need down here."

Shaking the fur to full size he noticed another note as it fluttered to the deck. He picked it up and read...*Please forgive me, but I was afraid I wouldn't go to Cachuma if I saw you first. I'll come back, amante, and we'll work things out.* The note was signed *Your Tosca, forever.*

Cassidy was crushed. After the confrontation with her on the bluff he had changed his mind about going with her. He had packed his gear, now eager to accompany her, maybe even make love in the woods, share morning coffee and bacon with her, then return as fully restored lovers. Bitterly disappointed he lay down on the bunk and covered himself with the birthday fur.

The pelt tickled his nostrils as he breathed in the damp night air. It was so quiet he could feel the blood squirt through his veins and his skin quiver with each constriction. His attention drifted to the dark corners of the old junk. He admired the fretwork and carved bulkheads. Hand labor, the craft of a private Chinese family who dared to lay the keel plank without so much as a rude sketch to go by, yet so intuitive that they always concluded with a product perfectly balanced at bow and stern, keel and topmast. He offered silent thanks to the family which had given birth to MARCO POLO.

His gaze shifted to the bronze helmet, the last component of the diving suit still in his possession. His eyes slid over the gleaming rounded surface of copper and steel, the two side windows for peripheral sight and the front one looking like the face of a Martian in a Flash Gordon comic book. The helmet was a work of art, form and function perfect.

Now perfectly relaxed he began to hum the tune of the new hisapiko, A HEAVY SILENCE FELL. Halfway through the melody he had made up his mind. It was his established pattern; when happy it was Hungarian or Yugoslavian music he wanted to hear. When melancholic only the Greek music could restore him. Tonight it would have to be Greek. He splashed cold water on his face then dressed in the white cottons; those cottons so symbolic of simplicity and freshness in a too-complicated world. Now the red hat and *opanky*. He was ready for Mr. Papanikolas.

As usual KYLIX was packed with noisy animated drinkers and diners. They grew quiet at first then blossomed into an excited buzz as Cassidy crossed the dance floor with the helmet cradled in his arms. He kicked a chair in place, then climbed up and fastened the helmet onto the spotlighted diving suit.

"Yasou, *Alexandros*! Looks like my ex-wife!" Satyri bellowed to the delight of his clientelle. "Hey, I'll be over in a minute!"

Cassidy needed a drink. He went to the bar and asked Yorgos for a beer. He watched as several patrons gathered by the diving suit and he reflected how important KYLIX and Satyri were to him. The two were halves, Satyri and his taberna.

"Hey boss, we're out of rice already," he heard the chef call from the kitchen.

"Give 'em extra dolmades and salad," Satyri answered, moving toward the bar where he stood beside Cassidy and poured himself a glass of retsina. "Hey, big night. Running out of food already."

"Great. Where are all the dancers?"

"Who knows. Sometimes you can't get rid of 'em, sometimes you can't find one. Hey, you look like shit lately. *Tekanis?*"

"Nothing's happening. Just work and woman trouble."

"You American guys don't know how to handle women. You're too good to 'em, they don't respect you. You gotta push 'em around. Let 'em know you got equipment, eh."

"Naw, this is different. When I'm working all my energy goes into it and most women can't accept that."

"Tosca, huh?"

"Yeah."

"Listen my friend, that girl is too young for you. I like Tosca, you know that. But at that age she's one person today, tomorrow another. You gotta watch out for number one, yourself. *Steen-eeah-sass!*" he shouted, toasting Cassidy's health. He placed a balancing hand on Alexander's shoulder and threw down the glass of retsina. "Come on, table time. We'll drink some ouzo and talk later."

Cassidy started for the dance floor while the Greek cruised by the bandstand with a request. The bouzouki player strummed a few riffs and the customers perked up. This was what they had really come for; to see the crazy Greek and his soulful dancing.

"OPA!" he shouted, and took the shoulder hold of the hisapiko. "We're the only ones, Alexandros. The only Greeks!"

"*Yasou*, boss, that's the way I like it."

The bouzouki got serious as it launched into A HEAVY SILENCE FELL. Sweet poignant music the Greeks understood by instinct. As they danced Satyri's brow furrowed, the bushy moustache quivered as he mumbled the lyrics and glanced sideways at Cassidy. "Hey, I'll make a Greek outta you yet, mother-fucker," he said, and squeezed Cassidy's shoulder sympathetically.

When the dance ended Cassidy made a move to leave the dance floor but Satyri got in his face. "Where the hell you going?" he said, matching Cassidy stride for stride.

"I'm out of sorts tonight, boss. See you later, huh."

"Hey, not till I do my table. I need some help and some noise. Besides, I got a special treat for you tonight. Stick around," he said, and gave Cassidy a curious smile.

At Satyri's signal the bouzouki slid right into the music, a boisterous song calculated to raise the adrenalin level for the table dance. The patrons stopped eating and talking and clapped their hands in cadence with the music. For probably the 8000th performance Satyri pulled it off without a hitch. Cassidy found it curious that he could make it look fresh and exciting yet another time. Catchy stuff, adrenalin.

The table dance finished, Satyri basked in the applause then rejoined Cassidy at the bar. "C'mere. I want you to meet a friend." He took Cassidy by the arm and pushed him toward a lone blond woman, early thirties, who sat and watched their approach.

"Katerini, this is Alexandros. You like Greeks, he's a Greek and he's horny. He wants to go home with you."

Katerini was stunned, as was Cassidy. She looked at Satyri with a tightly controlled face, then a slow smile spread across it. "You don't fool around, do you." she said to Satyri.

"Hey, why waste time. You like Greeks, I got you a nice Greek. Hey *malaka*..." he nudged Cassidy with his elbow and stared hard at Cassidy's crotch..."anything happenin' yet? Do something, okay."

"Jesus Christ, man! Kind of sudden, isn't it?" Cassidy said and grinned sheepishly.

"So, you're both alone. Both in a bad mood. What's the problem?"

"Well for one thing I've got a lady. Remember Tosca? Maybe Katerini has a boyfriend," Cassidy suggested and looked to her for support.

"So Tosca's up in the mountains probably farkleing around. Teach her a lesson. Show her who is boss."

"Look Katerini, I've got a girlfriend and we're really tight. He knows that, the bastard."

"Just trying to do a favor for two friends," Satyri offered, and moved closer to caress her shapely backside. "Hey poussy, poussy, come home with Satyri, huh," he purred, embarrassing both Cassidy and Katerini.

"Like I said before, boss, time to split. Nice to meet you, Ma'am. *Kahleen-eekhta.*"

She acknowledged his goodbye. Satyri fussed about his leaving but it felt good to be out in the fresh sea air. He looked around carefully and crossed to where the Morris Minor was parked. All he needed right now was for Padro to show up and complete his day.

But Cassidy felt good about the Katerini thing. It verified to him just how much he cared for Tosca. Katerini had been his first real test and he had passed it easily.

CHAPTER 14

▼

"OPA, Tosca!"

Standing there with her hand raised to knock, she was startled as Cassidy threw open the hatch to welcome her. She jumped aboard and threw her arms around his neck.

"It's so good to feel you close again, sweetheart."

"When did you get back?" he asked, finally releasing his grip on her.

"Late last night. Mom wouldn't let me come down."

"Jesus, I missed you, Tosca."

"Me too, *niño*. I won't ever go away again without you."

"I won't let you," he answered, and cleared his writing stuff off the bunk for her. "Your mom and I had coffee last night. We didn't expect you until tonight."

"Nobody wanted to stay longer. Too much going on with school and everything."

"Oh it's so good to have you back. Got time for breakfast?"

"Class starts at eight. I've got ten minutes to get up the bluff."

"Okay. I'll fix us a lunch then."

"Yeah, eleven-thirty on the bluff," she said, and paused in the hatchway to blow him a kiss. "The peanut shell is back, *amante*," she grinned, then stepped off onto the dock. Halfway up the bluff she stopped and waved again as he watched.

"Outrageous lady," he mumbled as she passed over the top of the bluff, still waving at him.

Below deck once more he poured a coffee and resumed work. It went well despite the fact that Tosca kept popping in and out of his consciousness. Eventually he regained his concentration and did some good work, until his eye caught the dial of the clock/radio.

"On my way darlin', on my way," he said, grabbing some fruit from the hanging basket, vegetables, peanut butter and bread, cheese and mayonnaise, and put them into his backpack.

She was waiting as he gained the top of the bluff, sitting there on the blanket with a friend. Cassidy waved and looked away to hide his surprise. Tosca's friend was badly disfigured, the obvious victim of a terrible accident of some kind.

"Alexander, this is my friend Carla. She's in my biology class.

"My pleasure, Carla."

Carla gave him a nervous smile then got to her feet. "Sorry, I've gotta go," she said. "See you in lab," she said to Tosca, then hobbled away toward the campus.

"I hope you don't mind. I told her about you and she wanted to meet you. She said I was making you up."

"Poor kid. What happened to her?"

"A fire. The furnace blew up at her house. So how's Simon coming along?"

The question surprised him being that Simon was such a bone of contention between them. He told her it was going well then changed the subject. "Angus Green and I had a talk about you and your father. I just wanted to understand, savvy? I want to share the pain with you, Tosca."

"I'm afraid for us, Alexander. Maybe we should move up to San Luis Obispo, or maybe Santa Cruz, huh?"

"Let's don't do anything radical. It'll work out."

"If you say so. Hey, look! What's going on down there?" Tosca said, pointing down to the harbor where a large white schooner was surrounded by sailors of the US Coast Guard. "Bet it's a drug bust."

"Could be. And they've got divers in the water. Probably tried to dump the stash overboard. Hey, that boat looks familiar."

"Can you see her name?"

"Her stern's swinging around...Yeah, I thought so. ACHILLEAS. Remember Joe Morgan? New Year's day, broken ear drum?"

"Right. Well I don't want him to go to jail but I hope they find the stuff. I hate dope."

"I'll check it out and let you know. Coming down after school?"

"I wouldn't miss it for anything, Alexander. I was only gone for a few days but it seemed like a whole month."

"Don't bother to bring your homework," he said, and pulled her down on the blanket to kiss and fondle.

"Don't *corazon*, you know how hot I get. I might miss class."

"*Corazon?*"

"It means heart. You are my heart, baby. But I really have to go now. We'll talk later."

It was midnight as MARCO POLO strained at her dock lines, creaking upward with each surge then settling slowly down as the tide retreated. The dock light knifed through the open porthole and onto the exhausted lovers, white torsos interlocked on the dark fur throw, eyes closed, hands still caressing each other. An empty wine bottle and several empty beer bottles remained on the galley table, remnants of the most incredible fantasy that either of them had ever experienced, fucking wildly topside in the open air with her strapped to the mainmast, her urgent pleas to the mythic Pheonician driving Cassidy onward as he probed her deeply and exhaustingly, all three of them enshrouded under the fur throw and sharing the uninhibited orgy.

As she re-lived the experience again she shuddered, her mouth opened slightly and her tongue moving from side to side to moisten her parched lips. "I've never been tied down before, *amante*. I was really smokin' wasn't I?" she said, giggling huskily.

"You were a goddess, darlin'. You're extra-special when you lose it like that."

"You too, Alexander, the best in the world."

"How could you know that? How many have you had anyway?"

"That's private. I'd never ask you that."

"Just makin' talk, babe. Don't get bent."

She sensed his annoyance and changed the topic. "Did you find out anything about that schooner?"

"Oh yeah, Morgan's a smuggler all right. He toured Mexico for a whole year before coming back stateside."

"How'd you find that out?"

"Remember Frank? The guy we took to the hospital? Frank says they were on their way to San Francisco when the eardrum broke, and that forced Morgan to change plans and go to LA instead."

"I don't follow you."

"Frank said they were dead broke, eating tortillas granola and peanut butter all the way back from Mexico. Yet when Morgan got back from LA a few days later he had a thick roll of bills, was driving a rented Ferarri, and took the crew to lunch at JOHN BUOY'S restaurant. Then for a final touch he gave them all a $500.00 bonus. Interesting, huh?"

"Yeah, sounds suspicious all right. So, did the Coast Guard divers find anything?"

"Frank says all they found was an old rusty bicycle and some fishing gear, so they gave it up. Hey, guess how many pages I got while you were gone?"

"Five. A dozen?"

"Guess again. Thirty! What do you think of that."

"Wonderful! How much longer do you think?"

"The way I'm going I'll have the first draft in a week. Soon we'll be as we once were, *niña*. No more problems, no more Simon Lindero."

"I was worried for a while. I thought I was going to lose you."

"No way, darlin'. So how about it? Can you stay the night?"

"You couldn't drive me away. This is my place, with you."

"Did you miss me while you were in the mountains?"

"Nooooo…" she toyed with him.

He pulled away from her just enough to see her face; to guage her reaction to his next question. "Did you make it with any of the guys up there?"

"All of them!" she waved her arms grandly. "I took them all on."

"Seriously?"

"Alexander!" she exclaimed, shocked when she realized he was only half-kidding. Her face turned sad in remembering. "Me and Carla were the only ones alone. The rest were all couples."

Cassidy apologized and promised that when he was done with Simon he would stick to her like glue; nothing would be able to shake him loose. She strained to kiss his lips, then yawning, scooted back into his groin.

"Set the alarm. I have to get up before mom does."

CHAPTER 15

▼

Several days later, as Cassidy was powering away at his story, Tosca came down from school and boarded MARCO POLO. She was carrying a large art folio and was struggling to maneuver it through the hatch.

"Come on, babe, you're letting the whole fog bank in," Cassidy complained, rubbing his hands together for warmth.

But Tosca was in such a great mood she wasn't about to be put down. Playfully, she cupped her hands over his eyes and said, "I've got something to show you."

He shifted impatiently in his chair and kept typing. "Come on, Tosca, sit down and behave. I've got some good stuff going here."

"And I've got some good stuff to show you. Look."

Cassidy watched as she put the folio up on the galley table and opened it. "Hey, isn't that Morgan's schooner?"

"Yeah. I did it as a class project. I met him last night. A really nice guy. Reminds me of you a lot."

"How'd you meet him?"

"KYLIX. Last night mom treated me to a bowl of the Greek's lemon soup and Morgan was having dinner at the big table."

"Wish you would have told me you were going."

"What for? I can't get you to go anywhere when you're working. Anyway, he wanted to learn a Greek dance."

"And you taught him one, right."

"A *sirto*, in exchange for this drawing. And I get to do the hull of ACHILLEAS when he puts her in drydock. That should make a swell sketch, huh?"

"Yeah. Different angle. So what's he like close up?"

"Hmmm, mellow, about 35. Probably the most handsome guy I've ever seen. A shame he's a doper. Tosca gestured with her hands as she talked, building Joe Morgan like a snowman. "He's got this gorgeous body, brown as chocolate. Great manners. Knows how to talk to a woman. I think he's got money, and let's see…Gold rimmed goggles, and he wears this big Aussie hat with the rim fastened up on one side and he's grown this big handlebar moustache."

"Sounds like you made him up."

"I know. Like Hollywood. Pretty exotic."

Cassidy felt a little disturbed by her ardor for Morgan but continued to work while she rambled on. "It's very strange, Alexander, but there's something about him. Like I feel as if I've always known him. It's unsettling."

"Yeah, some people have that facility," Cassidy observed absent-mindedly, barely listening to her now, more interested in his work.

"I told him about you and MARCO POLO," she said, and settled on the bunk with her homework. Her presence drew no further attention from him. His mind was back on Simon Lindero.

She was disappointed in his lack of interest in Joe Morgan; she had expected the writer in him to share her enthusiasm for one of life's unusual characters. She began to page through her sketch pad. He snapped a look at her, annoyed by the rustle of paper. Her breathing began to sound like explosions to him, her sighs like windstorms. He tried to ignore the distractions but failed, and turned back to the last pages hoping to regain his thrust by editing and re-editing. Finally frustrated, he put the manuscript aside. "I'm sorry, Tosca, I just can't concentrate with you here."

"Well…I don't know. What do you want me to do?"

"Could we try this. Maybe you could go home and let me finish and I can come up later."

She stared at him in shock. Rejected out of hand just as he had forewarned months ago. "All right, if you wish."

"Thanks for understanding," he said, and reached up to kiss her cheek absent-mindedly. "I'll be finished by 8:30."

Obviously this was not her choice but she went along with it because she was just plain burnt out. She put on the fur hat and wrapped herself in the cape. She opened the hatch and looked back with uncertainty; hard to accept that he had just kicked her out so causally.

She was weary of him. As she walked away each footstep echoed on the wooden dock and scattered the thick fog. The tears came and her shoulders heaved miserably. "It's the same as before the camping trip, dammit," she lamented, and disappeared into the gray mist.

Although an hour later than promised Cassidy did put Simon away and drove to Tosca's house. They had watched TV, a way to be together and yet take their minds off the growing problem. Now, lying beside her on the bed, he listened to her breathe in deep sleep. He reached under the bed and drew forth her drawing of the schooner ACHILLEAS. He stared at it for long moments and recalled her last words before she burrowed under the covers and went to sleep, "I don't understand, Alexander. Something familiar about that guy. I feel drawn to him."

Her comment disturbed Cassidy a lot. He slid the drawing back under the bed and snuggled up to her. But he had the wide-awakes and his attention settled on the mobile again. When he had asked her earlier why she had gotten it down from the closet her answer disturbed him profoundly. *It helps me to see things as they really are,* she had replied.

Mrs. Tosca had judged the mobile correctly when she had called it depressing. It struck Cassidy as pathetic also, as though its creator had cried out for help and understanding. About three feet tall, the mobile's 4 sides revolved around a center pole like a revolving kiosk. The 4 sides were covered with photos and drawings of Tosca in her mime costume of tails tophat and bow tie. There were 3 images of her on each side, one on top of another, 12 images in all. Though mentally tired and not functioning clearly he was determined to examine the mobile one more time to make certain his earlier appraisal had been reasonable. He reached out and moved the mobile with his finger.

The first side showed a very happy Tosca in tophat and tails, cane in hand. Her features were covered in white face, her lips and great almond-shaped eyes outlined in black, her cherry-red nose a dazzling accent. She strutted smartly, chin extended, walking cane in hand, delighted to be sharing her magic enchantment with all.

She approached a group of dogs and kids playing nearby. She doffed her tophat, bowed to the waist and clowned around. Kids and dogs responded by joining her in a wild circle dance.

Cassidy touched the mobile again and the 2nd side stopped before him. Tosca the Mime was ebuillient! On top of the world! She clicked her heels together, flipped the tophat high in the air and caught it on her head. Then with a devilish grin on her face she produced a kazoo from her sleeve, stuck it between her lips and pranced like an elfin while she tooted what was probably a happy carnival tune.

Cassidy grinned as moisture formed in his eyes, deeply moved by her simple childish outlook. In awe of her talent he moved the mobile to its 3rd side. She cavorted, did cartwheels, came to an exhilarating stop mere inches from the faces of three watching adults. They studied her outrageously grinning face as though she were an alien they couldn't understand. Unsmiling, they continued to stare with no comprehension. In the next picture her face had lost its radiance, turned away from her observers and toward the viewer with sadness. Tosca the Mime, the giver of pleasure, was now hesitant and doubtful like her audience.

He hesitated to look at the 4th side again but he nudged the mobile with his finger. Tosca had approached two other female mimes, her smile unsteady but hopeful. Cassidy felt her dread as the two mimes watched her approach with envy and suspicion. Then they were standing behind her back, whispering into their cupped hands as she flinched and waited to be hit over the head for some wrong-doing or other. The last picture showed Tosca with eyes downcast, tears streaking her face as the other mimes guffawed at her and slapped their thighs in mocking ridicule. This was pain he was looking at, not just gloom or melancholy. It would take a lot more time and thought before he could understand the mobile. In the end he would probably have to ask her about the meaning.

It was the violent jerking of her body against his own that brought him back to reality. He held his breath and listened to her mumble and shud-der...Mmmm...Mmmmmm. 'Hmmphhf', he thought with amusement, 'I guess the Phoenician came for her again'.

He eased himself off the bed so as not to awaken her, and left for the marina. It was 3:15 as he approached MARCO POLO. A lambent night, and clear, the kind that always filled him with awe and peace. But he had no sooner left Tosca than his writer's mind began to grapple with Simon Lindero again. Maybe he could get in a few good lines before drifting off to sleep.

He made the turn into his dock space and came to an abrupt halt, the hackles on his neck in a full defensive posture. Joe Morgan was sitting on his dock box. Flashing a quick vacant smile which vanished again as quickly, he pointed a finger at MARCO POLO and spoke, "Nice craft. Lotta good kharma. Hey, I appreciate you guys takin' Frank to the hospital. *Gracias.*"

"Yeah, Bair's cool. How's ACHILLEAS?"

Morgan said the schooner would have to go into drydock. Some of the planks had worked loose beating up the coast from Baha and she was taking on water. Again he flashed the quick vacant smile, an obvious affectation, and said he needed to score a lady before he could even consider going back to sea.

"Yeah. Well it's late," Cassidy answered, not in the mood to discuss farkleing at 4 o'clock in the morning. "See you around, huh."

"Sure, I gotta boogie too," Morgan answered, and slapped the large Aussie hat on his head as he turned away.

CHAPTER 16

▼

"Damn you, Simon!" Tosca exploded, checking her watch while she waited on the bluff, books in hand. It wasn't as though he had to come all the way from Goleta or Montecito; MARCO POLO was berthed a couple of hundred yards away. Pissed to the max she spread the blanket on the ground, sat down and waited.

Eventually her attention wandered to a roadway where the schooner ACHILLEAS hung balanced in the rubber sling of the travelling hoist, on its way to the boatyard for repairs. Walking alongside, nursing his boat every step of the way, was the tall man with the Aussie hat, Joe Morgan. Tosca was hypnotized by the tableau, and for the moment she forgot her problems with Alexander.

She watched the hoist operator shut off the engine, jump down to the tarmac, and after a heated discussion with Morgan he stomped angrily off to the SAND-SPIT CAFE.

Morgan climbed aboard the schooner as she pendulated in the rubber sling, and the big hat swivelled from side to side as he checked the security of ACHILLEAS' fastenings. Then recognizing Tosca even at that distance he removed the hat and waved it in greeting. She returned the greeting. They stood motionless and held each other's attention for a full ten seconds before she started for the marina to find Cassidy.

As she neared the harbor she experienced inner turmoil at the thought of Morgan, and purposely skirted the area where he waited. She entered the marina and marched straight down to MARCO POLO.

Cassidy was grotesquely asleep, arms and legs bent at such angles as to suggest a disturbed rest; empty coffee cup, half-eaten sandwich, brown apple core, all his writing paraphernalia askew. She eased down through the hatch, sat down and watched him sleep. She felt sad and hurt. Rejected once again.

She took an orange from his hanging fruit basket and put it into her backpack. She spread peanut butter on a slice of bread and went topside where she observed him a moment longer through the open hatch. "Jesus, what am I gonna do about this guy."

She chewed on the peanut butter bread while she considered her options, then left the marina and started back to campus. Somewhat curious, she scanned ACHILLEAS as she passed close by. It was still in the travelling hoist and Joe Morgan sat cross-legged on the deck.

"Hi," she offered shyly.

"Hello, crazy eyes. Would you believe the guy went to lunch and left us high and dry."

She broke into laughter at the pained expression on his face then split the sandwich in half and offered, "Share?"

"Thanks." He chewed the peanut butter laboriously, screwing his face into mock indignation as he chewed. "I've been eating this shit for the last month and I swore I'd never touch another peanut." Then sensing that she might be put off by his comment he added hastily, "I'd like to reciprocate. Can you handle JOHN BUOY's with me?"

"Sure! You bet!"

He jumped up onto the hoist's control panel and opened the engine cover, removed the coil wire and placed it into his pocket. "He can't go anywhere without that. Let him do the waiting."

She watched him closely, marvelling at his grace, until he leaped down to stand beside her. He took the remainder of the peanut butter and threw it beside the road. "That's for the bugs. Come on, we'll get you something nice, like shrimp or lobster. Something good for your health."

"Peanut butter has saved my life more than once. I've been living on it for the last four years."

Joe Morgan reached out for her and Tosca...with an uncharacteristic lack of objection considering he was a stranger...Tosca allowed him to hold aside her cape and admire her slender girl's beauty at first hand. "And it has done well by you. My oh my yes. Okay, peanut butter it is then."

"Oh no you don't! I'll take the lobster, thank you!" she grinned, and they started toward JOHN BUOY'S restaurant.

A half hour after Tosca left him Cassidy woke suddenly. As if by sub-conscious signal he sprang to his feet and faced the clock/radio. "Oh no, not again!"

he said, and moved toward the hatch to search the adobe bluffs. No one was there. "Oh Christ!" he agonized, and smashed his fist down hard against the bulkhead. "You blew it again, stupid."

There was nothing to be done about it now. He searched the bluffs one last time then returned to the manuscript, eyeing it with a mixture of hate and allegiance. "Might as well," he said, and took up the last page as he munched on the half-eaten sandwich, soon losing himself in the mechanics of the story. The entire afternoon zipped by in a haze of word and image and it was 3:15 before he heard her knock on the hatch of MARCO POLO.

"OPA! lady, come aboard."

"OPA! yourself."

"Sorry about lunch. Mad at me?"

"Huh uh," she answered, and kissed him on the cheek. Seeming to put little importance on the broken lunch date she removed her cape and sat beside him on the bunk. "I came down but you were out of it so I let you sleep."

"You should have woke me up. I'm really cookin', Tosca. Would you believe...I worked all last night clear through till ten-thirty this morning, then finally fell aleep. Jesus, I'm exhausted."

"I can't believe this. What's a book worth anyway?"

He was on the threshhold of a biting remark but managed only a rueful look. "Yeah, I keep forgetting it's not important to anyone else. Well anyway, I'm almost finished."

But even that promise did not allay her irritation. It would just happen again and again for as long as he had anything to write about. With her luck he would not be one of those 'one story writers'. She sat there next to him and felt a slight nausea; she didn't want to tolerate it anymore.

"Anything the matter?" he asked, sixth sense aroused.

"No. Why?"

"Just wondered. You seem different."

"Nope, same ol' Tosca."

A flip answer, it disturbed him. "Well I haven't eaten anything since early morning. Care for a helping of my boat stew?" he asked. She shook her head, avoided his eyes. "I thought you were fond of my world-famous boat stew," he took a stab at levity to conceal his sense of foreboding.

"I'm not hungry. I ran into Joe Morgan. He took me to lunch at JOHN BUOY's."

Cassidy looked away to hide his surprise. Afraid that the clumsy pause would reveal his jealousy he found himself saying one of those trite things that people are always sorry for later on.

"You and the sharpie from the dope boat?"

"Joe Morgan is the owner and captain of the ACHILLEAS, yes!"

"Okay, don't get excited. I guess the turkey's got money, huh?"

"Yes he has got money, no he is not a turkey. He's very mellow and he's in his particular space because that's the level his energy is concentrated in right now."

Cassidy was taken aback by both the strength of her rebuttal and the vague meta-physical content of it; a flat rejection of himself and a spirited defense of the stranger. "What's all this energy stuff?"

"The ultimate power in everything. We've all got it but most of us never realize it. It's manifested in motion, space, aura, and in more esoteric ways also."

He searched her face for a put on, a joke, but Tosca was serious, by god. He stared at her, bug-eyed, and waited for her to continue.

"You wouldn't understand him, Alexander. He's strange. He calls me crazy eyes."

"Sounds like one of those wild-eyed junkies you see twitching along on the breakwater, minds blown away by krank and shit."

"See! Just like he says! Stereotypes! Nobody ever gives anyone else the benefit of the doubt!"

"I thought you didn't like dopers and dealers."

"He couldn't possibly be a dealer. He's too nice a person. Besides, I asked him if he was and he said no."

"Well that's pretty dumb. He's not going to admit something like that," Cassidy smirked, and began to arrange his writing paraphernalia for another crack at Simon Lindero. She watched in disbelief as he activated the word processor and cracked his knuckles.

"I can't believe this!" she shouted. "All last night, all day today and here you go again. You need a reality check, my friend."

"Tosca, I can't compromise the work. It's got to be done."

"Why? Why does it *have* to be done. Besides you nobody cares if it gets done tomorrow or next week. Get real, Alexander." He felt the anger rise in him, then curiously a helplessness also. His mouth closed on the answer he had learned to fire back over the years. Even Tosca did not understand, though she did have the truth of it. Other than himself no one had ever given a damn. No one.

Regretful at the exchange she dropped to her knees and laid her head on his lap, a disturbed look on her face instead of the resolute one a few moments ago.

"Alexander, I love you so much and at this moment I need you more than ever. Please don't shut me out like this."

"Tosca, *niña*, I'm a writer, darlin', and that's all I want to be. Look, let's keep it together a few more days. I know what I'm talking about. I've been through this before. We can work it out."

"I'm listening," she said evenly.

"How about if I work days on the boat and then come to your house at night. Could you live with that for a week or so until I finish?"

"Now you're saying I can't even come down here to MARCO POLO!"

"But I can't work with you here! It's too small a space! Every sound or movement shatters my concentration!"

She was totally bummed out, helpless against the intractibility which governed his work. She wrapped herself in the cape and turned to go. "I just don't know what I can live with anymore. I don't know what to tell you."

"A few more days…Can we try, please?"

"I'll be at my house, Alexander. Goodbye."

The finality of her leaving was not lost on him. He shook his head in disappointment but returned to work as soon as she was gone. He was very close to the finish now; half a chapter plus the epilogue.

CHAPTER 17

▼

'483-7737…Cassidy drummed a rhythm on the wall of the telephone booth as he waited for her to answer. It was a glorious, fresh, outrageous morning! He wanted to run, jump, holler and roll in the grass, anything and everything! To stand quietly was the most difficult. He was finished with the god-damned thing! He was…"Hello," he heard a melodious voice on the other end of the line, and answered, "Hi, Marty. Alexander here."

"Well, where have you been for the last week?"

"Holed up. Jamming. Simon is finished. At least the first draft is."

"Great! So does a writer celebrate such things?"

"I still do. That's why I called, to ask you and her out to dinner."

"I'm cooking spaghetti. Why don't you come up here and celebrate with me and Chuck."

"Sure I'll bring the wine. What time?"

"Seven-thirty."

"I'll be there. Can I talk to Tosca?"

"She's not home."

Sensing her reluctance to discuss it further Cassidy cut it short. "Okay. See you tonight at seven-thirty."

He was still on a rush as he approached Tosca's house that evening, anxious to let her know that they were in the clear. It was an unbelievable high! He had been so wired on finishing with Simon that he had turned-to on MARCO POLO, airing out the bunk cushions, sleeping bags, blankets and pillows. He had flushed the bilges, spiffed up the galley and head, cleaned the portholes, all the things he had neglected for the past eight months. He was exhausted, yes, but it was a happy exhaustion.

Finishing a novel or a script wasn't that big a deal anymore, not like it used to be. But Simon Lindero was special somehow, and his best commercial effort so far, and it had caused way too much grief with Tosca. He was grateful to have concluded.

He realized there were complications now, specifically the sky-pilot of ACHILLEAS who was turning up in Tosca's world with regularity of late. Chance run-ins on the marina parking lot; and conversations as she passed the boatyard on her way to City College. A movie, coffee and croissant at the SAND-SPIT CAFE, then dinner and dance at ZELO'S a few days ago. No question that Morgan was trying to work her away from him though when Cassidy suggested this she insisted that they had not slept together but were just good friends and she was learning a good deal from him and had grown fond of him though she did not love him.

Cassidy was now anxious to give her his entire attention. He would smother her with care and regard! Overwhelm her with passion and expel the poacher-bastard Joe Morgan, reclaiming the halcyon days for himself and Tosca!

But something caught his eye as he crossed the patio to the kitchen door. An old black Volkswagen convertible stood in the carport. Cassidy had never seen it before.

"Hey, Chuck," he called out as Mrs. Tosca's boyfriend stood waiting at the kitchen door.

"Congratulations, man. Well done."

"Thanks. Hi Marty."

"OPA!" she said, pointing to the gallon of red wine he had brought. "Uncork it and we'll have a toast."

As Chuck saw to the decanting Alexander gave a cursory look around, fully expecting to see the owner of the black veedub. But there was no one else and the table had been set for three people.

"Nice old bug outside, though it looks like it could use a little love," Cassidy offered, priming Chuck.

"Yeah, but it's transportation. I gave it to Tina for school. It was just gathering dust in my garage."

"Nice thing for you to do," Cassidy answered, relieved that it had nothing to do with Joe Morgan. He took the glass of wine offered him and they all raised their glasses for a toast. "Author! Author!"

"After all that work I hope the book makes you rich and famous," Chuck added, clinking his glass against theirs.

After the toast Mrs. Tosca edged them into the living room to give her more space in the kitchen. They stood at the big window enjoying the sparkling lights below and the wine.

"Tosca won't be joining us then?"

"I doubt it," Chuck answered. "I understand that she hasn't spent a lot of time at home lately."

It was clumsy for the two men; they both knew what was on Cassidy's mind. "You might be in for some work on the Veedub. It does need a tune-up, and like that."

"I'm a lousy mechanic but I'll give it my best," Cassidy answered.

"Marta tells me you two are really stuck on each other."

"Yeah, if I haven't screwed it all up."

Glass in hand Mrs. Tosca joined them at the window. "Spaghetti's ready, guys," she said, and laced her arm through Chuck's in an intimate gesture. As Cassidy followed them to the table he listened and watched their attentions to each other. He felt left out, very vulnerable.

The spaghetti was delicious, balanced as it was by a green salad, garlic bread and the wine. A pleasant gathering, it picked up steam as it focused on politicians and their wicked ways. Thoroughly drunk, Chuck had to be tucked into the guest bed by Mrs. Tosca. Returning, she faced a dispirited Cassidy who sat staring at the darkened window in front of him.

"I'll take care of the dishes, Marty. It looks like Chuck could use a little TLC."

"He seldom drinks that much. Sure you don't mind?"

"Take a lesson from me. Stick close to him."

"I'm sorry you're having so much trouble. Maybe it'll all work out." She hesitated in the doorway and turned back to him.

"Angus Green told me about your talk."

"I didn't go there to pry. I just needed to know so I could maybe help."

"I tried to warn you off. But at least she is doing a lot better now. Her one lingering symptom is the fixation with security. She hasn't been able to deal with change or rejection since that happened to her."

Cassidy knew this to be true but that vulnerability was part of her attraction as far as Cassidy was concerned.

"Goodnight, Alexander. Leave the light on for her when you go."

It was several hours later when Joe Morgan brought Tosca home. Thankfully out of sight, Cassidy had gone to her bedroom to sleep off the wine, surrounded by her cushy blankets and stuffed animals. She studied his face in the soft light, then knelt to kiss him tenderly on the forehead. He stirred, opened his eyes and grinned in contentment. "OPA" she greeted him, then snuggled her arms around his neck.

"OPA, Tosca."

They remained that way for a whole wondrous thirty seconds, till the sadness that was destroying them worked its way to the surface. Quiet tears stuck in the corners of her eyes and would not flow. "Oh, Alexander…" she agonized as she lay with her head wedged against his own. "The novel? You've finished?"

"*Si, corazon.* Can you read tomorrow?" She shook her head and the contented look disappeared from his face. "Morgan?"

"We're going to the ARLINGTON. Berragamo and his mime troop are going to perform."

"I don't like it, Tosca," he said softly, trying to keep his voice down. "I mean, who do you want, me or him."

"You. I'd rather go with you if we had the money."

"Jesus Christ!" he fumed, angry, yet fully aware how important it was for her to see the king of mimes.

"I could be home by ten," she offered.

"Okay, I'll be here waiting. It's not right you should miss Berragamo."

His acquiescence pleased her. She kissed him passionately and he responded and they found themselves making love though this had not been her intention.

She watched him closely through slitted eyes as he caressed her body. She tracked him as he kissed her thighs, feet, arranged her long hair to frame her breasts, fingered her private places; rituals they had always relished while making love. But the look on her face, quizzical, amused, was troubling him. "Something's happenin' Tosca. What?"

"It's way weird," she answered, fidgeting uncomfortably, "but I know what you're going to do next even before you make a move." They continued making love but the comment had taken the edge off their love-making. It was the unsaid which troubled him "Are we gonna be all right, peanut?"

"Could we not talk about it right now?" she yawned, took off her clothes and threw them onto the pile. "Will you lie beside me till I fall asleep?"

"You bet, *niña.* Just like before."

She pressed her body back against his and fell asleep almost immediately. He savored every moment, finally leaving about 3 o'clock. As he walked down the steps to the Morris Minor he thought of the many moments sitting on those steps planning the future with her. He sat and watched the twinkling lights of Santa

Barbara below, and for the first time in months actually noticed the scent of the night-blooming jasmine in the Tosca flower beds.

"You were right, Tosca, I should have stayed in the garage."

Then, unwilling to tolerate the stress any longer he hurried down to the street as Bo Diddley's ruckus sounded from the big oak tree.

But the sadness only intensified in the closed spaces of MARCO POLO. He tossed and thrashed his sleeping bag as he struggled to sleep. He spent hours on the dark poop deck drinking coffee, listening to the buoys outside the harbor entrance, tracing the droplets of condensation as they rolled off the mast and shrouds; wondering at the nightly odyssey of the scavenger crabs as they scratched for food at the dock's waterline.

Just after dawn the big foghorn on Stearns Wharf began its baleful sound and still he was awake with his fixation on Tosca. Joe Morgan was getting the bigger share of her time these days while his own relationship with her was failing badly. They quarrelled when together. He questioned her moral fiber, she called him old-fashioned. He tried to keep busy editing old manuscripts, reworking old poems, writing to family and friends, anything to keep his mind off her. It didn't work.

She never came down to MARCO POLO that day either, her pattern lately. Finally he was unable to maintain, hurling his tee shirt at the clock/radio.

"God-damn it! Are you coming or not!"

Then, uncharacteristically for him, he scrambled topside as MARCO POLO rocked in the excessive wake of a passing craft, and he hollered furiously, "Slow down! The law says five knots in the harbor!"

The ten year-old skipper of the dinghy was frightened at the violence of his remark and Cassidy turned away, embarrassed. He returned to his fruitless pursuits and for the first time in his memory the screech of seagulls irritated rather than pleased him.

Suddenly his face lit up! Her footsteps! He recognized her pattern as she approached MARCO POLO and he threw open the hatch to welcome her. "OPA, Tosca!"

But it was only one startled tourist who had come close to admire the junk. "Sorry about that, man," Cassidy apologized as the tourist backed off to the main dock.

Still hopeful for a glimpse of her Cassidy scanned the harbor carefully. The big neon sign at JOHN BUOY'S caught his eye, a large indistinct puff of yellow in the foggy distance.

"Mmmm, I wonder…" he mused, and checked the clock to see if BUOY's was still serving lunch.

He went below, put on the red hat and a foul weather jacket, then headed toward JOHN BUOY's Restaurant. A surprising number of people were still there despite the bad weather, mostly grounded urchin divers and fishermen. They had no other place to go except home, so this would be their day for bullshit and swapping stories, and showing off scars from the monster shark that almost ate them alive out in the channel.

"Hey, Reggie, have you seen Tosca?" he asked the waitress, a woman who lived several docks down from him.

"Yeah. She was here earlier," Reggie answered, averting her eyes, not happy with the message she had to give him. "She had on that fantastic hat with the pea-cock feathers on it. Three days in a row now. I gotta say, he's one great tipper."

Cassidy's stomach was in knots. He stepped outside in the dank chill, nause-ated enough to throw up. He inhaled deeply of the fresh sea air and scanned the Yacht Club. He sat on the breakwater and watched the waves drive in ferociously, each overlapping its predecessor with a loud slap, KAAFOOOOOSH!, before withdrawing in a frothy hiss.

Somewhat refreshed, he wandered aimlessly from the breakwater to the bait shop, to the chandlery, to the office of the salty sea lawyer Chuck Kent; anything to take his mind off Tosca and Joe Morgan. He came to the back door of the SANDSPIT CAFE and pressed his forehead against the cold window glass. The cafe was closed, a single dreary light bulb glowing inside. He turned and made his way to the boatyard. Visibility was 50 feet, just enough to make out the twin black masts of ACHILLEAS dead ahead. There was no activity in the boatyard; the weather had ended all for the day. He let out a stifled gasp as he surveyed the thick gray billows of fog; her Veedub was nestled in close under the hull. Sweat rolled off him in a nervous reaction and he rubbed his arms and shoulders to calm himself.

"By God, she's aboard with him right now!"

His face distorted with anger he started for the schooner but taking a moment to reconsider he ran away from there, his rubber sandals slapping against the wet pavement.

"BITCH!" he shouted, the echo of his voice bouncing off the nearby stucco buildings.

Nothing happened in the boatyard for a few moments after he was gone. Then the rustling of feet and two indistinct forms appeared on the deck of ACHILLEAS.

"Hey, it might have been the foghorn, or maybe just seagulls honking," Morgan sought to explain the disturbance.

"No, it was him, I know it," Tosca insisted.

"Well if he's that stupid he's stuck with it. I'm not leaving."

"Joe..." she started to interrupt.

"No, listen to me now. These art guys are all egomaniacs. They think nobody else is worth a shit. I mean, look at you, you're a little treasure. You deserve better than that." He held her close, humming a tune as they rocked back and forth in the dank silence. "I really need someone like you, Tina. I mean, I travel a lot, meet a lot of girls. But you're the only one who has made me stop and think. You're a shining angel, kid, and I gave up on shining angels a long time ago. Didn't think there were any more out there."

"But you're gonna be leaving soon."

"Come with me," he offered.

"You mean to live with you?"

"Just you and me, crazy eyes. Travel, theater, no more peanut butter and no more bullshit from jokers like Cassidy. I'll treat you precious like you are."

"I'll think about it, okay."

"What's to think. I've wanted you from the first time I saw you on that ab boat. Why do you think I put in here for repairs? San Pedro's got a much better boatyard."

"But I've got school and stuff."

"You should get out of this place, Tina, it's way too mystic. Just crawlin' with tectonic jive. Anyway, we got much better schools where I come from. I'll give you a personal scholarship to Stanford or Berkeley if you can qualify."

"You'd do that for me?"

"My word on it. And the-wheels to get you to and from."

"Awesome! I've never had anything given to me before. But my mom wouldn't go for it. She says you can't trust a guy who drives around in a fancy car but doesn't even have a job."

"Tell her that's my business," he answered without rancor. "But how about you? Do you trust me?"

"Yes, I don't think you'd ever hurt me."

A whole head shorter than Morgan, Tosca raised her lips invitingly. He kissed her long and with passion, then flashing her the quick vacant smile he nuzzled her playfully nose-to-nose until his hat fell to the deck.

"And as for pain...That's always been optional, hasn't it? Come on, let's go below," he grinned suggestively.

Then gathering her up like so many feathers Morgan carried her down to the main cabin. To love, warmth, and untroubled pleasure.

CHAPTER 18

▼

"Dominique?"

"Yes. Who is this please?"

"Your old boyfriend. The one you swore you'd never forget," Cassidy joked, slumping in the garish light of the phone booth.

"Alexander! So good to hear your voice! It's been such a long time. Where are you?"

"Still in Santa Barbara," he answered, then remarked plaintively that he could sure use a friendly ear; that she herself had suggested he call anytime the need arose.

There was a clumsy silence on the other end of the line as she assessed this bit. Yes, she had made the offer, but only in the hope that it might keep him in touch, maybe help salvage their own recently busted romance. "You in some kind of trouble?" she probed uneasily.

"Yeah," he hesitated to clear his throat. "I met someone I like but it's not turning out right. It just seems to get harder each time."

Another long silence from her, then…"How old is she, Alexander?"

"Eighteen."

"Eighteen! My God, Alexander, don't you know better than that?"

"Better than what! So she's younger than you! So what!"

"For Christ's sake, Alexander, you've got a daughter who is that old!"

"Fuck you, Dominique! FUCK YOU!" he screamed, then threw the phone into its cradle and kicked the wall. "Fuck you!" he repeated, then walked back and forth vigorously as though to clear his troubled mind. He dialed the phone a second time. "Bair, listen, I know it's late, but…Oh Christ!"

"Take it easy, buddy boy. What's the problem?"

"I need to talk. Can you come down?"

"Gimme ten minutes. Build a pot of coffee."

"MARCO POLO in ten. Thanks Bair."

Cassidy opened the marina gate and crossed the gangplank down to the boat dock. He stared at the water and noticed the surface ripples of a school of minnows. Tosca had called them 'my babies', reaching out to stir the water, loving them as she did all animals. The recollection was painful as he shambled past the long line of tethered boats, all creaking in the morning tide, each one black and solitary in the silent fog.

He approached MARCO POLO and his mind was still on Tosca when a harsh voice sounded out of the gloom. "Well, I was afraid you wasn't gonna show up tonight, *hombre*."

The surprise, the closeness of Padro's voice caused Cassidy to jump back reflexively and lose his balance. He barely missed crashing into his dock box, pirouetting cleanly as he knifed into the water, avoiding MARCO POLO's protruding bow by half-a-foot. Padro doubled up in laughter at the sight of Alexander's close call and predicament.

"Hey, why don't you go hassle that guy on the big schooner!" Cassidy sputtered as he surfaced and looked around for his red hat. "He's the guy who is screwing her, not me."

"You're full of shit, you lyin' bastard!"

"I wish I was, Mister, but she's not mine anymore."

"It's not gonna be that easy, Cassidy. Get outta the water."

The water was cold and Cassidy's physical condition weakened by the strain of the last weeks. He looked around for a safe place to come out of the water but no matter where he might swim to Padro would get there faster. He grabbed for the dock and Padro aimed a kick which grazed his forehead. But this was Cassidy's environment. He knew the place better than his tormentor. Sputtering as though in trouble he submerged and swam down the long line of boats, away from MARCO POLO, while Padro followed on the dock from boat to boat, cussing Cassidy, trying in vain to catch sight of him. Still swimming underwater Cassidy doubled back to the junk and was climbing up on his dock before Padro realized he had been outwitted.

Half-frozen by the cold water and depleted by the effort to get away, Cassidy realized he was in deep trouble. Knife in hand, face distorted by hatred, Padro came on as Cassidy backed up toward the dock box and grabbed the oar kept there for his dinghy. His fear of the knife now lessened, Cassidy felt the adrenalin surge. He stopped and stood his ground.

"I told you she's not here. Put the knife down, man."

"Sure. After I seperate you from your *cojones*."

"Fuck you! I'm sick of your macho crap, and your daughter too! Come get it, you bastard! Come on!"

He swung the oar at Padro, forcing him backward, and continued to do so each time the knife was brandished. But Padro ducked under the oar and grabbed hold of its broad tip, slashing away at Cassidy as he held on. Cassidy used the oar as a pole and pushed with all his strength, forcing both of them into the water. Each man held on as they both disappeared beneath the surface but Padro lost his grip and surfaced, thrashing out wildly. Finding himself too close Cassidy swam away from the knife and left Padro sputtering, coughing up water.

"Hey, I can't swim!" he shouted in panic.

"Is that so. Well tonight you learn, *amigo*," Cassidy shouted, then dove beneath the surface and caught hold of Padro's leg. He yanked him under, held on till he heard the desperate gulping, then propelled him up to the surface. Padro thrashed around, trying to stay afloat but the experience had spooked him badly.

"I'll drown! Gimme a hand!" he cried, and Cassidy came close to assist.

"Throw the knife away first."

"I ain't got it," Padro wheezed, spewing water as he grabbed for the oar, nearly tearing it from Cassidy's grip.

"What the hell's going on here, boy?" Cassidy heard the welcome voice of Bair, just now approaching on the dock.

"Tosca's old man, and he's got a knife!" Cassidy warned, then using the oar he propelled Padro the last few feet to safety. Padro took hold of the dock but then lunged to slash at Cassidy with the blade.

"Pussy bastard!" he screamed, and Cassidy kicked out powerfully to drive him under the surface again.

"Let him up, Cassidy!" Bair shouted, watching as Alexander poked at Padro with the oar. "Don't do it!" he continued, searching anxiously for a sign of Padro.

"I haven't got him! He's down there somewhere! Hit the spotlights!" Cassidy shouted, then dove beneath the surface as the spotlights brightened the water around MARCO POLO. But it was Bair who finally dove in and snagged Padro, shoving him onto the dock as he spewed water, choking, barely conscious.

"Look buddy, this shit's gettin' outta hand. I thought you did it to him for sure," Bair said, spitting water, slicking his hair down against his scalp. "Knock it off."

Bair knelt down beside Padro and slapped his face to revive him.

"You stupid beaner! That was your last freebee, understand?" Anything happens to him I'll snap your neck like a twig. Hear me?" he held up the huge hands in Padro's face then slapped them forcefully down on Padro's chest, flattening him on the dock.

"Okay, okay," Padro sputtered weakly and crawled away as Bair flattened him again with a kick to the backside.

"It's finally cleared your cotton-pickin' brain. You ain't the meanest man alive. Remember that."

CHAPTER 19

▼

Except for the feeding frenzy of the seagulls the early harbor was deserted as Tosca bounced along sprightly, her breasts rolling inside the tight tee shirt, nipples pert from the brisk morning air.

"OPA!" she called out as she neared MARCO POLO and boarded.

Getting no return answer she peeked warily inside the hatch and stifled an exclamation at the trash and chaos inside. She studied Alexander as he slept, then stepped down into the cabin and kissed him lightly on the forehead. He stirred and sat upright, clearly surprised by her presence.

"Tosca, what are you doing here?"

"On my way to school. Thought I'd say hello."

"Got time to visit for a few minutes?"

The plaintive way he had asked this simplest of favors saddened her. "*Si*, Alejandro. How have you been?"

"Not so hot. I can't seem to get the hang of being single again."

She wanted to avoid talking about Joe Morgan so she asked about his work instead. "What are you doing with your time now that you're finished with Simon Lindero?"

"Just trying to survive. Listen, I know you don't want to but I think we need to talk about it."

"Sorry," she said, avoiding his eyes. "I have been seeing him."

"You've made up your mind then?"

"No, I'm still trying to understand my relationship with him. It's so weird."

"You love him or you don't. It's that simple."

"I'm really not sure. I just don't know."

"Well does he love you or is he just fooling around?"

"He says he does. I think he does."

"But you don't love him?" Cassidy asked, his hands to his mouth, staring at her in confusion. "Then how can you...God, Tosca, I can't believe a word you say anymore."

"I don't understand it either. I love you but I can't stop myself from going to him."

"You...love...me?" he repeated, dumbfounded.

"Yes, you. I can't stand making love to both of you guys. I'm going crazy!"

"What do you want me to do, Tosca. Just tell me."

Unfortunately there wasn't a ready solution for her. She raised her palms upward in that gesture of helplessness and shrugged. He asked if she was going to continue to see Morgan. Yes, they were going to the BILTMORE, she said, an answer that disturbed much more than most could have. The BILTMORE had been a favorite of his youth, essential California, a rambling resort of towers, verandas and antique interiors, even a private beach with its own wharf. As a teenager he had spent many an enchanted weekend there, sailing up from New-port Beach with his father and mother.

"See, it's because I don't have any dough," he said angrily. "That's why you're going with him."

"It isn't the money! I'm just trying to live my own life. You've experienced all this before. I'm just starting."

"Well I'd find out about such a dude if I were you. He could be a pimp, or a white slaver or something." She turned away to end the conversation but he wouldn't relent, taking hold of her chin and turning her around to face him. "I mean, has he got a real job? Where does he get the dough? Did you ever ask him?"

"He said he had a paper route. That's all he'd tell me."

"Jesus, Tosca, how can you be so dumb. Okay, here's the scoop on Mr. Big. His wife's got the money. They've got three grown kids who are all screwed up. They're both into other lovers. Both are self-centered sociopaths. The word is he has screwed his way from Vancouver to Argentina and just doesn't give a shit. If you think I'm just being a hard loser ask Frank. He's sailed with Morgan for the last six months."

"Joe told me all about that, but he says it's different this time. He wants to start over with me."

"Go ahead, Tosca, start over. But do it somewhere else. I can't handle it, knowing you two are over there fooling around in the boatyard. This is my home, Tosca. My home. Go somewhere else and make a fool out of yourself. I don't want to watch."

She sidled up to him and sat down on the bunk. Started to rub his forehead. "Alexander...I have really missed you. Can I lie with you for a few minutes."

Confused by this sudden change he grinned fleetingly but moved over to make room for her on the bunk. "I can't figure you out anymore, *niña*," he said, and was totally surprised when she started to undress. But desperate with skin hunger, excited by the prospect of lying with her again, he played it cool and began to take off his own clothes.

"I smell pretty raunchy. Can you handle it?"

"*Sí*, Alejandro," she answered, and rolled over to press her own body against his, staying that way till they both began to overwhelm the awkwardness they were feeling. "Hmmm, it's been so long. I've forgotten how good you feel."

"You too, peanut," he said hopefully. And though she didn't respond to 'peanut' he was still caught up in what they had once been to each other, and from all appearances might be again. He reacted to her sensuality, and she to his as they caressed each other.

"Hmmm, wonderful, Tosca. I've missed those eyes, and feeling your body against mine, and..."

"Alexander, maybe we should stop."

"I'm sorry?" he said, and drew back from her. "I don't get it."

"I only meant for us to be together. I don't think we should make love right now."

Realizing that she was unsure what it was she wanted at this point a strong sexual urge seized him. He would help her remember and show her how wonderful it had been for them. He covered her body with his own, and though struggling lightly at first she did finally respond despite herself. "Tosca, listen, we're gonna be all right. You'll see."

"Please, can't we wait till this all settles down a little."

But it was already too late. Obsessed, he plunged into her deeply, harder than usual, as though to punish her. She tried to stop him and recoiled as he came on to a quick, angry climax. He was through with her. She sobbed as they lay, not in anger but despair of sorts. This was a different Cassidy from the one she knew.

"I'm sorry, Tosca. I didn't mean to hurt you," he said softly, massaging her thighs and pelvic area, trying in vain to soothe her. She got up, and ignoring his attempt to gloss it over, put on her clothes quickly, avoiding eye contact with him. He watched her guiltily, asked when he could see her again. Humiliated, still in shock of sorts, she levelled on him and said maybe never after what he had just done to her.

"All right, enough of this humble shit! I'm gonna tell you something you need to hear!" he shouted, and jumping up he paced the cabin with no clothes on. "First you put me down for a cosmic walking dick. Okay, shit happens. Now you take off all your clothes and hop into my bunk, like…like you're going to the grocery store or something. Then you say *Alexander, I love you but don't make love to me.* Bullshit, lady, be honest with yourself! You've got an itchy place and you're not sure who you want to scratch it for you!"

"I'm trying to be honest about that! I told you I love you! Yes, I am unsure about Joe Morgan but I'm trying my best! I am!"

"My God, Tosca, what a rotten mess. It's sick."

She flinched at that comment, then stiffened. "I agree that I'm confused, but sick I'm not. I'm just more modern than you, that's all. We're trying to relate from altered points of view. You have to face it, Alexander, I'm not like you anymore. This is 2006 and I'm growing up. I'm changing."

"You're right, that's not my Tosca talking. Where'd you get that bullshit anyway?"

"It's not bullshit. Me and Joe talked it over. You just refuse to understand. To grow with me."

"Boy, you got that right. But I'll listen. Talk."

As she presented her point of view Cassidy realized he was indeed talking to a new Tosca. Same body, same face, but her reasoning and vernacular were now couched in the jargon of junkies and hipsters. He recognized it easily. Some of his oldest friends in the harbor were off-the-wall, harmless, but off-the-wall no less. He waited patiently for her to finish, then realizing he couldn't reach her he said softly, even desperately, "Darlin', that's quite a speech but do you really believe all that free love stuff? Instinct over commitment? Satisfaction over loyalty and honesty? Get real, Tosca, the sixties are dead! Deal with it."

"It may be dead for you but not for me. I'll go get Joe. He can make you understand."

"Man oh man, that's all I need, him aboard MARCO POLO. Jesus Christ, Tosca, don't you understand that you're just another fuck to him? He's a womanizer, working his way around the world, picking candy off the trees. Don't take my word for it. Ask Frank. Ask Satyri. Ask the sherrif, for God's sake!"

"I'll never get through to you. I might as well boogie on."

"Who you gonna boogie on with this time? Morgan? Padro again? Some new guy?"

Tosca paled at the comment. Her jaw dropped open in disbelief. Tears rolled down her cheeks and she backed away unsteadily. "I can't believe you said that to me, Alexander," she said and stumbled away in a fast walk, her shoulders rigid, jaw set.

As he watched her go Cassidy realized what an awful thing he had said to her. He rubbed his scalp vigorously and called her name as he ran after her. He snatched at her arm and tried to apologize but she broke his hold and walked faster.

"Tosca, that's the worse thing I ever said to anybody and I'm sorry. I apologize. I'm sorry, darlin'. Please?"

She stopped abruptly and faced him. There was no anger there, no forgiveness, just nothingness. She opened the marina gate and kept walking.

He leaned on the railing and watched her go. Then he started back toward MARCO POLO. "That's not my *niña*. She's gone beyond me somewhere," he mumbled, and boarding the junk he kicked the coiled hawser into the water.

Below deck, he reached into the storage locker back of the galley and withdrew a burlwood box; the box which used to hold uppers and downers in days past when he partied a lot. He turned the box upside down and shook it.

"Murphy's Law," he groused, and pitched the box back into the locker.

He was frustrated. He fidgeted. Then relieving his anxiety with a loudly shouted Aaaaarrrggghhh, SHIT!, he grabbed up a towel and headed for the bath house and a much-needed restorative cleansing.

CHAPTER 20

▼

"Hey Greco, who's doing the table tonight?" Cassidy primed the Greek as he approached the table where he and his Greek buddies were playing cards.

"What you talkin' about, *malaka*! Only Papanikolas can do that table. Hey, look, my boy Satyri. He's gonna spend Thanksgiving with me. Say hello to Uncle Alex, son."

"OPA Satyri! How you doing kid?" Cassidy greeted the boy and offered to shake hands. Embarrassed by the attention the boy stuck one finger in his ear and dug absent-mindedly, then turned away to gaze around KYLIX. "How long is he going to stay, boss?"

"The whole week," Satyri answered as he watched Cassidy lurch, half-drunk. "Hey, you got your good hat on, eh. Where you been?"

"The BLUEBIRD CAFE, the ENGLISH DEPARTMENT, MADISON BARE GARDEN. This is my last stop. I'm goin' home."

"I'll finish this hand and be over in a minute," Satyri promised, eyeing him curiously. It was one of only a half-dozen times that Satyri had seen him this snockered.

It was the middle of the week, fairly early, and the dinner crowd had already gone home for the night. Friends from the old country were still there, drinking, and like all native Greeks they were arguing about something. Cassidy stood alone at the bar and contemplated all the good years he had spent at KYLIX. It had become a necessity to him; a place of sanity where he could go to escape the *shithouse* out there. But tonight Cassidy was ill at ease and vulnerable. He stared at his image in the backbar mirror and for the first time in his life he felt old.

Observing Cassidy from the card game Satyri could not concentrate. He got to his feet and was halfway across the dance floor when the glass slipped from Cassidy's hand and shattered on the floor. Cassidy stared at it morosely but made no attempt to clean it up. Satyri motioned for Yorgos to clean it up then he poured two cups of strong Greek coffee and approached Cassidy.

"Sorry boss. As any fool can plainly see, I'm screwed up," Cassidy apologized, smiling ludicrously at the Greek.

"Hey, you all right?"

"Sure, Greco, all right."

"Here, drink this," Satyri said, and pushed the coffee closer. "So, problems with Tosca yet?" he asked, and Cassidy nodded affirmatively but said nothing. "They came in for dinner again last night. She was all dressed up, like a grownup, you know. Guy with the big crazy hat. Right?"

"Yeah, and a shit-eatin' smile."

"She shouldn't have brought him here," Satyri added. "Women like to rub it in, you know. Embarrass a guy, right."

"I wouldn't have thought Tosca would bring him here, to my own club. Definitely not cool."

"Aw, I seen it a thousand times. The young girls like to eat at the big restaurants. They want the Mercedes man, the ski man. I see 'em turn on all the time," Satyri said, pushing the ouzo bottle away as Cassidy reached for it.

"Come on, boss. One more to kill off a rotten day."

"Drink the coffee. You gotta drive home."

"Not so. I walked up from the marina."

"Smart. Do a hisapiko before you go?"

"Sure. But not HEAVY SILENCE, okay. I'm not into that one tonight."

Cassidy stumbled as he went to the dance floor to wait for Satyri. The sad bouzouki music was soon joined by the throaty sound of a male singer. Satyri looked troubled as he led the line of dancers. It was very often like that; an urgency Satyri was unable to explain, let alone control. Saddened by the lament of the hisapiko, Cassidy embraced the Greek as the music ended. "Gotta go, boss. Gotta go."

"Take it easy, huh. See you tomorrow night."

"Right. Hey…" Cassidy stopped alongside the show table and pointed to the teeth marks deeply etched in one corner of the top, the results of a thousand table dances. "Time to start on a different corner. Not much left of this one."

"No way! Took me a long time to get it just right."

"Your table, mah man. Your funeral."

On leaving KYLIX Cassidy returned to the marina, sat on the breakwater and marvelled at the shroud of stars which sparkled over the dark Pacific. Between the walk home and the strong Greek coffee he sobered up slightly. He thought (no, worried would be more correct) about the incident of several days ago aboard MARCO POLO; his taking of Tosca and the crude remark about boogieing on to Joe Morgan or Padro. Definitely uncool. His brain was heavy with guilt. He decided that he needed to apologize. He drove to APS where Mrs. Tosca answered the door in housecoat and a head full of curlers.

"Alexander, come in," she offered, though a bit apprehensive about his condition.

"It's all right, Marty. I'm not here to cause trouble."

"I know that. Have a seat."

"Sorry about the hour but I'd like to talk to her."

"She's not here. Anything I can help you with?"

"No, thank you. I'd like to wait for her if it's okay."

Mrs. Tosca gestured toward the living room. A large drawing of ACHILLEAS (the hull angle) stood propped against a chair. A blue windbreaker with ACHIL-LEAS stencilled across the back was draped over a chair. She was embarrassed as they both stared at watercolor and windbreaker. "I'm sorry about the way things turned out."

"Can't say you didn't warn me. You've been very nice to me Marty. I want to thank you."

"It worked out better than I thought it would. Yeah, change has always been hard on her," Mrs. Tosca paused, then added as proof, "Would you believe, the clothes pile is gone. She washed everything and hung it all up. I've been fussing at her and that pile for 3 years and now that she finally cleans it up I'm very disturbed. Something's happening to her. She's changing again."

Offering no comment Cassidy crossed to her room and switched on the light. There was a haunting emptiness where once the pile had covered a third of the room. He became light-headed. Nauseated. "Jesus," he whispered sadly and returned to the living room.

They sat for a while longer, the mood somber, depressing. Mrs. Tosca rocked her chair and racked her brain for an upbeat topic but finally gave it up.

"You shouldn't be driving, Alexander. Stay the night, why don't you."

"I'm all right. Thanks anyway."

It was deathly still after she went to bed. He sat staring at the darkness outside and his own reflection in the big glass window. "Hummph, funny man in the red hat. Old fashioned," he mocked, turning slightly to one side to check his profile in the window. He went to the kitchen table, took pencil and paper in hand, mumbling as he wrote...My lady Tosca

you will not find it today

it is where you left it yesterday.

Alexander/the dinosaur.

He taped the note to the kitchen door, then collapsed on the sofa.

It was 10:30 when he tumbled off the sofa. He cursed and made his way to the sink for a drink of water. After a dejected look at the kitchen clock he gave up and drove back to the marina, careful not to attract the attention of the police.

He drove slowly past the boatyard fence and stretched to see inside. As expected the Veedub was parked close by but the Ferarri was not in sight. All the weariness of the night's debauchery disappeared as the anger mounted in him.

"God-damn, I've got to see this with my own eyes."

He cut the lights and moved into a parking space near the boatyard fence where the bushes would shield the Morris Minor from approaching traffic.

A warm evening and quiet, the boat people and sailors already retired for the night. He became super-alert as he grappled with the possibilities. They could be at a movie, or dancing somewhere. A motel? He turned to scan the ridge of dark mountains to his right; they might be camped up there. Then he caught sight of the gleaming red machine as it glided slowly toward the boatyard, their easy laughter accompanied by music from the radio. He felt numb, strangely removed from the scenario as it unfolded before him, each movement and sound acted out exactly on cue. As in a vacuum he watched Morgan hold the car door open for her and kiss her long and passionately, the yellow harbor light framing them forever in his memory. He watched Morgan follow her up the ladder to ACHILLEAS' deck. Both paused on the ladder's rungs, her body flexing sensually as he slid his hands under her dress, over the taut muscles and into the warm moisture of her body. Cassidy went into shock of sorts as she backed down the ladder one step to accomodate Morgan's frantic lips, stretching up to kiss her groin and bare thighs.

"There you are, stupid. Now you can believe it," he whispered to himself, and a strange sense of nothingness came over him, like floating in a silent fog.

They were nowhere in sight as he came to his senses a moment later. He saw a dim light glimmer in the deck house of ACHILLEAS and then disappear altogether. He felt like true shit as all hope deserted him.

"We could have made it, Tosca, but you had to go and screw it up, didn't you," he reproached her, then fired up the Morris and drove away toward MARCO POLO.

The boatyard seemed deserted as he withdrew in the distance. There was no sound or movement at first. Then a car door closed softly on the Yacht Club side of the cyclone fence and a stealthy figure made its way to the gate, glanced in all directions, then ran for cover. Padro Tosca was determined. He read the layout of the boatyard in one expert scanning, satisfied that it was deserted.

He crossed over to ACHILLEAS, hunkered in close to the hull and listened to the sound of laughter and music coming from inside the hull. He found it difficult to control his rage. He bit his lip, causing it to bleed. Few things made him absolutely crazy anymore; communists, faggots, dope smugglers, and Castro too. He glanced around for some way to take his revenge, nothing terminal, just some little devilment to speed this jerk along his way. His hand reached around and touched the hilt of the big knife. Ewww, how he'd love to cut the bastard! He searched around for a more attainable possibility. Cans of paint, turpentine, other volatile chemicals littered the tarmac under the schooner's hull. Oh yeah! Burn the cocksucker! But he ruled that out quickly. There was no way he could ever hurt his little girl, no way. Then he noticed the long hull precariously balanced on its fore and aft cradles, supported on each side by adjustable wooden stanchions.

"Now this is something I can get into," he mused, rubbing his hands briskly together at the prospect. He gathered several sturdy ropes and tied them together, fastening one end to the bow cradle, then fed the other end through the cyclone fence and into the parking lot of the Santa Barbara Yacht Club.

He was ultra-careful as he crept back to the Jeep. To his twisted mind it was like the old days in Miami again, when he was a respected member of Colonel Alvarez' notorious *PATRIOTA*. There must be no witness to what he was about to do. He checked out the dark places. No living thing stirred. He pulled the rope through the fence a foot at a time so as not to make a chafing noise, then took several turns around the welded steel bumper of the Jeep, fastening it with a slip knot to the roll bar behind the driver's seat.

Padro was giddy, barely able to control himself as he touched the starter. He eased the Jeep along until the rope was taut. He stopped and revved quickly to prime the motor, then eased the clutch out and dragged the bow cradle out from under ACHILLEAS, causing her to crash down to the tarmac with a tremendous THUNK! He pulled the slipknot free and careened out onto Cabrillo Boulevard in a cloud of burnt rubber, disappearing into the night.

Joe Morgan was naked and confused as he emerged onto the deck of the slanting schooner. He hung onto the life rail and inched his way down to the bow and off onto the tarmac. He struggled to piece it together in his mind, not quite sure what might have happened. He saw the overturned bow cradle lying near the fence, heavy rope still attached, then he traced the rope back through the fence and the realization struck him.

"ASSHOLE!" he screamed it out, not knowing who at. "God! I can't believe this one!" He snapped a look back to where Tosca had just emerged in his oversized bathrobe, a bloody handkerchief held up to her face. "Hey, you all right, Tina?" he called out, and rushed to help her off the boat.

"Just a bloody nose. What happened? Why is the boat like this?"

"Some bastard yanked the bow cradle out from under her, it looks like. Maybe Cassidy?"

"Oh no, Joe, he wouldn't do anything like that."

"Who then? I mean, why?" Morgan scratched his head in perplexion as one of the other boat owners approached.

"Hell of a racket, man. What happened?"

"Somebody pulled her down. You happen to see anything?"

"Maybe," the sailor offered. Saw a guy peelin' rubber outta here."

"What was he driving?" Tosca asked quietly.

"Looked like a Jeep. Olive or maybe brown. He was headed toward Stearns Wharf."

"Hell I don't know anybody in this town who drives a Jeep."

"I do," Tosca offered. "My father."

Morgan's eyes burned into her's as he thought this over. "Where can I find him?"

"This time of the night he's usually down on Guiterrez Street, at the CLUB LATINO or The AZTECA. Want me to go with you?"

"I'll take care of it. You wait for me here," he said, dabbing at her nose with the handkerchief, helping her to negotiate the crazy angle of the unbalanced schooner.

It had been a good night down at the CLUB LATINO till this point, young Jésus Sola mused, chalking his cue stick, waiting for his turn to shoot. A busy night with many of his compadres playing cards, shooting pool and guzzling beer, a ping-gong game off in the distant corner, and his lying-bastard buddy Padro laying on the bullshit as usual.

But for some reason Padro was more light-hearted this night, inoffensive, boozing less than usual and not as aggressive. A pleasure to be with for a change.

He was an excellent shot, claiming to have learned the game from his father when he was only eight years old. The Sergeant-Major had sworn to make a man of him, shooting pool, hunting in the mountains, whoring, boozing. Yes, the Sergeant-Major had seen to his education all right. As Jésus watched closely Padro pumped the cue stick several tmes and cracked the cue ball smartly, then watched happily as several balls found the pockets.

"Just what the *barco* sounded like when she came down. *Estampido sonico*! ha ha," he said, and threw a five-spot on the table. "A couple of Coronas, eh, Jésus. And don't hurry cause I'm gonna clear the table while you're gone."

Jésus made his way to the bar, got the Coronas, and was on his way back to the pool table when he stopped suddenly. Concealed by a large plastic rhododendron, Joe Morgan sat watching the pool players from a corner booth. Jésus took note of the large Aussie hat but kept walking. He came near to Padro, put one of the Coronas on the rail of the table, and murmured, "*Alla esta el hombre con el sombrero grande.*"

Padro froze up for a moment but concealed his surprise. Barely an hour had passed since he had done the deed. How could the *gringo* have found out so quickly? He looked up at Morgan, held the challenge for a moment, then let fly with the shot he had lined up. A miss.

While Jésus took his turn Padro stood with his back to Morgan and swigged at the Corona repeatedly. He was losing his composure, pissed-off at the whispering of his companions and the glances of admiration directed at the *gringo*. Finally Morgan stood next to him, towering over all around.

"*Señors, por favor.* I'm looking for the cowardly dog who tried to wreck my schooner tonight. Anyone here know of such a dog?"

Padro strained to keep himself under control, then answered with a grin. "If we did know we could not tell you. Such a man would be in bad trouble with the police, right?"

"No *policia*. Just me and him," Morgan promised, then turned around to face the other men in the room. "*Señors*, if this *hijo de puta* shows up tell him I'll be waiting for him on the parking lot. No *policia*."

Padro was stunned by the maximum insult just hurled at him. He had not been called son-of-a-whore since his first days in Fidel's hospital. He seethed privately as the big man left by the back door but he did not follow immediately. The *gringo* had all the signs of great strength and experience. A man of juice.

CLUB LATINO went quiet except for the cash register up front and a female voice in agony on the juke box. Padro glanced at the circle of faces watching him expectantly. Faces watching for his next move. He managed a brave half-grin which went unanswered. He thrust the beer bottle in his mouth defiantly, tipped back his head and gulped, and when he put the empty bottle down a look of contempt had replaced the half-grin. He was on his own. He glared at those nearest him and pushed his way through on his way out to the parking lot.

He squinted to adjust his eyes to the dull light which bathed the parked autos. Joe Morgan stood leaning with one foot on the front bumper of the Jeep. Watching Padro he took off the sombrero and placed it on the hood of the Jeep, then approached Padro.

"You the one who pulled my boat down, mister?"

"Fuckin' right I did! Tryin' to ruin my daughter!" he shouted defiantly, and was about to further justify his action when Morgan slammed a hard fist in his face. Padro staggered backward, lost his balance and fell to the gravel. Morgan was on him quickly, pulled him to his feet and smashed him in the face repeatedly. Bleeding profusely through mouth and nose, Padro lowered his head and rammed hard into Morgan's gut, taking both of them to the ground in a tangle of arms and legs. Padro scrambled toward a nearby brick but Morgan wrested it away from him and threw it into the empty lot next door, then smashed Padro in the face a few more times.

"You creep! Don't ever come near my schooner again, *comprender?*" he shouted, then grabbed Padro by the arm and slammed him into the side of the nearest car.

Padro stayed on the ground this time. There was pain in his back. The wind had been knocked out of him. Faint from the lack of blood to his brain his ephemeral thoughts shimmered curiously back to Havana; deja vu; to a boxing match in the school gymnasium, an ugly happening he had blotted from his memory. An official gathering, the boxing ring deliniated by neat rows of folding chairs on all four sides, the chairs occupied by proud parents and fellow students.

The adolescent Padro shuddered in mortification from where he lay sprawled on the gym floor, the victim of a flurry of stiff punches and a strong shove from his opponent. He looked up into the cold eyes of the Sergeant-Major, sitting in the front row, resplendent in his proud uniform and gold braid. He despaired at the look of humiliation in those hard eyes, eyes which then shifted indifferently to stare at a vacant gym wall.

"Fuck you!" Padro mumbled, and spat at the uniformed apparition of his father as he slouched against the side of the car and swiped at his bloody face with his sleeve. "Asshole!"

"And fuck you too!" he shouted defiantly at Morgan as he watched every step Morgan took back to the Ferarri.

Padro pulled himself into a sitting position and saw his friends desert their watching places at the windows of CLUB LATINO. Back to their games and talk. He would never go back in there. He was disgraced and alone.

"My daughter, you motherfuckers! Mine!" he shouted, and spit up a huge gob of bloody mucous. Then he swore softly to himself…"Gonna get you for this, you *gringo* swine."

CHAPTER 21

▼

"Thanks for the dinner, Bair," Cassidy groused, watching glumly as his friend spread the Big Macs and french fries out on the galley table. "Makes me want to throw up."

"You're actin' pathetic, boy. Cut bait and get yourself an older woman."

"Fantastic idea, Bair. Let's see…How about someone 40 or 50 years old, recently lobotomized. A rich one with her tubes tied and no living kin to hassle me," Cassidy scoffed, then tossed a french fry in the air and caught it in his mouth.

"Just tryin' to help you, smart ass. Anyway, Mabel says for you to come up to our place for a few days. She's worried about you."

"Same difference. I take Tosca with me wherever I go."

Bair picked up the finished manuscript and paged through it as he wolfed down the hamburger. "Still sweeping? Cleanin' shithouses?"

"Yep. Got it down to ten hours a week now."

"It pisses me off seein' a guy with your brains cleaning up after people."

"So it goes. It's my own choice, Bair. It's cool."

"The book comin' along all right?"

"Yeah. Finished."

"Hey, maybe you can sell it, huh?"

"That's why I wrote the thing, my friend, so I can pay you back for all the cholesterol and Mad Cow."

"Hell, I wouldn't know how to act seeing your name on a book at the check-out stand," Bair said, and smiled a great proud smile. "What's it all about, any-way?"

"Right down your alley, my man. Schooners, a dope scam in Mexico. The protagonist is even patterned after you."

"You don't say," Bair snapped to attention. He picked up the manuscript and began to page through it. "What's patterned after me?"

"The p...r...o...t...a...g...o...n...i...s...t," Cassidy spelled it out for him. "He's my main guy. The skipper of my schooner."

"Man after my own heart," Bair grinned, clearly hooked now. "So what is it I do in this story?"

"Well, Simon Lindero, my protagonist, spots this salty old wood schooner for sale and falls in love with it. He hasn't got one thin dime but he's gonna have that schooner, one way or another, right. So he gets back into dealing dope just long enough to buy it, and incidentally, to rescue the heroine. He gives the bad guys a bad time just like you do."

"So..." Bair swelled up importantly..."I'm this Simon Randero?"

"LINdero. Yeah, except you're more conservative, not quite so hip and mellow as Simon is. You're more...more..." Cassidy stopped talking, his face turned pale as he stared hard at Bair. He grabbed the manuscript and pounded it into his hand. "Oh Jesus no. I can't believe I did that." he said, barely above a whisper.

"What can't you believe?" Bair asked, suddenly alert to Alexander's reaction. But Cassidy seemed to be in shock and could only stare at the bulkhead. Bair seized him by the shoulders and shook him stoutly. "Hey, what's goin' on here?"

Cassidy buried his face in his hands and thrust himself backwards against the teak bulkhead. Three, four times he banged against it until Bair lunged forward to stop him. "Are you nuts, boy?"

"I did it, Bair! I did it to Tosca myself! Aaawwww!"

"What did you do?"

"I made Joe Morgan a reality for her! Don't you see that!"

"Who's Joe Morgan?"

"Yeah. Remember the guy with the broken eardrum? That schooner's in the boatyard right now and Morgan's the skipper! He's the guy who has got my Tosca! Know what I'm saying?"

"Well God-damn. Christ-a-mighty," was all Bair could think to say, and still not clear as to what he might have had to do with it.

"And worse yet, in my story Simon ends up with Carolina."

"Who is this Cah-ro-leena?" Bair asked.

"She's the sweet young Mexican virgin that Simon rescues, just like that jerk has got my Tosca. I've got to warn her," Cassidy said, taking his good hat from the clothes locker and putting it on.

"You mean you're going there right now?"

"Yeah," Cassidy answered, a noticeable calm settling over him. "Relax, I'm all right," he said, and stuck the fingers of his right hand in Bair's face. "See. Steady as a rock."

"It's not your hand I'm worried about, boy, it's your head. Listen, I'll be down early in the morning to get you for breakfast. You stay close, hear me."

"Hey, I've never turned down a freebee yet. Later, huh."

Cassidy left him there on the poop deck of MARCO POLO and set out for Tosca's house. As the Morris Minor came to a stop on Tosca's carport she approached him warily. She stopped, watched him for several moments then looked at her feet. He came closer and took her hands in his own.

"Tosca, you didn't deserve the shit I loaded off on you the other day. I mean the thing about your father. Can you forgive me?"

"I'm trying, Alexander. I don't know what else to say to you. That was so gross."

"I know, and it'll never happen again, I promise you that. I was totally devastated myself," he said, and pulled her to him in a tenuous embrace.

She returned the embrace then stepped back to observe him.

"Why are you wearing the good hat? Where's the other one?"

"I lost it a couple of days ago."

"Oh," she said, visibly upset. She had made it to wear at dance festivals and parties. "I'll make you another. You'll ruin that one," she promised, and observing him closely she touched his arm in sympathy. "You look tired, Alexander."

"Yes, so tired lately."

Affectionately she linked her arm through his and led him to the sofa, but he seemed to not notice it. His mind was still busy with the Cah-ro-leena thing. "I've been trying to think my way through all this stuff, Alexander. I never really appreciated before how much we are into each other. The mementoes, music, dancing, books and poetry. Thrift stores and the KYLIX."

As she talked on his thoughts were elsewhere. He seemed to be listening but was impatient, a wild bottled-up look on his face as he sat stiffly poised.

"We need to talk. Joe has asked me to go away with him."

"Are you gonna do it?"

"I don't know. I can't make up my mind."

"He's already married."

"I know that."

"You mean you'd even consider it, knowing he has a wife and kids."

"I told him I'd think it over."

"Stay here with me, Carolina. I don't want you to go with him."

She cocked her head quizzically as he called her Carolina. He had said it matter-of-factly, as though in a trance.

"I know, Alexander, but we're in two entirely different places right now and you don't seem able to handle that."

"You want to be screwing more than one person, that's what it gets down to."

Her eyes blazed defensively as she struggled for composure. "I have to do what's right for me, Alexander. I'm on an advanced plane right now and you won't even try to understand."

"That's true. I can't understand that."

"I've grown, don't you see, and I'd like you to grow along with me. We've always learned from each other. It's all got to do with your inner freedom. An emotional awareness that will allow you to..."

"You are Carolina," he interrupted woodenly. She smiled and took it for a compliment with no other context.

"I know. You patterned her after me."

"Joe Morgan is Simon Lindero."

"Alexander..." she began, her voice uneasy as she began to sense his direction.

"My Simon Lindero is your Mr. Morgan. The ACHILLEAS and Simon's schooner both have twin black masts, both guys are smugglers, six-three, handsome and laid back," he continued. "The only difference is that Morgan's got a lot of dough."

She collapsed on the sofa to collect her thoughts as Cassidy pressed on like a prosecuting attorney.

"By your own admission you don't love him yet you have an overpowering urge to go to him. Your own words were...I feel as though I've always known him. Well I'll tell you what, *pobrecita*, you do know him! Intimately. You were my critic and I laid that story on you every day until you know him as well as I know him! I've created Joe Morgan for you right out of my own mind! He is Simon, Godammit! JOE MORGAN IS SIMON LINDERO!!!"

He waited for her reaction but it was something she was too stunned to give.

"Don't you find that amusing, Tosca? As much as I love you I've paved the way for my own replacement," he said, and jumped to his feet and paced keenly, eyes wild with anxiety. He laughed hysterically. "What did they used to call that in the nineteen sixties...a mind-fuck?"

Again he laughed the crazy laugh but too loudly this time and Mrs. Tosca shuffled into the room, puffy-eyed, roused from her sleep.

"What in the world is going on out here?"

"My fault, Marty. Sorry," he apologized. "I'll keep it down."

Mrs. Tosca shook her head uncertainly, waved goodnight and returned to bed.

"You got rid of the clothes pile. How come?"

"I'm not a child anymore," she answered, drained of emotion. "I'm going to bed."

"Can I tuck you in?"

She was leery of him now. Untrusting. A different feeling, one she had not felt toward him before. "You came here to hurt me. To rub my nose in it."

He started to object. My God! After all she had put him through! But he realized she was right; he had come to hurt her.

"Sorry, Tosca, I've had a bad couple of days," he said and moved toward the door. "Can I call you tomorrow?"

"If you like," she answered, and he left her sitting there, to consider the strange twist their affair had taken.

CHAPTER 22

▼

"Gosh, mom, look at that sky. Pretty bad, huh."

"The radio says it's the tail end of a hurricane in Mexico."

They were at the breakfast table nursing their coffees when the telephone startled them out of their after-breakfast lethargy. It was Alexander. He wanted to see her, to talk about last night.

Tosca glanced around to see if her mother was eavesdropping. She was. Tosca promised she'd come down to the junk after class. Cassidy mentioned that Bair was coming down for breakfast but after that he'd stay aboard to wait for her.

"What do you intend to do about him?" Mrs. Tosca inquired after she hung up the phone.

"I think I'm going back to him, Mom. Everything has gotten too complicated. I need the simplicity."

"As long as you've gone this far a clean break might solve a lot of problems."

"Maybe, but at least I always know where I stand with Alexander. Things have got way out of hand and I need to slow down."

"You might find you can't stop the process, honey. So, what's your day gonna be like?"

"Horrible. A mid-term. Lunch with Alexander. Some work on his new hat maybe, a mime performance at the-Elks, and I have to take the Bug down to Joe."

"What's wrong with it?"

"A gas leak. Mark says it could be dangerous."

"Is that fair to Joe, if you're going to dump him?"

"He's been on a lark with me. He got his money's worth."

"Justina! I don't like the sound of that."

"Sorry, Mom," Tosca apologized, hugging her at the door as she started for school. "Now don't forget, you might have to drive us to the Elks tonight."

Down at the marina MARCO POLO rocked under Bair's massive weight as he came aboard. Though it was unusual for Cassidy to get to eat out this was the second time in as many days that Bair had treated him. "Come on, skinny," Bair grinned, stabbing him in the stomach with an index finger. "Every time you have woman trouble you look like a bean pole. A sack of poor bones."

"Okay, let me put on some pants first."

While he waited for Cassidy Bair poked his head out of the hatch and scanned the darkening sky. "Damn Mexicans can really kick up a storm down there."

On the way to the SANDSPIT CAFE Bair rubbed his knuckles and winced painfully. "You know that old bromide about predicting the weather by the ache in your bones? Well that ain't no persiflog, better believe it."

"The word is persiflage."

"That's what I said...Persiflog."

"Where'd you hear that?"

"Like that, huh? Yeah, Mabel's always talkin' like that. Tryin' to impress me."

As they entered the dingy cafe Cassidy stopped suddenly. Joe Morgan sat there in his wide brimmed hat, coffee cup in hand and the newspaper spread out on the table. Bair noticed Alexander's reaction and understood at once. "That the stupid asshole?"

"He's not stupid," Alexander answered, and laid a hand on Bair's arm. "Come on. Let's go to ESAU's."

"Bullshit! I'll play it cool if that's what you want but I'll never stand aside for any man. Well, maybe Schwartzennegger."

Alexander followed him to an open booth which was behind and far enough away from Morgan. "It's a shame the damned schooner didn't fall on him," Bair groused, then brightened as the waitress approached with the coffee pot. "Mabel and me talked it over last night. She wants you up there for a few days so she can keep an eye on you. You might as well give her her way. She's worse'n the damn sherrif. She says either that or get yourself up to your kids' place for a visit. You need a change."

"I've been thinking about that. Keep an eye on MARCO POLO till I get back?"

"Hell yes. Even take her out for a run. Scrape some of them barnacles off'n her bottom, something else you ain't been takin' care of since you got in love."

Cassidy was ravenous and it showed in his manners much to Bair's amusement; Cassidy had always been the one to call Bair 'hog'.

"Boy, the way you're scarfin' up that chow I'd say I saved your ass from starvation."

"Probably. Hey, I've been thinking…When I sell the story I want to pay you for the dive suit. What's it worth?"

"Maybe fifteen hundred, but you ain't givin' me Jack Doodley."

"I'll get the money. I'll feel better about it."

"Suffer then, dummy, I ain't takin' a nickel. Call it a bonus. You were as good a tender as is."

"Why didn't you tell me that before. Hey, how are you doing'? Miss the diving?"

"Miss jumping in that freezing water 5 o'clock every morning? All those turds, plastic and oil floatin' around next to my face for 30 years? Hell yes I miss it, and I'm gonna keep on missin' it. Hey, I need a second opinion. Got time to check out an old Navy landing craft with me?"

"Sure, but what about MABEL N' ME. You don't need two boats."

"I'm gonna sell her. She's only good for fishin' and there ain't enough abs out there to fill a tooth. And I ain't exactly what you'd call chickenshit but them Great Whites are comin' in too close to suit me."

"Big market for urchins. Japanese love 'em."

"Japs are gonna eat us all outta house and home. Anyway, I could never get face to face with an urchin. Ugly little spiney things give me the creeps," Bair added, screwing up his face in horror.

"Why an LCVP?"

"I can let the ramp down in the water, dangle my feet, read a book or something."

"Dangle your feet in the…" Cassidy broke up laughing. "Boy you're weird. Okay, just make sure I get back to MARCO POLO by noon. Tosca's coming down."

"No sweat. Did you talk to her about the Carolina thing?"

"I laid a heavy trip on her. She threw me out."

"That's good. You're too gentle with her. You got to kick their butts once in a while."

Cassidy had heard him say something similar at least 20 times and always noted the look of satisfaction it gave him, but he couldn't recall a single instance where Bair had said it in front of Mabel. Just more 'persiflog'.

The old LCVP lay at anchor several hundred yards outside the harbor of Santa Barbara. They watched from the breakwater as she bobbed up and down on the choppy sea and tugged violently on her anchor buoy. "Won't be long now," Bair prophesied, measuring the gray sky. "Shit's gonna hit the fan this time."

"What's the forecast?"

"Harbormaster says we'll get it tonight but his head's down where his crack oughta be so don't expect any miracles outta him. C'mon, let's do it."

"I don't want to get caught out there. Can't it wait?"

"Naw, let's get it over with."

The yacht broker agreed with Cassidy about the timing but gave in to his old friend Bair. No point getting him pissed off, hardheaded as he was, CASH customer that he was. Besides, there was something Bair could help him with as long as he insisted on going out there today.

"Listen, Bair, I need to pull her drive shaft to get it straightened. I don't suppose you'd tow her in for me as long as you're going out there?"

"Couldn't wait for a typhoon, Charlie? Yeah, I'll tow it, you be good to me. Deal?"

"Got you. Take my Boston Whaler," Charlie suggested, and pulled a heavy tow rope from the closet. "Know how to tie a bowline," he kidded Bair, his mouth curling up humorously.

"Hell yes. Grab it by the shank, flip a loop over and under, pull it through and stuff it in a bag of chicken feathers. Right?" Bair answered, and gave Charlie the finger.

"Well I wouldn't stay out there too long in this blow or chicken feathers is what you might end up with."

The trip out to the buoy wasn't one you'd want to make every day. The blue colour was gone out of the water, replaced by the reflection of the dark angry sky. The wind waves churning up on the shale at Ledbetter Beach were short and powerful, the kind that make a wood boat groan with the miseries. But it was no way as bad as what was coming. Bair tied off the Boston Whaler and jumped up onto the LCVP.

"Damn, I haven't been aboard one of these old dogs since I was Navy."

"She looks a little rough, Bair. Might end up costing you some dough."

"True. But she'll make one hell of a boat for the islands. String a tarp across the cargo space, lower the ramp to the waterline and break out the barbecue pit. Great little camper. And look at that diesel! Only 50 hours on her, Charlie says."

"Hey, you could take Mabel's little Honda Car aboard and go to places like Pismo and Bodega Bay. That'd be cool. How much is he asking?"

"Sixty-Five Hundred, but business has been slow lately. Probably we can go talk him down," Bair said, and leaped up to the stern deck. "HEY!" he shouted with such alarm that Cassidy scrambled up to stand beside him.

"This is the first-time I've ever known you to do a thing like that, Bair."

The Boston Whaler had broken loose and was already 50 feet off the stern and moving in toward the breakwater.

"How are we going to get ashore now?"

"Anybody crazy enough to come out here in this weather...you can bet people are watchin' us. Might as well relax till ol' Charlie comes to get us."

"Jesus, I hope it doesn't take too long," Cassidy said, waving the canvas engine tarp. "I don't want to miss Tosca, though after last night she'll probably tell me to kiss off anyway."

But Tosca did not intend for him to kiss off. After the phone conversation of that morning she had decided to make him a gift. She had launched right into the hat project, a beautiful design she had pinched from a Della Francesca reproduction in one of her textbooks. Just a few minor adjustments and it would make the perfect reconciliation token for them. She drove to the marina, took the hat off the car seat and headed for the junk.

Approaching MARCO POLO she saw no evidence of his presence. The hatch was closed. No note was visible. Strange behavior considering his recent desperation for her company.

She approached the next boat where the neighbor was busy getting it ship-shape for the coming tempest. "S'cuse me, Sir, I was supposed to meet Alexander Cassidy down here. Have you seen him?"

"No, but you might check the bathhouse."

"Good idea. And if he comes will you tell him that Tosca was here and that I've something very important to tell him."

She left the marina and cupped her hands to holler over the wall of the bathhouse but there was no answer. She placed the hat on the car seat and sniffed at the lingering odor of raw gasoline. Fearful of an explosion or fire she closed her eyes, gritted her teeth and engaged the starter.

She drove the few hundred yards to the boatyard and parked next to the freshly painted hull of ACHILLEAS. There was no sign of Joe Morgan. Hair billowing in the wild wind she climbed the ladder to topside, rapping on the hull as she went.

"Permission to come aboard,"

Receiving no answer she repeated the courtesy again, "Permission! Permission!" louder this time.

"Yeah, go for it," she heard Morgan's faint answer from below deck. He scrambled topside and wrapped her in his arms as she stepped on deck, then kissed her flush on the mouth. "Hi, sweetheart. What's goin' on?"

"I'm in a real bind, Joe. Can you help me with the Veedub?"

"What's wrong with it?"

"A gas leak. Someone told me it'll blow me up."

"Hey, we can't have that. Sure, I'll check it out."

"Can I come get it at four-thirty?"

"I can't promise that because I'm trying to get ACHILLEAS ready for sea. The guy is gonna launch me tomorrow morning."

"Oh gosh. Well I've got rehearsal after school and it's supposed to rain tonight. What am I gonna do?"

"No problem. I'll give you a lift."

"Maybe you better not, Joe."

"Why not?"

"I'm going back to Alexander."

"Good for you and him, but where does that leave me?"

"I'm sorry, Joe. I never planned it this way. Don't be angry with me, huh?"

"Not angry, just surprised, disappointed. You're sure he'll forgive and forget?" Morgan asked, walking in tight impatient circles.

She shrugged, then gestured at the Veedub. "Sorry to bother you but I don't have any money for a mechanic."

"Come on, Tina, I like doing things for you."

Abundantly grateful, she hugged him then moved to a safe distance as he reached out for her. She practically slid down the ladder to the tarmac to avoid him, promising to return after class.

It was four-thirty on the button when she returned. Morgan's long torso was bent over and his head was down in the motor compartment of the Veedub. He straightened up and massaged his back as Mark drove up and honked the horn.

"Hey, is it finished?" Tosca asked, climbing over the door of Mark's sport car.

"No, but I'm working on it."

"Darn! Good thing I found a ride for tonight. Should I come back for it in the morning before class, or what?"

"It'll be ready later tonight. Stop by after the Elks and it will be waiting," he said meaningfully.

His persistence was embarrassing. She decided to make her intentions very clear. "Joe, I don't want to disappoint you but I think I love him. Honest."

"I figured as much when I saw the red hat in the car. But I've got a whole lot more to give anytime you're ready. Remember that."

"I've learned a lot from you, Joe. It's been good," she said, and gave him a hug. She climbed over the door of Mark's car and waved goodbye.

"I'm glad to see you back off that dude, Tina. He's pretty heavy company for you," Mark said as they drove away. "So, you've got a lift for tonight?"

"Yeah, the Elks always feed us after the show. Mom wouldn't miss it for anything."

"Break a leg, okay," Mark said, wishing her good luck in the manner of theater people. "And good luck with Mr. Cassidy."

Tosca said yes, she was supposed to have seen him earlier but they had somehow missed connections. Knowing his pattern she felt that he might show up at her house later that night.

And Alexander had indeed shown up at her house, but earlier than she had expected. Climbing the stairs to her house he thought he would never reach the top, he was that tired. He had not yet regained his verve since finishing with Simon, the first time that had ever happened since he started writing. Usually he would take several weeks off, a month maybe, then start work on the next project.

The cold cut right through his sweat shirt as he stood atop Alameda Padre Serra, the roiling clouds so close overhead. Hard to imagine that the peaceful town below would soon be reeling under the blows of another Pacific storm.

Her house was dark though it was barely seven-thirty. It was possible that Marty was sick or just overly tired, and had gone to bed early. But surely she would have left a light on for her daughter. Maybe Tosca had gone to bed early as well. He shuffled across the patio and rapped on the kitchen window. No answer. He moved to the window of her room and put his nose to the cold glass; no dark outline on her bed, no movement anywhere.

He moved to the edge of the property and observed the town below. She was certain to be down there with Morgan. And why not, he asked himself. The interloper was more handsome. Much more prosperous. He lived a far more interesting life, was younger and had a lot more time to give her, the ultimate luxury. Then his mood changed suddenly, the self-pity done with.

"Bullshit, Tosca! Up yours!" he shouted toward the empty house, then took the steps down three at a time, down to the Morris Minor and eventually to the KYLIX, the only place he felt wholly comfortable anymore.

CHAPTER 23

▼

"*Tekanis?*" Yorgos asked as Cassidy strode urgently from the dance floor, grabbed his retsina and downed it in one gulp. "He looks pissed off."

"Yeah, he's still got woman trouble."

Satyri watched with concern as Cassidy refilled his glass and drained half of that one too before turning away from the charafe. While this behavior wasn't offensive in any way neither was it normal for Cassidy. He had always maintained that wine robbed the dancer of his balance while beer did not. "I've never seen him act this crazy before. Bring me a glass," Satyri said, and moved toward Cassidy's table.

"Hey Greco! Have a drink," Cassidy offered, pulling out a chair for him, then clapping him on the shoulder. "Hey, where's your kid? I want to dance with the other table dancer!"

"Do it tomorrow. He's upstairs sleeping. I had to take him to the doctor. He's got a big fever. So, hangin' one on, are we?"

"Yeah. But one more and I'm gonna split. My ass is dragging."

Cassidy seized the charafe and poured Satyri's glass brimfull, then continued to pour on his forearm up to the elbow, soaking shirt sleeve and all. There was nothing Satyri could say; Cassidy and numerous other dancers had endured the same ritual many times good-naturedly. But Alexander continued to pour, saturating the table cloth and drowning out the vigil light. Then he toasted "*YAMAS!*" and clinked the charafe against Satyri's glass, downing the remains as the Greek smiled at him covertly.

"Hey, what's happening with you and Tosca?"

"Finished, boss, for sure," Cassidy replied, and at the remembrance his head lowered to his chest, stuporously, and remained that way till the Greek jostled his shoulder.

"Alexandros, you all right?"

"No, not all right," Cassidy coughed and cleared his throat to say more, but it wouldn't come as he struggled to swallow the dry lump in his throat.

"Come on. Let's dance my friend. A sirto'll pick up your spirits."

"No use. It doesn't help to dance anymore."

"That's bullshit, come on. We'll work it out."

"Naw," Cassidy answered, and moved toward the door. He was out the door and nearly to the curb before Satyri decided to follow him.

"Hey, it's only eight o'clock. Where you going?"

"MARCO POLO. See you tomorrow, boss."

Beaten down emotionally and physically, Cassidy took precaution to avoid the police as he drove; past the huge fig tree, down to Cabrillo Boulevard where he drove slowly along the beach, the longest and most nerve-wracking four blocks he had ever driven. Finally unable to deal with it he pulled to the curb in front of SAMBO'S ON THE BEACH, switched off the ignition and fell asleep.

An hour later he felt a thump on his backside. He struggled awake and squinted at the policeman's head framed in the open window; one of the beach patrol prodding with his baton.

"Got a problem, Mister?"

"Just resting, Officer. No problem."

Cassidy did his best to camouflage his unsteady voice but his thick slab-of-a-tongue gave him away.

"Sounds to me like you've got a snoot full," the cop said. Cassidy knew he was had. He waited contritely for the cop's next move. "Where do you live?"

"On a boat, in the marina."

"Leave the car here. Walk home."

"Yes sir, I'll walk home. Good idea."

"Be sure you do. That first DUI will cost about 5 grand."

As the cop watched Cassidy untangled from the Morris Minor and walked the three blocks to the marina. Approaching the gate he took hold of the handrail and stared at the dark water below. A small stingray inched along the bottom, lit by the fluorescent light, furling its batlike body as it hunted. He and Tosca had watched many of these ray fish together. He turned from the handrail, searched his pockets for change and pushed into the telephone booth where a huge moth careened chaotically in the garish light. His eldest daughter answered the phone. "Hi Pops, what a nice surprise."

"Hi Melanie. Sorry about the hour. I know it's pretty late."

"It's okay. A shame the other kids are all asleep."

"How are all you guys?"

"We're fine. Wish you were closer. We miss you."

"I know, baby. That's why I called. Think your mom would mind if I came up for a few days?"

"I'm sure it'd be okay. When would you be coming?"

"Three, four days. I'll call first."

"I'll tell mom. Will Tosca be with you?"

"Naw, we're finished, I think."

"Too bad. We were all anxious to meet her. So how are you doing as far as Gramma is concerned? Everything all right?"

"Pretty good but I miss her. It's just the idea that she's not here anymore. You know, something's missing."

"Yeah. Pops, you sound funny. You been drinking or something?"

"Just a tad. God! I can't squeeze anything by you!"

"Be careful on that boat. Don't fall in the water."

"Yes, mother."

"Take a long walk before you get on the boat. It'll help."

"Yes, mother. So, I'll see you soon. Tell everybody I called and I love them dearly."

"Okay, Pops. Love you too."

The harbor was deserted as he walked along and fish-gulped the fresh air. The tourists fishermen students and boat people were all settled in for the night, and with the impending storm the harbor would see minimum use for the next few days. The fishermen would take a welcome break, the students would park closer to campus, the tourists would be marooned in their motel rooms with their TV sets.

Cassidy was stimulated by the whistle of the wind and sound of boats banging against their docks, an excitement that had become second nature to him. Poorly fastened boats would break away from their docks tonight and unsecured sails would unravel and rip to shreds in the gale force winds. Rain would blow in from hard-driven angles and swirl into sparkling helixes. Some of the boats anchored outside the seawall would drag anchor and pound up on the beach where they would be picked clean of all bronze and brass fittings by the beachcombers of Santa Barbara. It was the same each time. People never seemed to learn.

His direction took him close by the cruising Harbor Patrol. Motor running, headlights framing him, they waited patiently while he negotiated the crosswalk. He was well-known to them as MARCO POLO's design was the butt of many jokes by the tupperware-loving boaters, as well as a tourist attraction.

"Big blow comin' Alexander. MARCO POLO ready?"

"Yeah, she's ready. I'm going down there now."

"Hey, last day for the dock rent. I noticed your name's still up on the board."

"Thanks for reminding me. I'll take care of it right now. I can't afford the penalty."

"Julie's still in the office. She'll take your money."

As Cassidy continued to the harbormaster's office he realized he would have to pass the boatyard. It made him uneasy and had a sobering effect but there was no way around it. As expected, the Veedub was parked there, outside by the Ferrari. He felt betrayed and stared at the freshly painted hull of ACHILLEAS, secure once more in her fore and aft cradles. He knew Tosca was below deck. Felt it in his heart. Nothing ever changes but the name of the girl and the reason it won't work, he thought sadly, and moved on.

Aboard the junk he tried to relax as she strained at her dock lines. He was tense as he laid on the bunk and stared at the overhead, thinking about the busted relationship and the incredibly dumb violence of Tosca's father.

"Jesus! Never again," he swore, and shifted his body to find that one perfect position which would calm his churning gut and ease the pain. It was not to be had. Her spirit was everywhere; doing homework on the bunk, sharing pita bread and hot milk, screwing so wildly on the galley table that it almost broke loose from the stanchion. He turned on FM and got Vivaldi (her favorite concerto for oboe and cello). He turned off the radio and tried silence…deafening. Pet mice, clothes pile, Hot Springs Creek, all her bizarre touch bases. His mind wafted over them like a tortured ghost that wouldn't give it up.

In desperation he got to his feet and changed into the white India cottons. He grabbed the red hat, secured the hatch and went back ashore. Only the Greek could defeat the wild spectres that were plaguing him tonight. He would spend the night with Satyri and son in the apartment above the KYLIX.

He was caught totally off guard as he entered KYLIX. It was boisterous and radiating great energy though it had been quiet and half-empty just an hour ago.

"Alexandros! YASOU!" Satyri called out. "Can't stay away, huh? You like my KYLIX! Come on, have a drink. We'll do the table."

"No, no, I've sobered up once already tonight. Hey, where'd all these folks come from?"

"I don't know but I'm not complaining. Helps with the child support, you know. Hey, the sailor with the big hat, he's back in the corner eating dinner. He asked about you and Tosca."

"What's he want?"

"Go find out. Holler if you need help," Satyri offered.

Cassidy removed his jacket as he made his way back to the corner booth, back by the patio doors. As he drew near Morgan nodded and pulled a chair out for him. "Buy you a drink?" he asked as Cassidy sat down.

"No thanks, too much already. Satyri said you wanted to talk."

"Yeah, I called Tina's house but I guess she's still at the Elks. I'm shipping out in the morning and I just wanted to tell her the Bug is ready."

"She's not going with you?"

"No."

Cassidy felt elated but answered obliquely to cover his surprise. "Better think it over. Hell of a storm building out there."

"I know that. I'll just lay in at San Luis until it blows out. Any port'll do as long as it's away from Santa Barbara."

"Why so anxious all of a sudden?"

"I believe in kharma, you know, and this town's got some bad vibes for me. I mean, like her old man. I mean who'd be vile enough to wreck an old wood schooner! The man's a god-damn lunatic!"

"You've got that right."

"Anyway, I just wanted to say…treat that lady well and you've got an angel forever."

Cassidy felt a surge of anger. The colossal nerve of the man! As if he and Tosca could pick it up again, just like that!

"I'd appreciate it if you'd tell her goodbye for me," Morgan continued, "just in case I don't get to…Oh oh, be cool now. Here she comes and boy she looks way pissed off."

They both tracked Tosca as she drew near, hostility on her face, suspicious of them being together. "May I join the party?" she taunted them.

"Sure honey," Morgan answered, and scooted over to make room for her. "How'd it go at the Elks?"

"Fine," she answered brusquely, and the blue/green eyes darted back and forth between them, adding to their sense of guilt. She offered nothing further and Morgan broke the silence.

"I called your house. The Bug's ready, and I'm takin' ACHILLEAS out of here bright and early. I didn't want to go without saying goodbye."

"Oh?" Tosca hesitated, her glance skipping from one to the other for an explanation.

"Excuse me. Time for the table dance," Cassidy said, and made his way to the big table where Satyri watched his approach.

"Everything okay back there?" Satyri asked.

"No problem. He just wanted to let Tosca know he's leaving Santa Barbara tomorrow."

"Great! Everything's all right then! Tell you what, Alexandros, I like Tosca. She's a good kid, know what I mean. I'll talk to her. Make her treat you better, okay."

"Nothing you or me can do about that one."

"Bullshit! This girl listens to Satyri, you better believe it. Listen, I'll lend you some dough. Take her down to Acapulco, Take her to a big club, you know, a classy resort. Women love that."

"Yeah, I bet she would at that. She's never been away from Santa Barbara. Huh uh, I don't think so. I could never pay you back."

"So what's new eh. Pay it back when you can, right. I got plenty dough."

"I appreciate the thought, boss. *Efkhareesto*," he thanked the Greek.

"Any time. Gotta take care of my friends, you know. Hey, look at 'em. This is a great crowd, havin' a good time. Got the Thanksgiving spirit. I like a hot crowd. Makes it easier to do my table when they don't just sit there like dummies. Come on, a sip of ouzo and we'll do the table."

"Okay, just one," Cassidy agreed, and drained the shot glass Satyri poured for him. "Awww, that shit's bad," he complained, grabbing at his throat. "No wonder you Greeks are always pissed off."

"Aaaallll right! Ready for the hisapiko? I feel like a million bucks! OPA!" Satyri shouted, and filled all the other glasses at the big table, toasting, "*YAMAS!*" Then he clinked his glass against all the others, downed the drink, and smashed his wine glass upon the votive candle. "All right, I mean we're gonna party big time. On your feet everybody!" he shouted, and waved a dozen dancers out to the dance floor.

Grinning widely behind the bushy moustache, thoroughly enjoying his role, Satyri clapped his hands rhythmically as he moved between his patrons to the dance floor. At his signal the musicians began to play the party favorite, ZORBA. Dancing beside him Cassidy felt the enormous energy he radiated sometimes, on a special night. This was such a night. Satyri was pure machismo, wet and warm with perspiration. All the world was beautiful! Even the Turks were good guys tonight!

"OPA Alexandros! Everything's all right, okay? OPA!"

Cassidy had never seen him execute the dance more perfectly. The intricate patterns, sudden tricky moves calculated to fake his followers out of position, yet not so completely as to discourage them or mar the beauty of the dance. Satyri hummed the music privately, eyes mere slits, sweat beading across his forehead. As the dance ended the patrons responded with a barrage of shrill whistles, yelling, and pounded their wine and beer bottles against the table tops in unison as they shouted OPA! *en masse*. It was a madhouse.

Smiling, using his shirttail for a towel, Satyri mopped the sweat from his forehead. He took the microphone from the bandstand, and walked among his patrons to thank them for their hyper-reaction.

"You cause this to happen! Did you know that? I love a crazy crowd! I love the people of Santa Barbara! OPA!" he roared to their approval, and twirled his worry beads around an index finger.

"Tell you what...This is a special night, know what I mean. You know, you can feel it in the air. Good night like this, a special crowd, I tell jokes. But I gotta tell you...don't take it personal. I don't get offended, nobody gets offended, okay. One thing I like about this country we do jokes on each other, right, even the President. Lotta places you get shot in the head for less."

He hesitated until the applause told him jokes were in order. Definitely a joke night.

"Okay, there are these 3 guys standing on a street corner, right, and they're talkin' things over. They're foreigners, a Greek, an Arab, and a Jew. They're talkin' religion, politics, you know. A horse fly circles around the Greek's head, bzzz, bzzz. Greek gets bent all outta shape, right. He goes, *'pssssst, pssssst,* get away you dirty bug!' and swats at the fly with his hand. The fly does a zigzag and goes for the Jew, *bzzz, bzzzz.* The Jew ducks and gently pushes the fly away with his hat. 'Git avay, bug, git avay'.

So the fly does another zigzag, buzzes the Arab. Arab is like radar, see, watching real close...watchin' the fly...ZAP! his hand flashes out, he's got the fly. Nonchalantly puts the fly in his mouth, eats him, right. Well, the Jew and the Greek don't quite know what to make of this, you know. They look at each other. Shrug. The Arab is nuts. Right?

So they start talking again. Another fly buzzes around. Same thing happens again! Crazy Arab goes after this one and eats him too! The Greek and the Jew are flabbergasted.

But they're hangin' out, see. European guys hang out on street corners at night and talk about stuff and look at girls, right. So they're talkin'...talkin'...another fly comes around. Heads for the Greek. Greek sees him coming, swats at him, 'God-dam fly! Get outta here!" He drives the fly away. Fly zigzaggs over to the Jew. Jew watches him real close...like radar he follows the fly...watching...watching... ZAP! He's got the fly! Turns to the Arab. Sticks his closed fist up into the Arab's face, grins, says, 'Hey, vant to buy a nice fat fly, huh?"

They loved the joke, they loved the Greek. As they thundered an ovation he stood there grinning. "OPA! OPA!" he responded, clapping his hands.

He could remember jokes not so well received; nights he had miscalculated and waited in vain for the applause. Embarrassing. Tonight everything was great, his body strong, mind working like a jackhammer, sweat rolling off his forehead.

"Aaaallll right! Time for the greatest table dancer in the world! Very few of us left, you know. Used to be you'd find three, four Greeks doing the table dance down in the PLAKA, the night club section of Athens. I mean every night. They all wanted to lift tables. Now all they want to do is rock n' roll with the American girls," he mused sadly. "Nobody wants to do the table anymore. I'm the only one left. The only crazy Greek. OPA!"

He was right, of course. Nobody could do TWO tables like Satyri, the Athe-nian, a man who had performed the dance at the LINCOLN CENTER and CARNEGIE HALL with the NATIONAL TOURING COMPANY OF GREECE when that august company could not find a Greek in Greece to do the table. He had also performed for NBC-TV, prime time.

The bouzouki started the music. Satyri approached the table, teasingly, cau-tiously, as though he and the table had a dialogue going. He feinted at the table like a bull fighter, turned his back and circled it with arrogance and indifference, glared at it. He dropped suddenly to his knees in a sliding graceful motion, gripped a corner of the table with his teeth and rose to his full height, arms out-stretched to the side for balance, and danced away with the table held firmly in his teeth.

His fingers snapped the rhythm and his feet shifted smoothly like a ballroom dancer as he covered the perimeter of the dance floor. After a few turns around he returned to the center, directly under the Art Deco ball of mirrors where he spun like a dervish, the red tablecloth flying out horizontally until he slowed the spin, stopped, dropped to his knees and SPAT the table out onto the dance floor.

He acknowledged the wild applause, then danced over to a second table loaded with dinner plates, salads, wine bottles, glasses and ash trays, votive can-dles and purses of the lady diners. As Satyri chatted a moment with the ladies at this table, assuring them he would bring their purses back when the dance was over, Cassidy assessed the weight of the two tables at a hundred pounds and it worried him. The ladies grabbed their purses which reduced the weight to about ninety pounds. Still too much. Satyri dropped to his knees, clamped his jaws together and lifted the loaded table very slowly, not so much concerned about food and drink spilling as the pointed ash trays and candle wax which might disfigure the handsome face if overturned.

The musicians banged away on bouzouki clarinet and keyboard as Satyri arranged the second table on top of the first one for perfect balance. He fussed with it, readjusting everything one last time. He dropped to his knees. The crowd noise diminished expectantly. He chewed on the corner of the table for the perfect fit, the exact leverage. The jaws clamped in place, he positioned his legs and lifted both tables slowly, surely, one table leg braced against his torso for support. He was up! The trickiest part was over!

Unrestrained applause greeted him as he circled the dance floor, arms outstretched to the side for balance, wine glasses and carafes brushing against the ceiling light shades, approaching Cassidy on the second time around. But he broke stride slightly as he spotted a blur of activity outside the patio doors, and pointed a finger of warning toward Padro Tosca, wobbly drunk, pistol raised to fire at Joe Morgan who was sitting no more than five feet to one side.

Alerted, Morgan kicked the door closed against Padro, deflecting the gun, causing it to discharge wildly. The terrified customers ducked for cover and sent up a cacophony of screams, but their cries paled compared to the one coming from Satyri. His eyes bulged and the veins in his neck were distended with shock as he stood stiff-legged with the table locked in his jaws. An animal roar burst through his clenched teeth, filling KYLIX with its power. Both hands clutched at his chest in a desperate embrace and the blood seeped between his interlocked fingers. Frozen in place, all were transfixed by the tableau and the relentless scream of agony. Then suddenly there was a sharp CRACK of wood as Satyri bit through the corner of the table, dumping the tables and contents in a tumbled heap on the floor. The chaos peaked to a crescendo as he stood with the table corner still locked in his teeth. His eyes wavered and lost their focus. His body trembled and the animal roar reduced to a bare grunt. Surrounded by ninety shocked patrons, none of whom could help him, the Greek finally collapsed as his life blood drained down to colour the dance floor of KYLIX.

CHAPTER 24

▼

The patrons had wasted no time in leaving after the incident. It had stunned them all, the suddenness...the finality.

Though they had heeded Captain Bateman's request to vacate KYLIX and go to their homes a few of them had loitered outside on the sidewalk, apparently feeling the need for some kind of additional closure. They withdrew eventually as did the authorities and except for the lone squad car out front the neighborhood had returned to normal.

Alexander Cassidy and Yorgos Papanikolas were alone at the bar now, silent, sipping ouzo beneath the melancholic glow of red blue and gold ceiling spotlights. An unreal light. Almost violent.

Yorgos sat at the counter with his head cupped in both hands. Cassidy glanced at him covertly as a single loud sniffle broke the silence. "You okay, Yorgos?"

Yorgos grabbed his gut abruptly, got down off the barstool and stood behind Cassidy, clasping a hand to his shoulder.

"Gotta go, Alekko. Can't stand this shit anymore."

"I'm good here, Yorgos. Go home."

"You're sure. I mean, the kid'll be all right with my family until Erica gets here."

"I'll take care of it. Bateman left her a message. She's gonna call this number."

"Bateman gonna get pissed if I leave?"

"Naw, it's cool. Go on home."

"Okay, you know where I live. *Kahleeneekhta.*"

The KYLIX felt oppressive after the door closed behind Yorgos. For the first time since he knew the place Cassidy was alone there and it was deathly quiet, uncharacteristically so. He downed what ouzo was still in the glass. The fire was in his throat, then spread quickly to his innards. He took a club-like hold on the bottle, got down from the barstool and moved aimlessly between the tables, four chairs to each with red-checkered tablecloths, the votive candles now extinguished.

He stopped, gazed around listlessly. Exhaustion overcame him. He dropped heavily into the nearest chair, put his forearms on the table and rested his head. Time passed him by as though in a vacuum. His ears felt hot, the back of his neck cold. The dead weight on his arms caused them to tingle. He adjusted them in response and became distantly aware of upending the ouzo bottle. He snapped awake and put the ouzo bottle upright.

He allowed his gaze to drift around KYLIX; to the hundred empty wine wickers hung in a decorative line around the walls; to the revolving Art Deco ball of mirrors which hung from the ceiling above the dance floor. As in a daze he focused on the coloured prisms of light which reflected from the mirrored ball down onto the dance floor, a hypnotic circle of moving reds greens blues and white, silent and never-ending. Then abruptly he got to his feet and made his way to the kitchen where he lowered his head to the sink and splashed cold water in his face.

Somewhat relieved Cassidy wandered uncertainly around KYLIX while waiting for the expected phone call. He studied the Greek figures on the muralled walls. He might as well have been standing in a taberna in Athens as one in Santa Barbara, California. There were classic ruins, shepherds in the fields, ancient patriarchs at the backgammon board. Young men, drunk and carefree dancing in a taberna; fishermen on their boats, and his own favorite…the portrait of a beautiful girl on the kylix, or drinking cup. The trademark.

Suddenly he was startled out of his reverie by the table, still askew, one leg shattered by the impact. Nausea seized him. He lifted the sagging table, braced it with a chair and backed away. He stared at the dark spot on the dance floor, still evident though Yorgos had worked hard to remove all the traces.

Cassidy's face lost its composure by degrees and settled into a pained expression. He knelt down and pressed his fingertips across the spot in curiosity. His mouth opened as though to speak then closed without a sound. He tried again and the intimate soulful words of the Greek love song A HEAVY SILENCE FELL punched out haltingly one word at a time…*Épefté vathia shopé…sto palio* mas vaso."

He faltered, stopped singing. The muscles in his jaw tightened and determination replaced the pained expression. He tipped the bottle and saturated the spot with ouzo, allowing time for the powerful liquor to permeate the wood. He grabbed a tablecloth and scrubbed frantically but nothing happened. The spot was stubborn. More ouzo, more frenetic scrubbing but again to no avail.

"*FÉ-YÉH-TÉH!*" he shouted, but the stain would no 'go away'.

Angrily he got to his feet and hurled the tablecloth down at the stain just as his obsession was interrupted by the harsh ring of the telephone.

He crossed to the bar and watched the phone ring several more times then snapped a look at the wall clock. It was three a.m. in Santa Barbara, six a.m. in Philadelphia. He picked up the receiver with a certain dread.

"Satyri, that you?" a woman's voice enquired.

"No, it's me, Cassidy. It's been a long time, Erica. How are you?"

"There was a message on my machine from a Captain Bateman. He said it was urgent. What the hell's going on out there?"

"Bad news, I'm afraid. Satyri was killed tonight."

Cassidy waited for the usual outcry of grief but got only silence from the other end. "Erica?"

Finally…"Oh my God, which Satyri? Is my son all right?"

"Yes Ma'am, he's upstairs sleeping. He doesn't know yet. I'll stay with him till you get here."

"What happened? Jealous husband?"

"No, some crazy shot him while he was doing the table dance."

"I knew it. I always told him it was no place for a child to be."

"Erica, the man is dead."

"I warned him. He never did pay any attention to what I said."

"Yes Ma'am. So what do you want to do about the boy?"

"Christ! I'll have to take off work and all that crap. I don't know. I'll check it out and call you back."

"You do that," Cassidy answered, a bit angry at her callousness. "Get me the flight number and time and I'll pick you up at the terminal, or else Yorgos will," he said, and slammed the phone back into its cradle. "God, what a mistake that one was."

Cassidy took another pull on the ouzo as he turned to the backbar. He stared at the pyramid of beer and wine glasses stacked there, next to a small globe of the world on which a Greek sailor's hat rested significantly. The deep rich colours of the window murals sparkled as they were backlit by the outside street lights.

"Uncle Alex," the small squeaky voice startled him, "where's papou?"

Cassidy turned to look at little Satyri, pyjama clad, golden hair askew, eyes swollen by sleep and fever. "Papou?" he repeated.

Cassidy choked up at first, not sure what he should tell him. The small voice reminded him that there would be much bigger losers by Satyri's death than himself Tosca and the others. He hesitated. What could he possibly tell the kid?

"Uh, he's gone up to Saint Barbara's Orthodox to help the priest. He told me to stay with you until he gets back. Okay?"

"But when…When is he coming?"

"Pretty soon now. Why don't we go back upstairs and when he gets here I'll ask him to come up and tuck you. Okay?"

The boy appeared to be satisfied with the lie. Still half asleep he licked his dry lips and his attention shifted around KYLIX, to the dark corners and the spell-binding coloured lights. He was hypnotized by the kaleidoscopic patterns of colour reflected from the Art Deco ball of mirrors. Finally his gaze settled on the miniature table his father had built for him. His own table.

Cassidy felt the boy's forehead. It was hot. "I bet you're thirsty. Want some water?"

He nodded, then downed the glassful given him. Cassidy lifted him in his arms and started upstairs. "Come on, back to bed. Your mom's coming. Did you know that?"

"Momma?"

"Uh huh. She's coming tomorrow."

Cassidy searched his face for a reaction as he laid him on the bed and snugged the cover up under his chin. The boy had accepted the whole deception, thank god. His eyes were heavy with sleep, already closing as Cassidy left the room.

Once downstairs Cassidy walked out on the patio to guage the sky and listen to the storm wind. He locked the patio doors and the side door. He switched off the dance floor spotlights, bathroom and kitchen lights, then finally the Art Deco ball of mirrors. He was somehow disturbed without the revolving prisms. He punched the switch on again and felt better for it.

He was at the front door now, reaching out to throw the dead bolt when a handsome, strangely familiar face stared back through the glass at him, startled, her hand already pulling on the door handle.

"Uh, sorry but we're closed."

"It's still on," she said, and pointed up at the electric sign above the door which showed the inside of a kylix. The tondo at the bottom of the kylix was painted the marvelous orange of the ancient Greeks. Against the orange, depicted in black silhouette, a drunken satyr with hard penis was chasing a young *maenad* who was in full flight, yet still smiling. Above the kylix bold black letters announced…KYLIX TABERNA.

"May I come in?" the girl asked.

"I don't mean to be abrupt but it's not a good time."

"Please? Just one quick look."

Alexander looked at her boldly. Something about her intrigued him. She stood her ground and looked up at the sign as a few raindrops fell on her face. "She's my twin, just like they said."

He leaned out and followed her point. She and the *maenad* on the sign were look-alikes, exact in profile. The long black hair pulled into a chignon, prominent forehead and classic nose, small shapely lips. The rounded chin petite yet well defined, eyes large and almond shaped.

"This is incredible!" Cassidy replied enthusiastically. "Are you a Greek?"

"Yes."

"*Éhlatéh méhsa,*" he offered deferentially, and stood aside.

"*Efkhareesto, parapolee,*" she thanked him and entered. As she passed through and surveyed the interior spaces of KYLIX she put a hand to her heart and said, "It's fantastic, just like they said."

"Who said?"

"My teacher and some of the dancers at City College. I take Greek dancing there."

Cassidy hit the light switches for her and the murals came alive with voluptuousness.

"Absolutely! I love this place," she added.

"What's your name?"

"Lia. Actually, Malia Economos, but they call me Lia."

"Mmmm, nice. Mine's Alexander."

He gestured to the big table and recovered the ouzo bottle from the bar. "Old enough to drink?"

"No, and I don't," she answered. "But I'm frozen. Anything hot to drink?"

"Chef's gone home."

"How about hot milk?"

"I can do that. Back in a minute."

As he stood at the stove with the milk Cassidy spotted Satyri's worry beads on the salad board and put them into his pocket. When he returned she was standing raptly in front of the kylix mural by the dance floor, checking it out, not seeming to be aware of him. Astounding!, he thought. In his past association with dealers, museums and private collectors, he had literally seen hundreds of such faces on the black/orange Attic and Apulian vases, but he had never dreamed that some day one of them would come marching through the front door.

"No question about it, Lia, that's you."

"I know, and my mom too. She looks the same, and my grandmother also."

"Mmmm, gorgeous family. Excuse me. The milk oughta be ready."

He continued to watch her through the swinging doors of the kitchen as she passed in front of Bair's old diving suit, awed by its size and weird design. *What a sweetheart,* he mused. Satyri would have liked her bigtime. A shame she had to discover KYLIX this night of all nights.

He poured the milk and joined her at the big table where she was reading the dust jacket of one of the LP albums kept at KYLIX for sale.

"Oh yeah, I love Theodorakis' stuff," she said.

"Right. A fine composer."

"Thanks for the milk. It's getting cold out there."

Cassidy nodded and watched her small mouth ingest the milk, and the worry beads whirled around his finger. "What are you into up at City College? What's your major?"

"Just general studies. It's my freshman year."

"You live in Santa Barbara?"

"Pasadena. This is my first time away from home. I mean, really away. How about you?"

"I live on a boat in the harbor."

"How cool. I park down there for school. Bet I pass by your boat every day. Well, I better get back to the apartment. Looks like a big storm, huh?"

"Yeah, it's supposed to be a big one."

"Do you work here or are you just one of the dancers?"

"Dancer. I do a pretty good hisapiko."

"Why don't you come to class sometime. They allow guests who know how to dance and we can sure use the help. There's about forty of us in the class."

"I'll do that. When and where?"

"The gym. Every Thursday at three-thirty."

"See you there, day after tomorrow."

"No street shoes. They scratch the floor."

"I have opanky."

"Right. *Kahleeneekhta.* I really appreciate you showing me around."

"My pleasure. Good night, Lia."

The KYLIX was depressing after she left. Cassidy's thoughts were back to Satyri and the night's happenings, so surreal and startling. Cassidy would never forget his friend's last moments; the look of disbelief, the scream of defiance. But at least Padro Tosca was not going to get away with this one. Captain Bateman informed them that his men had apprehended Padro, reeling drunkenly on the railroad tracks near Fess Parker's resort, heading for an area thick with undergrowth that had once been a hobo jungle. Good news, but no help for Satyri.

The stark ring of the telephone interrupted him once again. Thinking it was probably Erica with the flight information he picked up the receiver and acknowledged.

"Alexander, Marty here. Tina asked me to call you and apologize for running away. She…"

"I wouldn't call it running away, Mrs. Tosca. There wasn't anything she could have done. No one could help him."

"She said 'running away', Alexander. He's her father and she feels responsible. I'm experiencing the same thing."

"Please don't, Marty. What happened had nothing to do with you. Especially you."

"I appreciate that. What…? Hold on a minute," she said, and Cassidy could hear several voices in the background. "Angus is here. He says he'll catch up with you tomorrow after things quiet down."

"I don't know where I'm gonna be. I'll call him. Listen Marty, I'm expecting the boy's mother to call here. I'll talk to you tomorrow. And tell your daughter to just take it easy."

Sitting there at the bar Cassidy thought about the enormous burden of guilt that Tosca would be carrying around. Sure the pain would diminish with time but it was going to be one awful ordeal for someone as emotional as she was, already troubled as she was. He wanted to help her but thought it was such a personal thing she would have to deal with it alone.

He was exhausted. He closed his eyes and let his mind rest. But an image materialized. The ball of mirrors turning, Satyri and Tosca doing their favorite couples dance, a Yugoslavian Kolo number called Sukachko. He imagined the chorus of Balkan girls as they harmonized 'Dunai dunai dunai vey, dunai vovo ladno,' and Satyri whirling her with such speed and centrifugal force that her torso and legs became airborne and parallel to the floor, and she would have gone hurtling through space except for his strong arms cupped around her shoulders. Eventually the image faded, the music subsided and Cassidy was face-to-face with his troubling reality again. Could there ever be a rapproachment for him and Tosca? Were they finished as lovers? There was no way to be certain but he suspected that their time of sweetness had probably passed. The events of the past month had nudged her over the edge of innoccence, and himself too where she was concerned. And then a disturbing thought swept over him all at once and he broke out in a nauseous sweating! It had actually been in his power to have Padro put away after the attack on him at Hot Springs. Satyri need not have become ensnared in the violence at all. Damn!

"Hey, enough of that negative stuff, Cassidy," he reproached himself, and began to turn the lights off again, coming finally to the switch for the revolving ball of mirrors.

The switch was on a muralled wall, with Satyri dressed in a black leather vest and pants, white shirt, bushy moustache and a full shock of coal black hair. The mural showed him dancing with a single table gripped in his teeth, arms outstretched to the sides for balance. As if for the first time Cassidy stared dumbly at the mural, suddenly aware that he had never questioned the logic of dancing with a table clutched in your mouth. Why? What kind of cultural symbolism would cause you to dance around with a godamn table clutched in your teeth? The significance escaped him. He pondered over the possible origin of it.

He took a deep breath and swallowed hard to suppress the sadness before it took him over again. He raised the ouzo bottle high and stared long and hard at Satyri's likeness, then thought to himself, 'To Malia Economos, boss, and farkeling too'. He then took a final swig from the bottle before hurling it at the base of the mural, shattering the bottle, splashing the remaining ouzo up onto the Greek's dancing legs.

"OPA boss. *Kaleeneekhta*," he said softly as moisture filled his eyes. He switched off the Art Deco ball of mirrors, plunging KYLIX into near darkness, then shuffled up the stairs to wait for Satyri's mother. Outside the storm continued its gradual buildup against Santa Barbara.

EPILOGUE

▼

The stand of pine trees which had dominated the bluffs at City College for more than a century were under assault once again, as were the ancient cypresses at EAST BEACH CEMETERY, the site where Satyri would likely have his final resting place.

The BIRD REFUGE, usually teeming with various exotic species, was chaotic and without a single tennant, while the harbor's perrenial survivor (the seagull) had instinctively shifted its roost to the gables of inland buildings, there to wait for the tranquillity which always followed the chaos.

Down in the harbor the wind raged against boat and building and sent up a shrieking babel. The preliminary rainfall was sporadic, even gentle, but the recurring lightning, thunder, and dirty boiling sky reminded one that the big wild stuff was nearby and approaching fast.

It was eight a.m, as Mrs. Tosca drove up with Tina and parked next to the dock where ACHILLEAS had been launched earlier that morning. Expecting them, Joe Morgan stepped over the handrail and met her halfway.

"Morning, Tina," he said, kissing her lightly on the cheek. "The Bug's ready to go, honey," he said, looking sad, finding it difficult to face her squarely.

"Thanks, Joe. I really appreciate it."

Tosca hesitated, then looked up at him and burst into tears suddenly. He pulled her close and they stayed that way as the rain pelted them with single heavy drops.

"Sorry," she said, wiping at her tears. "I just feel so terrible."

"Hey, it's nobody's fault, Tina. It's just the kharma in this damn place. I should have split when I first experienced it."

"Is the car all right?" Mrs. Tosca interjected, hollering through the half-open window.

"Yeah, Mom. I'll see you back at the house," Tosca said, and waved as her mother backed up and drove away. Tosca opened her car door to get in but Morgan stood there with his arms extended toward her.

"Listen, I know how upset you are right now but I'd give anything to have you aboard when I sail out of here. Give it a chance. We can leave your mother a note with my address."

"I can't, Joe, what with Satyri and stuff, and Alexander. We're all gonna be a mess for a while. But it'll be impossible to forget you, I want you to know that."

"Yeah, where have I heard that one before", he said, then turned away from her in frustration.

"Joe Morgan!"

"Sorry, Babe, I'm just a poor loser. I don't know what to do about this," he said, wringing his hands, shuffling back and forth nervously. "I don't know what to do."

"Joe…Please?" she said imploringly. "So what time are you leaving?"

"In a few minutes. Waiting for Frank to come aboard. Come on, I'll walk you to the Bug."

It was time to say goodbye. They both squirmed as they faced each other for the last time. They had been through a lot in a very short space of time. She reached out to kiss him on the lips but was very careful to avoid his body.

"Sorry about the grief you had with my father," she offered, sliding behind the wheel of the Bug.

"Yeah, a close one for both me and my schooner. Hey…" he said, pointing at the red hat on the car seat, "tell him I didn't mean him any harm, okay. Stuff just happens."

"I'll tell him."

He reached into the car and touched her face tenderly, brushing each eyebrow with a fingertip. "One green one blue. Christ! For the first time in my life I'm in deep trouble. Don't forget me, huh."

He closed the car door then ran for cover as fierce lightning burned through the sky and the rain began to pour down on Santa Barbara.

Tosca was relieved to have settled her dual relationship and its attendant anguish for her and Alexander. But there was still Satyri and that would likely take a long time, maybe even a different town.

"Whatever it takes," she sighed, and drove to the parking lot nearest MARCO POLO, to wait for the rain to let up a little. But her wait was in vain. The storm had commenced in earnest.

"Oh well..." she mused, shrugging her shoulders. And taking the hat under her black cape she set out on a lady-like sprint through the downpour, toward MARCO POLO and her lover.

FIN

Photo credit to: Rob Shackelford

The author was born and raised in St. Louis, MO.

Attended Washington University, Saint Louis, MO.

Moved to California and lived in the harbor at Santa Barbara on a Chinese junk.

Special thanks to helpmates: Lance Richardson

Titus Woods

Sanford Dorbin

978-0-595-40067-6
0-595-40067-1

Printed in the United States
54145LVS00006B/46-75

9 780595 400676